travels
with
jim

Jill Evans

an imprint of Sunbury Press, Inc.
Mechanicsburg, PA USA

an imprint of Sunbury Press, Inc.
Mechanicsburg, PA USA

For information about special discounts for bulk purchases, please contact Sunbury Press Orders Dept. at (855) 338-8359 or orders@sunburypress.com.

To request one of our authors for speaking engagements or book signings, please contact Sunbury Press Publicity Dept. at publicity@sunburypress.com.

FIRST BROWN POSEY PRESS EDITION: December 2023

Set in Adobe Garamond Pro | Interior design by Crystal Devine | Cover by Igor Andric | Edited by Lawrence Knorr.

Publisher's Cataloging-in-Publication Data
Names: Evans, Jill, author.
Title: Travels with Jim / Jill Evans.
Description: First trade paperback edition. | Mechanicsburg, PA : Brown Posey Press, 2023.
Summary: *Travels with Jim* follows two young adults, Jim and Sorrie, who travel across America to explore their place in the world. Jim hops trains in a search for his father. He encounters Sorrie, a girl who comes from affluence but trades a life of comfort to escape from something she cannot name. Together they traverse the grittiness of life and discover that being with each other might be more important than their freedom.
Identifiers: ISBN : 979-8-88819-163-7 (paperback).
Subjects: FICTION / Literary | FICTION / Coming of Age | YOUNG ADULT FICTION / Urban and Sreet Lit.

Product of the United States of America
0 1 1 2 3 5 8 13 21 34 55

For the Love of Books!

To my extraordinary children and also to my
cousin Victor, the original mountain man

Contents

1

Virginia

THERE'S A FADED red boxcar in a field outside Richmond, Virginia. On hot days, the interior heats up with a dense sogginess that makes the air so humid and thick that anyone standing inside might think they'd been dropped into a true believer's version of a fiery hell. Only it's not hell; it's just a lonely old junker in a field in Virginia, and on a summer morning in 1993, anyone looking inside wouldn't find the devil. They'd just find Jim.

In the breaking daylight, Jim crouched against the boxcar wall and studied the black lines on his railroad atlas. The lines resembled fine-waxed threads against the faded paper and wove a series of crisscrosses from California to Maine. With eight years on the road, Jim knew the oily seats of the local diners and the garbage-strewn alleyways of every town. He knew the best dive bars where a man could get a foamy beer, and he knew the musky aromas of a dozen seasoned women who wanted to make him their friend. Jim loved them all, and it didn't matter if they loved him back. He was a traveling man.

Still, Jim knew freight schedules changed, and trains got cut for lack of cargo. A phone call home confirmed an uneasy feeling Jim carried in his gut: his Mom was sick, and he had to find a reliable route to Montana that was safe and quick. But as much as he hoped to get there, he needed money for food and cigarettes and had to figure out where he would find it.

Jim shoved the map into his sack and rubbed his head. A night of drinking with a group of roof riders from South America had taken its toll. His bones crackled like wet tinder on a blazing fire, and he held an achiness that made his back hurt and his stomach growl. Jim needed food, or every hop would mean a visit to the woods to heed the call of nature instead of a quick journey west.

Jim lifted his cramped legs and stood up to stretch. His muscles loosened in the expansiveness of his outstretched arms, but time wasn't on his side. Even though he was only twenty-three, he'd been traveling for years and carried an old man's weariness, and it was moments like these that he questioned why he was still chasing four a.m. shadows. Loneliness often grabbed at his insides, but he had no desire to stop. Unlike some others he'd met on the road who had no place to go and nothing to live for, Jim was on a mission, and that mission was to find his father.

Jim hiked his knapsack onto his shoulders, walked toward the car door, and jumped out. In doing so, he barely missed a thorny rose bush that clawed at his pant leg. He stopped to examine the fabric and then looked up. The mist had burned off the trees, and the stark yellow and blue streaks across the sky told him it was after sunrise—too late for the cows to go to pasture but too early for the grinding sounds of cars taking drivers to work.

Scanning the horizon, Jim fished out a dime-store compass and held it to the light. He spun around the way a seafarer might have circled a hundred years ago and stopped when the needle pointed northwest. Looking up, he saw a crop field and the outline of a road. This was the way out.

With his heavy black boots and lean frame, Jim cut a path through the plant stalks and soon smelled the pungent odor of hay. As tiny translucent particles floated in the sun's rays, an army of gnats arose and clouded Jim's sight. He swept the bugs aside and noticed farm buildings in the distance. Farms meant people and garbage cans filled with food scraps and sympathetic housewives who could be flattered into handing a gaunt hobo a slice of day-old bread.

But the buildings were deserted, and the road was crusty against his boots, leading to nothing for miles. So, he decided to change direction only to find long stretches of fields with fences and burly clumps of trees but little else except for a rusty tractor and a herd of indifferent cows.

Stopping near a line of mailboxes, Jim got his canteen from his knapsack and took a swig. The water was warm but satisfying. As he placed the cap onto the lid, he saw something glistening in the distance: an open garbage can against a weathered farmhouse. He drew closer and noticed a white bag with a fast-food logo. With one swift jerk, he snatched the crumpled pouch from the can and took off down the road.

Once secured behind a rock wall, Jim ripped open the bag and discovered a half-eaten hamburger and a pack of fries. He checked for any green spots and then shoved the food into his mouth; it wasn't much, but he'd had worse. A stale burger tasted as good as prime rib if that's all there was to eat.

After he finished, Jim resumed walking but didn't recognize the scenery. He'd traveled to Virginia from Florida by hitching a series of rides, and when the last driver for the night turned off, Jim got out. He met the roof riders a short time later, and they offered to share a bottle of vodka; the night was lost to madness after that.

It was day now, and Jim found himself on a road he didn't know in a town he couldn't name. The street was paved but had gravel ditches with old tree roots that someone had cut away. Jim kept walking, hopeful to hear train whistles, but the only sounds were the high-pitched trilling of insects and the echo of his boots on the blacktop.

As he approached a patch of woods, he heard the crack of a heavy branch. Jim's radar went up. There was another crack, and he stopped.

Was he being followed?

He moved slowly now, his boots an extension of the blacktop, heel quietly rolling into a foot, picking up, putting down, as his eyes scanned the brush the same way a soldier on patrol might look for the enemy. The scenery moved with an ocean-like sway, but as soon as he stopped, so did the wave. Jim squinted but didn't see anything. He strained his ears to listen, but there was only the soft motion of the wind against the leaves. It reminded him of the nights he'd spent in a patch of Adirondacks woods where he heard the sound of babies crying in the trees until he realized it was only catbirds. But there were no catbirds now—just a gentle breeze. His nose filled with the scent of pine, and he was lost in that memory when a very human noise jolted him back to reality. Was it weeping?

Jim moved closer. Yes, someone was definitely crying; first sobbing, then snuffling, then the low hum of sadness.

Could someone be tracking him?

Jim took a deep breath and bolted forward. A body shot up as hands clawed through the bushes, around trees, and past wildflowers. Jim chased the figure and reached out with his arms. He sprang up and managed to clasp a leg, which kicked and wiggled free. Jim was in fast pursuit, more for his safety than out of curiosity. Lunging forward, he grabbed onto something. Instead of catching one leg, Jim snagged two. The force of the movement sent both of them tumbling down a knoll. Breathing heavily, Jim looked up to see who he'd caught.

She was short and stocky with bright red hair and crimson high tops, and she kept saying, "Get your hands off me!" as she punched the air to push Jim away.

Jim grabbed her wrists and tried to block the sharpness of her nails. "I'm not going to hurt you," he said.

It was then that she opened her eyes. They were big and blue, and it was clear from the raspiness in her breath that she was frightened.

Jim let go and held out his palms in a show of peace. "Are you calm now?"

The girl bolted up again, but Jim yanked her back down and pinned her to the ground. "How about now?" She wasn't going anywhere; he was practically sitting on her.

"Why are you doing this?" She said, gasping for air.

Jim surveyed the bushes around her, turned, and looked to his back. "First, tell me if you have any friends nearby because I don't like it when someone I just met baits me with a question while their buddy sneaks up and sticks a shank against my neck."

"What are you talking about? I don't have friends," the girl said in disbelief. "But I *do* have a knife, and I know how to use it, so you better get off of me," she struggled to get out from under his firm grip. "You have no idea who you're messing with."

"Oh?" Jim moved off of her and allowed her to sit up. He couldn't resist challenging her question. "Who am I messing with?"

"I don't have to tell you anything." The girl turned her focus to her knapsack as her fingers tried releasing a catch lock on the front, but she had difficulty pressing it hard enough to unfasten it.

"You aren't going to open it that way."

"I'm making sure there won't be any funny business." The girl continued to fumble with the clasp.

"I'm not any funny business," Jim said as he leaned against a rock and lit a cigarette. "I'm just a guy passing through, which I have to be doing directly." He took a rusty pocket watch from his pants and glanced at the time: *9 A.M.* Damn. He had to find a train but worried about the girl's safety. She didn't know what she was doing, and her black shirt with a picture of a stack of books on it and expensive high tops told him she wasn't a street kid. She had money, which made Jim's thoughts go into overdrive.

Maybe he could turn their conversation into something more profitable. "What's your name?" Jim asked.

The girl stopped fumbling with her pack. "Why should I tell you anything?" She frowned.

"You don't have to; I'm just asking, is all," Jim shrugged. "I'll be on my way soon enough."

"Well, be on your way then," the girl waved dismissively.

Jim chuckled. He would have, but he wasn't about to pass on his next meal ticket. "It would be fine if I knew who I was talking to. Can you tell me your name?"

Book Girl brushed the leaves from her white pants, and Jim couldn't help but wonder if she imagined the leaves were him as she replied, "Why don't you just go away?" She smiled as she'd finally mastered the catch on her knapsack, opened it, and extracted a pocket knife. She fiddled with the edge of the closed blade to get it open, but her shaky fingers couldn't grip the smooth edge of the metal.

"You're not doing it right." Jim extended his hand, but Book Girl continued to try to wiggle the blade loose with no luck.

"You're not going to stab me, are you?" She asked after finally deciding to quit.

"As long as you don't stab me," Jim said.

Seemingly reluctant, Book Girl handed over the knife, and Jim put his thumb on the outer stud, guided the blade out, and then handed it back.

"Thanks," she said, fingering the sharp blade. *"Is this a dagger which I see before me?"*

"What the hell are you talking about?" Jim's brow furrowed.

"It's a line from Shakespeare's *Macbeth*." Book Girl struggled to close the knife.

Jim took it from her hands, pressed the lock, and guided the blade into its casing. "There." He handed it back.

Book Girl took it carefully. "Thanks," she said before studying his movements. Jim thought she might be looking to see if he had a knife hidden somewhere.

"So, what's your name?" Jim asked again.

Book Girl shook her head. "It's stupid."

Jim put a hand over his mouth and suppressed a laugh. "Your name is Stupid?"

"No. My name is Sorrie."

"What kind of a name is that?"

"It's the name my parents gave me, is all."

"Were they sorry you were born?"

"How should I know? I told you my name, and now you tell me yours."

"It's Jim."

"Well, what kind of a name is 'Jim'?"

Jim paused. "It's the kind of name a father gives a kid before he disappears and goes on the road," he said. "I've been searching for him for eight years now. Some say he's dead, but I don't believe it." The words brought up images that never left Jim's sleep: four a.m. train whistles; eighteen-wheelers moving through the mist; the shadows on the backs of buildings; the glow of a street lamp and a figure underneath; the click-clack of the shoes that never arrived—the father only myth provided.

"How are you going to find him?" Sorrie asked.

"I hop on freight trains and go coast to coast and back again. I'll find my dad someday—maybe wandering down a road or in the back of a dive bar. He's out there, and I'll find him. I know he's waiting for me so that he can get back."

"Get back to what?"

Jim didn't answer but asked, "Aren't you going to tell me where you come from?"

"If it's all the same to you, I don't want to discuss it."

The girl's body grew rigid as she stood up. Jim felt a twinge of nervousness. He didn't want to lose an opportunity. "Where you headed anyway? Maybe I can help."

Sorrie's expression turned hard. "It's none of your business where I'm going or what I've been through. I don't need anybody telling me what to do."

Jim backed up. "Whoa, don't go all princess on me. I'm just trying to see if we can help each other. After all, I helped you with your knife, right? Maybe I can help you in other ways."

"A knife is just a knife. It's not the same as trying to get somewhere. You can't help me, and neither can anyone else. Besides, I know exactly where I'm headed. What do you know about it anyway?" Sorrie fixed her shirt and hiked her knapsack over her shoulders. She climbed the knoll's incline and bolted down the road.

By the time Jim got up, she was gone. Just blacktop and a yellow stripe leading off into infinity. "So much for money." Jim ran his fingers through his curly hair. He picked up his belongings from the ground and started for the road. Noticing that the laces on one of his boots were loose, Jim bent down to tie it. As he did, he spied something sparkling in a patch of leaves: a pink change purse with an embroidered red heart. Jim glanced up the road to see if the girl was still there, then snapped it open. It contained sixty-five dollars in crumpled bills and was enough to go straight through. Stuffing the purse into his pocket, Jim wondered if, in his travels, he'd ever run across her again and whether he'd have the guts to tell her he pocketed her money.

* * *

The trip into town didn't take long, but by the time Jim reached the concrete sidewalk of the main drag, he was tired, and his legs ached from walking; his stomach was a churning sea. He surveyed the landscape: the tallest structure had a bell tower and a clock that read ten. A brick building sat on a corner and had the hue of ripe cherries. The letters over the door said, "Reds," and a neon cocktail sign was visible in the window. Jim felt the urge to go in and spend Sorrie's money on a few shots of Tennessee whiskey, but eating was the better option. He scanned the street and noticed a yellow awning over what looked to be a hardware store. Beyond that was a glistening line of silver supermarket carts.

He made his way in its direction when he noticed something else: there, sitting on a bench across the street, was Sorrie. Her head hung low, and her shoulders slumped toward the ground. The purple backpack rested next to her. Jim reached into his pocket and caressed the purse. He was irritated by what she said, but square was square. Besides, she could help him in other ways.

Jim walked over to where she sat. She looked up; her face was stained with tears. "I lied to you. I don't know where I'm going, and I seem to have lost all my money, and I'm scared. I can't go home forever but can't figure out what to do because all my money's gone."

Jim sat beside her. "Listen, I don't know what happened to you, but it's pretty clear you could use a friend."

Sorrie glanced toward her knapsack and fingered a plastic lizard clipped to the strap. "So, now you're going to be my friend?"

"That's for the future to decide, but just to show you that I want to help you, I have something for you." Jim reached into his pocket. "I think you forgot this." He handed her the purse. "You dropped it on the ground when you took off."

Sorrie snatched it from Jim and counted the money. She looked up. "You kept this for me?"

Jim shook his head. "I'm not that generous. I would've kept it for myself, but when I saw you, I knew I had to return it."

Sorrie wiped a tear from her cheek. "Why didn't you just take it anyway?"

Jim ran his hand over the top of his hair. "I would have, considering it's a big country, and our paths probably would have never crossed again, but now that I see you, I didn't want to keep what rightly belongs to you, especially since I'm not a thief."

"Then what are you?"

"I'm a guy who rides the rails hoping to find his father someday."

"I thought you said he was dead."

"That's what some people think, but I know he's out there somewhere wandering the highway."

"You mean you don't have a home?"

"I bed at my Momma's place in Montana, but I consider my home the road."

The girl looked down. "I appreciate you helping me, and I'm sorry for doubting you. Is there something I can do to say thanks?"

A smile came over Jim's face. "Yeah," he said. "Buy me a hot breakfast."

* * *

The coffee shop was small, and it smelled like fresh bacon and onions. A man pointed for them to sit at a table near the window. When the waitress came over to take their orders, she eyed Jim and Sorrie's dirty clothes and asked if they had enough money to pay for the meal. Sorrie opened her change purse wide enough to flash a twenty-dollar bill. Their food was delivered in short order.

"Where you from?" Jim asked as he scooped scrambled eggs onto a slice of buttered toast and bit into it. His strength had returned, and he was feeling invincible.

"Why do you need to know?" Sorrie eyed her plate of pancakes and began pouring maple syrup all over the top. Jim smelled the woody sweetness as a thread of thick brown liquid cascaded down the side of the stack.

"I'm asking, is all. You bought me breakfast, so I figured we could have a conversation. Besides, I don't string with no lowlifes."

"We moved a lot when I was little but settled outside Richmond a few years ago."

You don't sound like a Southern girl."

"I'm not," Sorrie snapped back.

"I'm just asking. You come from money?"

Sorrie played with the sugar packs. "What makes you say that?"

Jim stopped chewing but didn't look up. "Let's just say the girls I hang out with don't have fancy T-shirts with pictures of books on them and expensive shoes. Your clothes aren't worn, so you belong somewhere else."

"My parents have money, but it's not mine."

"How much they got?" Jim swallowed and looked up.

"That's a rude question," Sorrie said. Jim shrugged, and she continued. "I have no claim to it, at least not after I ran away."

"You ran from a nice house in Richmond with food and a warm bed?" Jim couldn't believe anyone would give up the comforts of a rich home for a life on the road. "Why'd you run?"

"That's none of your business."

"I don't mean nothing by it." Jim finished his breakfast and leaned back in his chair. He busied himself with lighting a cigarette, took a drag, and exhaled; the smoke curled from his mouth, and he had trouble seeing through the gray cloud.

"Let's just say there are some things more important than comfort."

"I can only think of one thing better than a soft bed and three squares a day, and that's finding my father."

"Why don't you just go to your mother's house and wait for him?"

Jim rolled the book of matches between his fingers. "It ain't like that." He paused. "Where you going anyway?"

"I was trying to head west by bus, but I didn't have enough money."

"Don't you have one of those cards you put into a machine?"

"No, I never had one of those. I took all the money I had and left."

Jim sensed that she might not be telling the truth but decided to change the subject. "Why go west?"

"I have an uncle who lives in Nebraska."

"Nebraska's quite a hike. It's no wonder you didn't have enough money."

"How do you know how much money I have?"

"Lady, I saw the purse and opened it. I counted the money."

Sorrie shifted in her seat and looked down. "You had no right to do that," she said.

"Right or not right, I did it, so there's no point in complaining. Besides, why didn't you ask your friends if you didn't have enough money?"

"I don't have any friends, at least not real friends."

Jim stamped out his cigarette in an ashtray. "I never really liked friends," he confessed. "Friends let you down. They'd just as soon cut you as kiss you when it comes to the important things."

"What are the important things?" Sorrie asked.

Jim leaned back and thought. "A dry place to sleep. A few dollars for whiskey, a pack of smokes." A smile came to Jim's face as his mind dipped into his pool of memories. "An angel offering a good meal. A sunny day on a cannonball. A beautiful woman."

"I'm disappointed if whiskey and women are all you think about."

Jim leaned forward and low. "Lady, you aren't the first to be disappointed with me." There was a pause in the conversation, and Jim wondered how he might convince Sorrie to go with him. After all, Nebraska was between where he was and where he was going. "How do you think you're getting to Nebraska, seeing that you seem to want to get there so fast?"

Sorrie's eyes welled up. She fished out a hand mirror from her pack and held it up to her face. Noticing a small patch of mud on her cheek, she tried to wipe it off with the edge of her shirt, but to no avail. "I don't know. I've never done this before. I want a bath and some clean clothes. My skin itches from all the dust, and my hair's dirty. I feel like cootie spit."

Jim rubbed his chin. Those sixty-five dollars would more than cover a pack of cigarettes and a bottle of Old Crow—and they might be able to pick up a spare job here or there along the way. "I can take you, but my going rate is a few packs of smokes, some food, and maybe some whiskey or beer. We'll be hopping freight, so if you think you smell now, just wait."

Sorrie paused. "What's the difference between freight and going by regular train?"

"That's easy. Freight's free. My services aren't, but you'll save money."

"Can I trust you?"

Jim smiled the way the devil might smile just before he took someone's soul. "If you can't trust me, just don't go. But you won't get there alone. For every one of me, there will be ten thieves itching to rob you. Besides, to me, it's a business contract."

"I don't know," Sorrie said.

Jim's heart dropped out of his chest. He'd already been with this girl most of the morning, and if he didn't hook her now, he might have to spend the rest of the day begging for money. "Listen, my father was a songwriter and wrote this song about a lost girl. You remind me of her."

"Your father wrote songs?"

"You could say that. My father wrote them going on twenty years ago."

"I wouldn't know his songs. I'm not that old."

"How many birthdays have you got?"

"Eighteen."

"Well, hell, girl, you're legal."

"That's not a problem?"

"We're talking, aren't we? Listen, I won't jump you or nothing. But you have to promise you won't say I kidnapped you because if you get mad at me and start tossing that around, I'll leave you where you sleep. Is it a deal?"

* * *

Soon, they were standing outside the coffee shop. The heaviness of grease hung in the air, along with the rich aroma of coffee. As Jim adjusted his backpack, he sensed something was wrong.

"Maybe if you can tell me where I can get a train, we can part ways here," Sorrie said.

"Why did you flip all of a sudden? I thought we had a deal. Besides, you said you didn't have enough money to get there."

"Not for a bus, maybe, but I'll pay for however far I get on the train."

Jim kicked his foot against the cement curb. "Then what? What if you get stuck in Kentucky or Tennessee or something? Where are you going to find another nice guy like me?"

"What about that speech about leaving me where I sleep?"

"Listen, I'm sorry," Jim put his hands into his pockets and hung his head. "It makes me mad when somebody wants to go one way but then changes their mind, especially if I'm settled on helping them. I've already burned a lot of time today, so I guess you could say I've got an investment in you." He stood close to the road, and a speeding car went by, beeping as it passed. Jim ignored it. Sorrie was his best ticket, so he had to convince her his offer was genuine. "I gave you back your purse, right? Just from our talk, I don't think you can go it alone. I mean, I found you crying in a ditch, but maybe that was fate, see? Maybe you have some guardian angel who told me to find you. But listen, I don't have time to waste, so decide if you want to come; I have to be moving along." Jim knew Montana was waiting, and it was now that he regretted not keeping the purse.

Sorrie dug the tip of one of her high tops into the gravel. "Why should I pay you for taking me in a direction you were going to go in the first place?"

"Never mind about me. Let's talk about you because, from the looks of things, you weren't going in any direction except maybe spinning around in circles."

Sorrie stood in front of him and said nothing.

Then suddenly, Jim reached out and grabbed her backpack. "You think you can get there without me? Let's see what you got. A hobo needs to carry certain supplies."

"Hey! Stop that!" Sorrie cried, but Jim tossed her sleeping bag aside and unzipped the backpack.

"You're sleeping gear looks okay, but what's in here?" He examined the contents of her sack and took out a pair of turquoise leggings. "Don't need these," he said as he tossed them into a garbage can. "There's no hat, no gloves."

"I have gloves," Sorrie insisted as she clawed at the backpack, but Jim continued to block her with his backside.

"*These* are gloves?" Jim snorted as he extracted a pair of orange knit gloves. "They're so damn thin, I can see through the little pockets of yarn."

"Those are from Martin's," Sorrie shot back as he tossed the pair into the bin.

"Let's see what else you got." He pulled out an expensive lace blouse. "Oh, that will keep you warm in the West Virginia hills." Out it went, into the garbage. He reached his hand in and pulled out a box of tampons. "Well, what have we got here?"

Sorrie grabbed the box and bag from his hands. "Those are *mine*," she said, turning her back on him and fishing her clothes out of the garbage.

"You think you'll get there by yourself? You won't get past Kentucky. I know what I'm doing and what you'll need," Jim said. "You'll need a warm jacket, good boots, leather gloves, and a good hat. We're talking about the road here," he said. "Army-Navy surplus if we're lucky. Most likely used boots from a thrift store."

Sorrie stopped and defiantly looked at Jim. "All right, all right, I'll go."

But then, Jim had a different thought—one he had wondered about ever since he met Sorrie: maybe she had something more to offer than money.

He lowered his face and grew serious. "I'll take you, but you need to promise me something."

"That I won't say I was kidnapped?" Sorrie asked smugly.

"No, it's something else."

Sorrie was still arranging her belongings, and only half looked up. "What? Liquor? Cigarettes?"

"No, something else."

Sorrie stopped what she was doing and stared at Jim. "You're not asking me to . . ." Her voice trailed off, and Jim could tell she couldn't form the words.

"No, not that," he said, and there was silence. Then, finally, Jim turned his back, pivoted around, and glared into her eyes. "You can read?"

Sorrie nodded.

He reached into his sack and pulled out a faded paperback with a picture of Jim's father on the cover. Sorrie glanced at the title: *The Lords and the New Creatures*. "Can you read this to me?"

Sorrie took it from his hands. It was a book of poetry. She leafed through the pages and stopped at places where there were small drawings. She ran her fingers around the outline of the sketches. "You mean you can't read?"

"I can read words, but they get all jumbled up in my brain, and sometimes I see them like they're backward. Plus, I don't understand the meanings. Can you explain the words and help me make sense of them?" Jim asked, pointing to the book.

"Of course I can."

"I want you to be sure. This and cigarettes and maybe some food and beer?"

"I said I could." Sorrie closed her knapsack and hiked it onto her back.

Jim looked down at the book with the face of a man Jim only knew from the stories his mother told him. "When we get to our next stop," he said, "we'll get you some proper clothes."

2

On the Road from Richmond

Ｆ Jɪᴍ ʜᴀᴅ an enduring love affair, it was with trains. It wasn't just the roar of the old cannonballs shooting down the tracks or the rush of adrenalin when he shimmied up the side of a car. It was the attack of the senses. It was the choking taste of diesel, the crunch of pebbles, and the cottonmouth dryness in his throat when he felt a rush of steam as it shot out of the old boilers. It was graffiti-littered cars and the fast movers in the middle of the hump yards and all the clanging steel from gigantic chunks of rails slamming into rails to little spits of bolts being flung into aluminum coffee cans. It was the harsh, scrapping sound of trains rubbing against each other, but it was also how an unhurried locomotive had a knack for slowing life down. It took on a type of musical rhythm with the other gritty noises of the day, like whistles and air brakes and the ear-splitting silences before it all turned awake again. It was home, family, and comfort in a vast open expanse of noise mixed with stillness where no one could tell him what to do.

And if there was a reason to have this girl come with him, it was because she could understand the words he couldn't, so when Sorrie said she'd help him read the poetry book, it was one more sign that he'd made the right decision. After that, all Jim could think about were the black words embossed on the white pages of a book he could barely read and never entirely understood.

Jim carried this hope with him as he and Sorrie traveled along the railroad tracks to find a freight yard to get them to a city where they could connect to an even bigger city to take them west.

They found a single train line outside of town and spent the next few hours walking along the edges with Jim assuring Sorrie that one track led to two, then three, and on and on until they'd be near the yard.

But it wound up taking hours. The path was steep, and the incline dropped off in certain places. Jim knew one slip-up would have them falling into the mud-covered ditch below or tripping onto the tracks and getting swept away by some demonic black coal car.

They finally reached a flat trail where their shoes cut a path through the reeds, transforming the plants into a straight line against the earth. Jim noticed Sorrie was breathing heavily. She drew in large chunks of air and asked, "Will we ever get there?"

"We're going in the right direction, and if you see tracks, they'll eventually lead us to a freight yard," Jim reassured her. Sorrie kept asking, and Jim kept answering until the conversation stopped and the air filled with the buzzing of insects and the crunching of shoes on a landscape of spiked weeds. Jim guided Sorrie up jagged slopes by grabbing her hand and holding her waist. When he touched the skin between the gap in her shirt and pants, he found it was smooth but solid, and Jim hoped he'd never have to fight her.

They maneuvered around rocks, railroad ties, and pieces of twisted metal. The air was hot and thick, and at one point, Jim stripped down to a black shirt and cargo pants while Sorrie removed her shirt and discreetly slipped into a white V-neck tee. Jim offered Sorrie a red bandana as he plopped a G.I. Boonie hat onto his head.

After an hour, they stopped to rest and drink water, and Sorrie thanked Jim for having the foresight to fill their canteens at the coffee shop. Jim doused his head and then asked Sorrie why she'd run away.

Sorrie took a swig from her canteen. "I don't like being controlled."

"What kind of control? Did your parents lock you in the basement or something?"

"They tried to control everything about me: my hair style, the clothes I wore, the friends I had, the schools I went to—everything from when I was a little girl."

This was something Jim couldn't wrap his thoughts around. How can someone deny another person's freedom? "I don't see how they could do that."

"They never gave me a chance to make my own decisions. They were constantly disappointed in the choices I made."

"They can't control you if you don't live there," Jim said.

"Exactly. So, one night, I packed up my things, sat on the front porch steps, and gazed into the dark, trying to get up the courage to leave." Sorrie stopped to adjust her backpack. "I was sitting there and remembered something I'd read that said to go into the future, you need to forget the past. I was getting up the courage to run, but then I got distracted by a group of kids walking down the street. They were loud, and a girl with dark hair kept taunting a small boy with them by calling him names and pushing him into the road. It gave me more strength because it was like that dark-haired girl was my parents." Sorrie began walking again. She briefly turned to Jim. "I could have been that kid; I felt like yelling at the girl, but I didn't want the noise to disturb my parents. After the group disappeared down the street, I walked into town to see about a bus ticket, but like I told you, I didn't have enough money."

"It seems to me you're free now. As long as you don't live there or need their money, they can't control you."

Sorrie looked down at the dirt. She snapped a plant reed from its roots and twisted it. "I used to try to ignore them. I'd go into my room and read books, but of course, my mom would always have a schedule of things to do, so I'd have to tear myself away from what I loved best to go to ballet lessons or learn the piano, or some such thing."

Jim was intrigued. "What kind of books?"

"Any kind. I always dreamed about going places, and books helped get me there."

Jim smiled but doubted her story; he went along anyway. Not questioning Sorrie meant heading west without the problem of money. "I guess if that's what you say. Did you leave because you were pregnant or something?"

Sorrie's eyes met Jim's. They were hard, and Jim prepared himself for the sting of a slap across his face. "No, I'm not pregnant. I told you my parents wanted to manage my whole life because they screwed up their lives, so they thought they'd get it right with me. But enough about me. I have a question for you."

"Shoot."

"Where did you come from when you found that patch of woods? Were you stalking me?"

Sorrie's comment surprised him. Jim was prepared for an avalanche of questions about the poetry book, but that's different from what he got, so he decided to tell the truth. "Don't know exactly. I had a hangover and lost my way."

"But why that patch? Did you see me sleeping there? Were you going to rape me?"

"Rape you? Lady, I never raped anyone in my life. I thought you were something else in those woods. I already told you I was feeling bad. Besides, it's against my policy to go fishing people out of whatever trouble they're in; I figure it's always better to let them stay there. At least then they won't blame me for their grief."

Sorrie relaxed her shoulders. "I'm not the type to come after anyone. I don't believe in fighting. I slept in that ditch all night, and then you came along. I got scared, especially after you grabbed me. But afterward, I saw that you didn't look healthy. When you gave me my money, and after I got to know you, I realized you knew a lot, like you've learned it from the road and could maybe help me get through."

"I learned it from the road. I didn't lie. I've been looking for my father since I was fifteen."

Sorrie tilted her head. "How old are you anyway?"

"I'm twenty-three."

"That's young."

Jim glanced into Sorrie's eyes and didn't blink. "Not for me," he said.

* * *

A few miles later, they came to more than one set of tracks, and then another, and Jim knew they were near the end. The terrain was old territory for him now; he knew the freight yard was close.

The steel rails were stacked along several pilings of ballast against a slight incline and stretched around the bend. A fine pebble mixture formed the track's foundation. It made balancing difficult, but the alternative was to slog through the soupy mud on either side of the tracks.

Jim walked along where the rails and sleepers sat; he instructed Sorrie to stay closer to the mud because he didn't want her stepping near the tracks where a train might barrel down behind her.

"Won't I hear it?" Sorrie asked.

"No," he said, "you might not hear it. In this terrain, the trees can absorb noise, so depending on how fast the engine is going, you might not hear it until it hits you. So, consider that your first lesson in learning to ride the rails."

They walked further, and Jim noticed Sorrie struggling against the clay soil. She fought to free her sneakers, but each time her legs rose, her sneakers emitted a sucking noise and threw her off balance.

While Sorrie stopped to clean the brown muck off her shoes, Jim hurried toward the freight yard, but when he noticed Sorrie wasn't with him, he stopped running and waited for her.

"You up for this?" He asked. If she couldn't run fast enough to hop a moving train, he wouldn't be able to take her, and his plans would be shot to hell.

She nodded. "I think so."

The cars in the freight yard were only half full of goods, so Jim had no trouble deciding if he could get a ride. The yard held all types of cars, from coal cars to tankers to sealed boxcars, all lined up in an organized mess. Some sat on short strings of track uncoupled and apart from the larger cars and engines, while others sat idle in covered shelters in different parts of the yard.

The freights were naked against the afternoon heat, and each car acted like a radiator in the blazing temperatures. Jim tried to take a path away from the oil smell of the engines, but he could tell Sorrie was struggling. Jim moved quicker as a coughing Sorrie ran to catch up. When he ran across a yardhand or an engineer, most of them barely glanced from their clipboards. Those who paid more than a passing eye fired off a "Get outta here, ya street bum" before Jim disappeared behind more cars and flashing signals.

He stopped to gage the darkness of a few boxcars, but after he noticed their doors were closed, he abandoned them and ran down the line. Sorrie didn't know it, but the fever of the yard with its screeching and clanking and steel wheels braying into the wind drove him—like an alcoholic in a sea of open liquor bottles.

He chased the old life as he ran between the strings of cars until his need for energy stopped. Once he did, he felt the air in one big whoosh, and at that moment, Jim had an irresistible urge to hug the whole damn freight yard.

A breathless Sorrie snapped him back to reality.

"How do you know which one to take?" She asked, panting.

"Sometimes you don't. It might depend on what track it's on or whether it has power, and sometimes, they talk to you like they know where you're headed. But sometimes you have to guess like I'm doing now." Jim turned to Sorrie. "There's one thing you learn pretty quickly in a freight yard: you can spend more time waiting for a ride than actually getting one."

He glanced at a car, then returned and surveyed Sorrie's clothes. "Going to wear those jeans?" he asked, eyeing Sorrie's ultra-tight white pants. "Your shirt looks okay, but those pants won't let you jump, so loose jeans and boots are better."

"I have nothing else," Sorrie said. "You promised we'd find a store, and I could pick out some clothes. Besides, from what I've seen, plenty of cars are in front of us. Why can't we just hop on one of these?"

Jim pointed to the cars in their immediate vicinity. "Well, if you had the hankering to go up north, I'd say hop on this one, and, if you were headed down south, then take a stab at that one, but otherwise," Jim winked, "you got to ride the train that's going your way." He peered toward another line of cars, then stopped and thought momentarily. "What to wear? Well, like I said: loose jeans, gloves, don't matter if they have fingers, a dark shirt—maybe even loose flannel—and," Jim surveyed Sorrie's sneakers, "boots—industrial if you got 'em."

"But I hate grunge," Sorrie whined.

"You need boots, not them sneaker things. You need black leather or shoes with bottoms like a rubber tire. It'll get cold and rough on a train. Your feet need to grip whatever you're climbing on, and sometimes, what you're climbing is oily and wet. You'll be able to jump better, and the thickness of the soles will keep your feet warm." Jim was restless; he wanted Sorrie to be ready to go. Jim looked past the cars along the lines, and as he did, the warm breeze blew his hair into his eyes, and he had to whisk it away to see.

"In southern heat, you're talking about leather boots keeping my feet warm? It's about ninety-nine degrees. That's why I have sneakers, and if I weren't wearing sneakers, I'd be wearing flip-flops," Sorrie glanced down at her shoes. The mud had dried, and she rubbed the sneakers against each other, trying to scrap off the clumps of dirt.

"It's hot here, but we'll be in the mountains soon, and it gets mighty cold up there." Jim could see Sorrie was sizing him up, wondering if she should have come. He looked in her direction and was about to speak when an image beyond her face caught his eye. "That's the one," Jim yelled and tore across the yard.

Sorrie ran after him, trying to keep up.

"This is the one we want," he said, "going to be going soon, too." He glanced around. There were railroad people in the yard; anyone could come by and kick them off the train, so Jim decided to wait. "Tell you what, we need to catch this baby just as it's leaving the yard, so come with me." He took Sorrie's hand and led her down a slight embankment near where the tracks thinned out. He used the extra time to explain how she should throw her gear in first, then grab onto the edge and roll her legs and hips onto the floor. In this way, she'd be able to use the momentum of her body to hoist herself up.

Jim heard a short whistle and told Sorrie to wait until the train began its run out of the yard. The engine pulled a string of coal cars and closed hoppers past them until a series of boxcars passed. When Jim saw the first open boxcar, he grabbed the edge and hoisted himself in. The train went slowly, so Jim got a good grip and rolled onto the train.

Sorrie ran beside as the train picked up speed. She grabbed for the door but had trouble holding on. As the train went faster, Sorrie sped up, breathing heavier and heavier.

"Grab on!" Jim yelled as a second whistle sounded. He motioned for the door and reached for Sorrie's hand to place it where he pointed.

Quickening her pace, Sorrie gasped for air and mouthed, "Help me" as she flailed her arm and tried to grab the side of the car.

"Grab the frame and hold on. Swing your leg up," Jim yelled. "And get rid of that damn knapsack. Throw it onto the train *now*."

But Sorrie didn't do as instructed. Instead, she tried to clutch anything she could hold on to and pull herself up. When she couldn't get her footing or swing her body, Jim demonstrated with his arms, but he was afraid of leaning too far out, fearing he might roll head-first down the steep incline next to the tracks. She threw her leg up, and Jim grabbed her heel and tried to latch it to the lip of the floor railing. Instead, Sorrie gripped the door edges and strained to hook her legs but kept missing. As the train gained speed, she began to slip off the side.

"I don't think you're ready. Go home," Jim yelled above the noise of the engine. It was against his judgment to take her now, money or no money, seeing how uncoordinated she was. Hell, she might get them both killed.

The more Jim yelled, the more he noticed how her whitened knuckles gripped the car's edge. The train's momentum slowed before it jerked back up to speed, which allowed Sorrie to firm up her grip.

"I have nowhere else to go!" She shouted, her voice increasingly desperate.

The train bucked harder, and Jim realized Sorrie might tumble down the embankment or get swept into the wash of passing freight. Jim thought she could get killed out there and was annoyed with her clumsiness. And then, doing something he promised himself he would never do—rescue a stray—Jim angled himself and grabbed under her arms to hoist her into the boxcar.

As he lifted her, the train slowed, then jerked again, and Sorrie lurched back. Jim reached out and held onto the thin fabric of her T-shirt, then pulled her up and away from the opening. The familiar sound of a steel floor being shaken echoed in the space as Sorrie's body hit the metal. She landed on a stack of crates in the corner. The interior stunk like wet paper, and the floor was covered in slime, but Sorrie was safe and with Jim.

He released his grip. "That was really stupid," he said. "You could have gotten yourself killed—and probably me, too. You don't know anything about catching out."

"That was really stupid?" Sorrie yelled as she pushed Jim back. "You could have killed me jerking my neck like that."

"Listen, you," Jim grabbed Sorrie's arm. "I was trying to save you. One more second, and you would've gone flying into a signal post, or didn't you realize that?" He released her, folded his legs up into his chest, and glanced out the opening. He eyed Sorrie to see if she was okay, then reminded himself that he was only in it for the money and the book.

"It was my first time," Sorrie reminded him, "I'll get better, I promise. I know you were trying to help." She struggled to make herself comfortable as she leaned against the boxcar wall. Her white pants were now covered in black grime. She tried to brush the dirt away and, in doing so, muddied her hands, which she wiped across the dirty pants.

Noticing her clumsiness, Jim found a piece of cardboard and told her to put it under her.

"Tell me," Jim asked, "What'd you mean when you said you had nowhere to go?"

"I just wanted you to take me. Besides, I told you that my uncle in Nebraska will care for me. He knows what my parents are like."

"It doesn't make sense. Are you risking your life to get to Nebraska over a bunch of parents telling you what to do? A little more time and you'd be off to college."

"They already picked a school even after I told them I didn't want to go there. They called the dean of students and asked if they could do anything to increase my chances of getting in." Sorrie stopped and looked directly at Jim. Why are you so interested in my life, anyway? All you're interested in is the money, right?" Sorrie adjusted her knapsack to lean against it.

Jim extracted a green poncho from his bag and sat on it. "You're right. I don't care, but if we travel together, it would be nice to know what type of person I'm traveling with."

Sorrie shrugged and picked at her fingernails. "I won't be able to go to their school now if I'm going to Nebraska."

"Maybe if you show that you can do it by yourself, they'll give you more credit and leave you alone," Jim said.

Sorrie stared at him, her blue eyes glistening in the darkness of the car. "You don't know my parents. They'll send someone after me to bring me home. They'll track me down to the ends of the earth. Both of them are ruthless. If an employee in their company tells them they found another job and my parents know where it is, they'll call the owner and say what a terrible employee the person was. They're monsters."

"Is this something I have to worry about?" Jim asked, but Sorrie didn't answer. Jim leaned back and questioned whether he'd get into trouble taking her to Nebraska. Still, another thought crossed his mind: maybe her wealthy parents would offer a reward, and he could cash in on it. Jim could only wonder.

He watched the light dance off her cheeks as he gazed at her from a distance. She wasn't what he would call pretty, but there was an aura of sophistication about her that most girls he knew didn't have.

Jim put aside his thoughts of money. "Say listen," he said, "what about the book you promised to read?" Jim fished it out and handed it to her.

She examined the light. "I don't think I can read it here. It's too dark."

Jim motioned for her to move closer to the open boxcar door.

Sorrie hesitated. "Before I come over there, I want to know how you'll keep the door from sliding on top of me. Jim searched for a railroad spike and pinned it into the boxcar opening with a nearby brick. "Why did you do that?"

Jim smiled. "To keep the door from closing. Don't worry. It's safe."

"You're not going to push me out, are you?"

"I want you to explain the poetry in the book, so why would I push you out?"

"Just asking."

Jim suddenly had an idea. "Let's do this. You can point out the words as you read to me, and I can learn to read better." Jim looked down at the cover to avoid Sorrie's gaze. He desperately wanted to know the same things his father knew.

"I can do that," Sorrie said. She turned to the first page and cracked the binder. She looked at the title and, using her index finger, traced out the words as she began, then paused. "Who is this guy on the cover, by the way? Is he the author?"

"That's my father."

"Your father wrote this book of poetry?"

"Yeah, he's a poet and an artist. He's also a rock star. Haven't you ever heard of Jim Morrison?"

Sorrie went back to looking at the cover of the book. "I don't know who that is."

Jim wondered if she was looking at the same cover he was. "He's one of the greatest rockers of all time. How does a smart girl like you not know that?"

Sorrie shrugged. "I don't watch television or listen to music. Maybe I saw his picture once in an old *Life* magazine, but I don't remember."

"It doesn't matter. It only matters to me." Jim rested his elbow on his knapsack and watched Sorrie move her fingers across the letters. He silently mouthed the sounds she spoke and tried memorizing the passages.

As he heard the verses spill out into the air, the smell of cardboard and humidity melted away, and Jim saw a vision of his father smiling at him. Jim smiled back. He felt the wispiness of Sorrie's breath on his cheek. There were poems about the city and sex and death. She spoke deliberately, often repeating whole pages because some of the verses were so brief, with so few words that she couldn't catch the meaning immediately. Jim smiled. He was enjoying the way the poetry flowed when Sorrie suddenly stopped.

"I don't get it," she said.

"Get what?" Jim was alarmed that her tone had changed.

"They're just words. They have no connected meaning. The thoughts aren't strung together in any logic, and besides, it's just about madness and killing and death."

Jim sat up and had a queasy feeling in his stomach; he might have made a mistake taking her. "You're the big expert. You're supposed to know stuff like this. That's why I brought you along—so you could pronounce the big words and help me understand what the poetry was trying to say."

"I never said I was an expert at this. I studied all types of poetry in school, but never poems without meaning."

"Maybe you're not thinking hard enough." Jim envisioned the back of a man walking away, and frustration set in. "Maybe you're not as smart as you make yourself out to be."

Sorrie gazed into Jim's eyes, and Jim could see she was annoyed. "Listen, I don't question why you want me to read these poems or this book, so don't question how smart I am."

Jim lowered his head. "Sorry."

"What I mean is that I don't know what this poem about Oswald is about. He goes from a taxi to a rooming house, and then it talks about killing, then movie houses. It doesn't make any sense." Sorrie re-read the poem. Her eyes lit up. "No, wait. As I remember from school, Oswald— the man who killed President Kennedy—was arrested in a movie theatre. But it could also have a secret meaning. Maybe it's like those desperation poems where he's just a tragic figure, like the poems T.S. Eliot wrote, like nihilistic poems."

"Nihilistic? What's that?" Jim asked.

"As if life has no meaning. People are just living, and even living has no meaning. There's nothing to hold onto. In this poem, not only is Oswald the victim, but so are the President and the officer. Oswald runs into a movie house, which symbolizes seeing his life on film as if it could only exist there." Sorrie examined the pages and shook her head. "I get it now. I just had to open my eyes and see it."

"It makes sense, doesn't it?" Jim felt vindicated. "It's the words my father loved, and I want to hear more." Jim gently lifted the book from Sorrie's lap and placed it back into her hands. She continued reading.

It didn't matter if Sorrie realized the meaning of the words. Jim understood them. There was confusion. Jim's father sang about it, and Young Jim lived it daily between the freight yards, flophouses, and weekly drunken sprees. Good moments meant food and beer and cigarettes and a smooth ride. Bad moments meant snarling dogs and bulls and getting tossed off a train head-first into a pile of weeds. Jim was enjoying one of the good moments.

He listened to the poems and watched Sorrie's hands glide across the page. She stopped every so often to explain the passages. Every phrase was a window: the summer, sleep, even the air outside. Sorrie stopped at times to allow Jim to mouth the syllables. She read about fear and attraction, dreams and emotions, and with each passing poem, Jim's confidence in the words grew. He was getting to know his father through the poetry in the book. Even though Jim felt inferior in the light of Sorrie's intelligence, he relaxed, knowing that once he could read and have a pot of money, her part in his life would be over.

3

Virginia into Coal Country

SORRIE READ FOR half an hour, often returning to passages because Jim said he didn't understand the meaning of the words. One of the poems, "We all live in the city," made Jim sit up because it mentioned bars and pawnshops. Sorrie recited a passage about prostitution and people with diseases, and Jim shook his head and stared at the floor.

"God, what my father must have lived through having the genius to write a poem like that. He knew. He knew."

Sorrie stopped reading. "Why are you sad all of a sudden?" She asked.

"I'm not sad. I'm never sad. My father knew what it was like for the people stuck on skid row."

"I don't understand why they're stuck. Why do they live in a tent on the street when they can return to their families?"

"You, of all people, should know the answer to that question. Didn't you tell me you weren't going back to your folks? Same with the people on the street. My father saw it in his mind's eye: the street's their family, but they got to do stuff they would never have considered doing to buy drugs or food. They need the drugs to numb them to keep hanging onto that life."

Sorrie closed the book and searched for the words until she said, "What are they hanging onto?"

Jim lifted his head and lit a cigarette. "They survive, and they got to do stuff a man like me doesn't like to talk about."

"It's okay, I can take it," Sorrie said. Jim smirked but said nothing. Sorrie continued to press. "Did you ever do what they do?"

Jim leaned back against the wall. "I don't need to. I have a purpose, and I stick to it. I travel to find my father, and I bed at my mom's place when I'm not on the road. If I have to spend the night in a city, I just hide behind a dumpster in an alley and watch what goes down in the street." Jim looked up and pointed to Sorrie. "And I keep myself clean—not like those wankers who don't care about how they smell and never bother to scrub themselves. A road bum can get dirty quickly by climbing trains and sleeping in ditches. I keep myself clean because I got a mission, but they got nothing, so be glad I decided to take you because that's what you'd be up against without me."

Sorrie put the book aside. "You took me for the money. That's like being my worker, and I'm your boss."

Jim smiled. "You think you own me? Stand in line, princess, because you've got a lot to learn about me."

* * *

They were up to a poem that had no name but talked about someone blinded by the sun who plucks their eyes out. Sorrie mentioned the Greek tragedy *Oedipus*, and she asked Jim if he knew the legend. He didn't, so she explained the story of the boy born to his parents, who gave him away.

"When he was grown, he unknowingly killed his father and married his mother, then gouged out his eyes once he learned the truth," she explained.

"Serves him right for killing his father," Jim said.

Sorrie closed the book and looked Jim straight in the eyes. "It's about being blinded by the truth. The same way the poem talks about eyes burning and the compulsion to pull them out."

"I don't understand all you just explained about the kid who plucks out his eyes."

"Just imagine if the family you grew up with wasn't real."

Jim laughed. "That foster family I had was out there, for sure, and when I was with Momma, it wasn't much better. Of course, by then, my father was on the road someplace, but Momma made amends by propping his picture on a chair at dinnertime, and we'd just stare at him with nothing to say."

"How many do you have in your family?"

"I got a brother and a sister," Jim said, "and Momma, of course."

"Are they all Jim Morrison's kids?"

Jim paused, then fidgeted with the cellophane on a pack of cigarettes. "My brother and sister got the same dad back in Montana," Jim extracted a lighter from his pocket. "Listen, can we get off this? I'd be much obliged if you'd read more poems."

"Clear something up first. You said you had a foster family. When did that happen?"

"I was nine when I was put into foster care in Florida, but I'd rather not talk about it if it were all the same to you. Besides, your Greek story doesn't outshine my father's writing. My dad's poems are better if you ask me."

"*Oedipus* is a classic."

"And Jim Morrison's poems aren't?"

"But wasn't he a rock star? Why didn't your mom go after the money he earned?"

"Because she had nothing to show except a lot of personal stuff. They never lived together or anything. They just hung out at his concerts, and she told me they got married once, but she doesn't have a certificate to prove it."

"It seems to me that your Momma is pretty short on evidence."

Jim's mood shifted from contentment to annoyance, and a sour taste coated his mouth. "It's not up to you to judge, and while we're at it, it's none of your concern. I know he's out there, and I'll find him."

"I wouldn't have any idea where to find someone who doesn't want to be found, and it would be something if you discover he's not your father."

"Of course, he's my father, and I know he's out there. It doesn't matter if the world doesn't know because I know," Jim motioned to his chest. "He's my dad in here, and I aim to find him. That's why I visit honky-tonks and dive bars. When I bed in the woods, I also look for him there. But right now, I'm traveling to Montana because my mom's dying. My dad left a big trunk of stuff; I know my brother will burn it if I don't get to it first. I was headed there when I met you, but we got to move fast."

"I hope to be there when you find him."

Jim responded by asking Sorrie to read more poems. Her comments bothered him, but in his mind, Jim asked himself if she was right. *What if Jim Morrison wasn't his father and his mother wasn't his mother?* Could that explain why he was sent to live with a family in Florida? Could they be his birth parents?

No. What's real is real, Jim folded his arms. The truth was what you felt in your gut.

But what did Sorrie say? "All you know is what your parents told you."

Jim scoffed at the notion. *Of course, Jim Morrison is my father. There was an inscription in the book. There could be no other way for it.*

* * *

The hours ticked by, and Richmond was a memory as the train roared into the far country toward West Virginia. The sky grew dark, and Jim showed Sorrie how to make a quick meal by combining water with a powdered breakfast mix in a clear plastic bag. They dined on the shake and a few candy bars Sorrie had in her knapsack.

The train labored up a mountain, gently rocking against the rail bed. It snaked higher into the belly of coal country, and Jim could sense the air getting thinner and the temperature dropping. He and Sorrie changed into warmer clothes and covered themselves with their sleeping bags as they leaned against the boxcar wall. Jim was used to the sudden shift in altitude and temperature, but Sorrie was shivering, and it reminded Jim that she didn't know the first thing about street life.

He turned it over in his head. Sorrie knew books, while Jim was laughed at for how he stumbled over words when asked to read. Sorrie could read plenty and talked like she knew stuff. Jim never spoke to anyone unless it was about his father's music, and he got used to keeping his head down and staring at the speckled floor tiles as he walked through the school. He never looked anyone in the eyes, least of all his classmates.

Jim felt at home under his sleeping bag, but Sorrie was fussy. She whined that Jim ate all her candy bars and complained about the grittiness of the powder and how the water it was mixed with was musty and gave her a stomachache. "You'll learn to like it after a few days without," Jim said.

"I'd rather eat a piece of moldy bread," Sorrie answered.

"No, you wouldn't," Jim shot back. "You'd be sick to your stomach in the corner, and then I'd have to gag on that awful puke smell running up my nose."

Sorrie buried her head in her knapsack. It was late, and the cool air turned thinner. Both could make out their breath in the darkness of the car. Sorrie tried to keep her fingers warm by moving them around in her coat pockets but finally emerged from her sleeping gear and took out the gloves Jim said were inadequate. She placed her hands inside and stretched the fabric to create air pockets.

Seeing her struggle, Jim said, "That weave lets the cold air in. Also, that's the wrong type of gloves for the mountains." Jim shook his head. "Try bundling up in your sleeping gear and putting your hands between your legs or under your arms to warm them up. You can always put them between my legs, but I don't think you want to."

"Sitting close to you is as far as I go. By the way, when do we get off?" She asked.

"I'll let you know." Jim peered out into the darkness. He wanted to get as far west as possible, but he could see the thin air and cold were affecting Sorrie more than she admitted.

"I'm hungry and have to go to the bathroom," she said, bouncing on her heels.

"We don't even know where we are," he protested.

"But I have to go," she said, "It's *urgent*."

Jim waved his hand. "I don't have any newspaper to cover up the poop, but you can just go over there in the corner on the cardboard and then throw it outside. I promise I won't peek."

"I'd rather die," Sorrie murmured. "It's going to be bad."

Jim got irritated. "Listen, this is the life you signed up for. You got to get tough and suck it up. We got to get west, so go over there in the corner."

Sorrie let out a sign of desperation. "You don't understand. It's going to be awful. I've never done anything like this. I know you know this route because you said you traveled everywhere. Can we stop? Since you're the guide I hired, you need to do what I say."

"I do things when I'm good and ready," Jim said. He looked over at Sorrie, who was shaking. He sighed. "Okay, the first slow pass, and we'll jump." Jim wasn't going to give Sorrie the satisfaction of winning, but she was right. He'd been traveling these routes for years and knew that anywhere along the way, there'd be small villages and an angel or two willing to help out. But Jim was anxious to be on his way, and any miscalculation would mean slugging through the mountains on foot. He needed Sorrie to read the book, but he doubted whether she could continue with him on the road.

A few minutes later, the train jerked, spit out a puff of smoke, and settled into a sluggish gait. They assembled their gear, and Jim escorted Sorrie to the door. "Jump," he said.

She turned back to look at him. "I hope you'll jump right after me and not leave me there."

"Don't worry. I'll be right behind." A few seconds later, they sailed together out of the boxcar, down an embankment, and straight into the middle of nowhere.

After finding a patch of trees and surrounding brush, Sorrie got her wish to relieve herself while Jim stood away. Once she signaled she was done, he made it clear they'd have to spend the night in the woods, so both hunkered down until morning.

The sun woke them, but so did an army of ants crawling on Jim and Sorrie's sleeping bags. While Jim brushed them away, Sorrie stood and shimmied, which made Jim laugh and Sorrie turn red.

After gathering their belongings, they traveled along the mountainous alleyways of slag and dirt until they reached a small building at the corner of a road near a railroad crossing. There were no street signs, just a dilapidated, whitewashed store in an area that smelled like coal.

As Jim glanced around, he noticed none of the houses that dotted the landscape were white. Instead, everything had a dim gray from the years of settled dust, as if every paint chip had escaped into the wind and left a shadow.

The few people who sat on their porches in the early hour had the same pall as the houses. Their bodies sloped downward as if they were sinking into the earth from the weight of the tiny coal crystals that settled on their skin.

"I hope you know what you got us into." Jim turned to the store and peered into the window.

"What do you mean by that?" Sorrie asked.

"Sometimes, if you get off too soon, you might have to wait days for the right train to take you out. There's also a risk that the cars going through these parts are closed hoppers or coal cars—meaning they can't carry anyone—least of all two bindle stiffs like us."

Sorrie frowned. "What's a bindle stiff?"

"A tramp, you know, a hobo. Someone who carries their own bed."

"I never considered myself a hobo."

"You don't want to be a hobo, so go home," Jim said, and just as he said it, the elderly owner of the store walked up carrying a silver object in his hands.

"You folks aren't familiar," he said as his shaky hand inserted the key into the lock.

"Just passing through," Jim offered. He knew when to say enough to let the person he was talking to know he wasn't there to cause trouble. "Just here to buy food and be on our way."

"Hope so," the old man said as he led them into the store and switched on the light. "Not much here. Just some boxed stuff and pop. I sell papers mostly and lottery tickets, but walk around if you'd like."

Jim sensed the old man's eyes following them in the store, so he told Sorrie not to look around too much. Sorrie bought crackers and soap, and both asked to use the bathroom. The owner was cordial but not friendly and questioned where they had come from and where they were headed.

"To Nebraska; we're hopping freight," Jim said.

The store owner began fidgeting with a jar of candy sticks on the countertop. "There isn't much passing through. My best advice is that you and your friend keep walking west and not stop in any towns until you're clear of the mountains."

"That's a hell of a long hump," Jim said.

The owner continued arranging the candy sticks and then shook a bin of root beer barrels to loosen them from sticking to each other. Jim picked up the aroma of licorice as the owner flipped the candies from side to side. "You won't find any friendly faces in this place; we kind of like to keep to our own, if you know what I mean."

Jim took this as a warning not to come back, so as soon as Sorrie returned from the bathroom, they paid for their groceries and left. Jim noticed that the old man never took his eyes off them.

Sorrie turned to wave goodbye, but Jim whispered, "Just keep walking."

"I don't see anybody," Sorrie said.

"Just keep walking. We're being watched. We need to get out of here as soon as possible." Jim glanced at the nearby houses, where he saw the corners of window shades curled upward to reveal suspicious eyes the size of headlights peering from behind the glass. He began to quicken his pace.

"Why are we running all of a sudden?" A clueless Sorrie asked.

"We're not running," Jim corrected her. "I'm worried some locals might get suspicious and call the police." And no sooner had Jim said it than a white police car stopped in front of them, and an officer got out.

"What's going on guys?" The officer asked.

Jim stopped walking and held his arm out to block Sorrie from moving ahead. "Nothing, officer. We were just on the way out of town."

"How long have you been here? We did have a break-in down on Market Street a few days ago. Know anything about that?"

Sorrie moved past Jim. "Look, we're just passing through," she said. "We arrived early this morning and needed to stop for supplies."

"How'd you even find this place? I don't see a car." The officer glanced down the street and then turned his attention back to Jim.

"We've been walking," Jim said, then Sorrie interrupted.

"We hopped freight and got off a mile from here."

The officer smirked and put his hands on his hips. "Now, you're not telling me you broke the law, right? Because I can't condone that and might have to inform the freight companies to be on the lookout for you two."

Jim jumped in. "She's not saying that, officer. We were passing through but needed to stop and buy supplies." Jim looked for a name tag on the officer's shirt to address him more formally, but he could only see a badge with numbers.

"Do you two have any identification on you?"

Jim pulled his wallet from his pocket and produced a fake Florida driver's license with a made-up name. Sorrie pulled a student card from her knapsack. The police officer studied the two documents and handed them back. "Well, Mr. Jake and Miss Sorrie, is that how I pronounce your first name?" Sorrie nodded. "I'll be asking you to pass on through and not to stop. We got some old people in these houses who don't take kindly to bums and hobos. You get my meaning?"

Jim adjusted his knapsack. "We'll be leaving directly," Jim said. "We weren't aiming to bother anyone."

The policeman headed back to his car but hesitated. He turned to Jim. "You sure you didn't have anything to do with that break-in on Market Street?"

Jim opened his wallet and put his fake license back into a slot. "I don't know anything about that. I can't even tell you what got broken into or where Market Street is."

The officer opened his car door. "That's the old man's place where you bought your supplies. He was the one who called me." Jim shook his head and watched as the officer returned to his car and drove off. Right after he did, Jim looked at Sorrie.

"You need to learn to keep your head down and say only three things: 'hello,' 'goodbye,' and 'thank you' if you want some advice from the man you're paying to keep you alive."

"What did I do?"

"Never talk to cops or give them information. Pretend you're a stone, and let me do the talking," Jim said.

"I have a voice, and I'm going to use it."

"Don't try using it where we can get into trouble. It's my ass just as much as it is yours." Jim moved away from Sorrie, and as he did, he noticed something in the distance: a man was sitting in a rocking chair on the porch of a house. Jim wondered why he hadn't seen the man before. He squinted and watched the man rock back and forth in his chair. The man struck a match, held it up to a cigarette in his mouth, lit it, and then blew out the flame from a corner of his mouth. His features looked vaguely familiar in the firelight, and Jim wondered if he'd ever seen him in his travels. He was tempted to walk over and introduce himself but decided against it. He could hear an imaginary watch ticking and knew it was time to leave.

They walked a few miles and found a farmer selling home-churned peanut butter and snacked on the spread and the box of crackers Sorrie bought from the store. By midday, they rested inside a covered wooden bridge with pink and white graffiti on the walls. Above the sound of flowing water, Sorrie asked for Jim's book of poetry and read more poems.

"You read a lot?" Jim asked.

"I'm a regular bookworm. I crawl in and out of books and stories," Sorrie said. "I love words."

"You have lots of friends in school being so smart and rich?"

"No. I was a loner, and I wasn't one of the popular kids. I never gossiped like everyone else. The kids treated me like I didn't exist, but one day, I decided to start smiling as I walked down the halls. I just smiled at everyone. They next day, I overheard a conversation from two classmates talking about how nice they thought I was even though I didn't know them. They didn't realize I was faking it; it was like a voice inside my head saying, 'smile, smile.'"

"Yeah, I'm always listening to voices in my head too." Jim scanned the inside of the bridge. He'd heard about this bridge in his travels but could never find it until now. The rays of sun coming through the gaps in the wall's slats exposed the dust floating in the air. It wasn't as fancy as some of the other bridges he was used to bedding down in. Still, it was comfortable, and Jim made a mental note to remember its location if he was in these parts and needed shelter from the rain. He barely heard Sorrie's sentence.

"I guess you're just thinking about things. Figuring stuff out."

Jim straightened up. Maybe he and Sorrie weren't that far apart. "Figuring stuff out, yeah—but for all the wrong reasons. I didn't speak to any of those classroom lugs in school because I'd get in trouble for saying something. That's how I learned when to shut up."

Sorrie fanned the pages of the book. Jim felt the breeze on his cheek. "I did the same." She said. "It wasn't easy having money. Everyone expected you to go to the most expensive schools or give money to the latest happening, and when you didn't, they'd ridicule you."

"I don't know what that word means—ridicule."

"You know, make fun of you. Anyway, I told you I enjoy reading, especially coffee table books."

Jim lit a cigarette. "What's a coffee table book? A book made out of a table?"

Sorrie didn't look amused. "It's a book with a lot of pictures you put on a coffee table," she said.

Jim dragged on his cigarette. He exhaled, and as he did, he popped his mouth to form opaque Os that drifted off and melted away. "We never had coffee tables, just a side table where Momma put her glass of beer. We never had books either, even in the foster home. They didn't read books, just scandal magazines from the store and *T.V. Guide.* So, I never learned to read too well, but I remember songs. I have all my father's lyrics right here in my head." Jim tapped his temple.

"Tell me about some of the words."

"You know that story you told about the guy who plucked his eyes out? It reminds me of the lyrics from one of my father's songs." Jim cleared his throat and sang a song about a child who didn't belong to his father or mother. "That's like what you said about perception and accepting what people tell you."

"I guess it's what you see and how it affects you," Sorrie said.

"In one, my father talks about not being your parent's child. Then you read poems about the bad things in life, like his songs. They deal with darkness and danger."

"Well, the symbol of darkness reminds me of Plato's *Allegory of the Cave,* where prisoners are chained to a wall, and there's a fire to the back of them, and they can't turn around to see reality. Only the wall. When people pass behind, all they see are the shadows, not what's real, so if they see a figure on the wall, they're not seeing the person but the shadow."

"Exactly!" Jim said. "Like my father's poetry talks about shadows. It's like we only see what we want to see. Kind of like making up a world that doesn't exist."

"So, with your dad, I wonder if it's your true life or something your mom told you? And I don't understand why you keep traveling to find him even though he's dead."

Rather than get angry, Jim asked, "How do you know he's dead? Did you see his body or something? Only one or two people saw his body, and they could have lied. He was buried before anyone even knew he was dead, so how do you know?"

Sorrie dug her fingers into the edge of her shirt. "Someone was there, right? They were witnesses."

"Look at the facts: my father was being hounded by the cops, the drug dealers, the news people; everyone wanted a piece of him. What better way to leave all that than by faking your death? It makes perfect sense. He's out there, and I aim to find him." Jim closed his eyes. The image of the man on the porch came back to him. He wondered . . .

4

The Town in the Woods

Following the train tracks that ran parallel to the water, they got lucky with a hop on a piggyback and were headed west. Along the way, Sorrie reminded Jim that he promised to stop somewhere for clothes. Even if he was hell-bent on not taking her all the way, he wanted to ensure she had what she needed for the road.

The next hop took all night but got them to a larger town where the size of the buildings told Jim there was something worth discovering. Sure enough, not too long after they exited the train, they stumbled onto a secondhand clothing store tucked into the side of a building a mile from the yard and a stone's throw from a cozy patch of woods where a fella might get an afternoon nap if the mosquitoes didn't keep him up.

The store was covered with peeling handbills and faded blue lettering spelling "smoke shop" and "tailoring." However, there were no businesses like that in the building. Jim mouthed the words, pronouncing the sounds of the letters until he was satisfied he was reading them correctly.

While Sorrie poked around inside, Jim remained outdoors. He wanted to check their bearings and catch a smoke. He kept tabs on her by occasionally glancing through the streaked glass window and watching her flip through the clothing racks. She pulled some black shirts and pants from the wire hangers and showed them to a middle-aged woman. The woman wore red lipstick and had a lit cigarette dangling from her mouth. Sorrie and the woman spoke, and Sorrie put a few pieces back on the rack. She found more choices and looked up as Jim followed her movements; when she noticed him staring, she lifted the clothes to show him, but he put his head down. Women's clothes were a woman's concern, and he wasn't familiar with styling, sizes, or what might look good. He was used to seeing girls wear stuff to keep them warm on the road.

The woman directed Sorrie to a closet-sized dressing room. Turning away, Jim glanced down the street. The short hops made him hungry. The chances of finding a place to dumpster dive without being noticed were slim to none. Jim scanned the few stores in the distance. His eyes weren't used to direct sunlight, and he had to hide his head in his chest and squint to focus.

The town center seemed like any other small village with red and white brick buildings and American flags, but Jim spotted a supermarket sign and a row of carts. He flicked his cigarette into the road. If it weren't for this girl, Chicago would have been in his sights by now; saying good-bye here might be a good option. Then Jim realized he couldn't do it the same way he couldn't pass up a quarter embedded in the asphalt on a hot summer day. No matter how much he had in his pocket, Jim stopped and pried the coin loose with his finger. Once it was safely in his hand, he felt like the wealthiest man in the world. Scoring Sorrie to read the book and provide cash was like that coin.

Jim glanced through the glass and saw Sorrie paying for her used clothing. He watched her take a crisp five-dollar bill from her red purse and wondered how much she had left. Everything was adding up fast.

Sorrie exited the store wearing a dark T-shirt and loose denim pants. "I got this T-shirt and pants and some other stuff. It cost me twelve dollars."

Jim laughed. Even though her hips were ample, the pants were too big, and the shirt said "Atlas Tire Iron" on the front.

"What's so funny?" Sorrie asked.

"You think the pants could have gotten any bigger?" He spun her around, grabbed a handful of material covering her thigh, and wiggled it. "They could've fit another leg in there."

"Well, you told me to buy something loose," she protested. "The store didn't have girl pants in my size, so I had to pick from the men's rack. Besides, the side and back pockets will be good if I need to hide stuff."

Jim hadn't thought about that. He looked down at her feet. "You still have those dirty sneakers? I told you to get some boots."

"The boots are in the bag." Sorrie held up a brown paper bag and seemed quite pleased with herself. Jim, however, wasn't impressed and started walking toward the supermarket. Sorrie shuffled alongside him. "Any reason to walk this way?" She asked.

"Food," Jim said. "And we need to get it pretty quick. It's better not to linger—especially since it's almost noon—and I don't know when we'll catch a ride out. So, we have to look for any opportunity. Local folks have a way of noticing strangers."

Sorrie squinted as she looked at the sky. "The lady in the store told me tomorrow's going to rain and to watch where we were hiking because flooding is all over the Midwest." Jim had yet to hear about the weather and made a mental note to remember the flooding; they might have to change their route, and any chance of him getting Sorrie to Nebraska through the middle of the country might need to be reconsidered.

As they entered the supermarket through the sliding glass doors, shoppers eyed them with curiosity, then suspicion. Obvious to Jim but oblivious to Sorrie, the locals instinctively knew strangers, and to prove it, the conversation got low, and the stares got hard. There was a momentary glitch as if Jim and Sorrie were enveloped in thickened gelatin while nothing else moved. They stepped into the produce aisle and time-shifted back, returning everyone to their business.

"So, how strong are you?" Jim asked.

Sorrie looked perplexed. "I don't know. I don't lift weights if that's what you mean. Why do you ask?"

Rephrasing, Jim said, "I mean, how much money have you got left?"

"Let me ask you a question. How much money have you got left?" Sorrie said.

"You first," Jim countered.

"Not much after the shopping trip, maybe a few bucks. And you?"

"Well, I guess that makes you the prizewinner because I got nothing, so it looks like you're buying," Jim turned right and walked into the canned goods aisle. Despite his irritation, he was beginning to like this girl. She had spunk and a wiry smile, and her smile was genuine, unlike the grins he'd seen on the road. Maybe he had misjudged her, and she was a friend in disguise. But then another voice inside him said: *Give her time; she's not jaded yet. They all become poisoned. Give it a while*, and Jim knew this voice spoke from experience.

Heading toward the canned goods, Jim picked up a container of fruit. Sorrie followed behind; he picked up another, then another. Jim juggled them before depositing the cans in a vacant space on a shelf in the aisle. He walked a little farther, grabbed a package of bologna, and then went to where the bread was stacked.

Bewildered, Sorrie asked, "What about me? Don't I get to choose something?"

"Go ahead. You got the whole store. Just do it," Jim answered.

"That's okay. I'll stay with you," Sorrie said as Jim picked out a small loaf of bread. "Is this dinner?"

"What do you think?" Jim turned his back on Sorrie and walked down the dairy aisle. Finding a green hand-held basket abandoned on the floor near the eggs, he put the groceries in it and added a quart of chocolate milk. Toward the end, he grabbed a box of donuts, then turned to Sorrie and said, "I hope you got enough money for this." Hastily, Sorrie grabbed a container of peach yogurt and quickened her pace to catch up.

The clerk at the cash register didn't know what to make of the odd couple standing in front of her: Jim, with his dark clothing and skinny frame, and Sorrie, with a brown paper bag and a black T-shirt. Jim took the food out of the basket, and just as the cashier rang up the last item, Sorrie placed her yogurt on the belt.

When it came time to pay, Jim looked at Sorrie as she pulled some money from the pink purse and gave it to the cashier.

"You're seventy-five cents short," the cashier said.

Sorrie searched her pockets for change and, finding none, leaned over and whispered, "That's all I have. We're traveling freight, and I have no more until Nebraska. You can take my yogurt off, but I'm starving."

The cashier stared at Sorrie. "If you think I believe that one sister, you might as well try selling me a bridge. Now, do I have to call the manager?"

Sorrie searched her pockets and then felt inside the zippered compartments of her knapsack. She found a quarter and threw it on the belt. Her eyes filled with tears. "That's as much as I have. I was kicked out of my house because my mom's crazy, and I spent all my money on food. I can send you the rest when I get to my uncle's house, but I'm clear out of money, and so is my traveling friend. I didn't realize how much the food would be."

The woman grabbed the quarter and put it into a change slot in the cash register. She didn't look up. "Go on," she said. Jim threw everything into a plastic bag and hurried out. No one stopped them as they left.

The town square wasn't an ideal place to eat because it was out in the open, but Jim was so hungry that as soon as they sat down at a red picnic table, he tore into the bread and bologna, alternately eating and swallowing with the help of some gulps of chocolate milk. He offered food to Sorrie; she took bread and a few slices of meat and delicately arranged a sandwich. "You're so damn neat," Jim said.

Sorrie didn't look up. "That's the way I was raised."

"Well, I wasn't raised that way," Jim savaged the corner of his sandwich. When he was done eating, he pulled out his railroad atlas to find a route around the flooding, reasoning that they might have to stop at some camps and get an idea of how bad it was around Nebraska.

Curious, Sorrie asked, "What are you looking at?"

"It's a railroad atlas charting all the train lines. I need to find a route around the Midwest flooding. Some years, I have to go a thousand miles out of my way to avoid weather disasters: floods, tornadoes, hurricanes. I hope it's not the case this time, especially since it's late in the season."

"I hope you can get me there soon. I have to find out what my parents are up to and if they're coming after me." Sorrie's voice trailed off. She decided to change the subject. "You're neat too. You used your napkin in that coffee shop and folded it. You must have learned manners somewhere."

Surprised that Sorrie had remembered this gesture, Jim said, "I guess I got some learning from somewhere, but that's a lot of brain time worrying about me being a gentleman when you should be thinking about Nebraska." Jim closed his book, reached for a donut, took a bite, and asked, "Was that all the money you had?"

Sorrie looked Jim in the eye. "I have a twenty-dollar bill, but I didn't want to break it."

"I can't say I approve," Jim said, "but there's nothing like stealing from the poor and giving to the poorer."

"Kind of like the Artful Dodger in *Oliver Twist*. Sorrie finished her sandwich and ate her yogurt.

"The artful what?" Jim asked.

"The Artful Dodger. He's a character in the story. He's good at picking pockets and stealing from people. Eventually, he gets caught but is quite cunning, so it takes a while."

"Is that what you think you are? A person in a book?"

"We're all living in our own stories and plots. Like your story. It's quite romantic, but is it true?" Sorrie finished eating and placed her garbage in a nearby wire wastebasket.

Jim paused. "I already told you. My mom has lots of his stuff: letters, photos, even a jacket. She told me all about him because she used to go around the country and follow him everywhere he played. She has backstage passes to his concerts, and there's photos of her and Jim together."

Sorrie frowned and squinted her eyes. "How do you know she wasn't just a fan?"

"I know because she told me, and I believed her."

"Did you ever meet him?"

"I never got to meet him, and I don't think of him as a rock star, just my father. But I know him."

"But you said you never met him."

"Just because we weren't introduced doesn't mean I don't know him inside." Jim pointed to his heart. "I know his songs and thoughts, and I plan on knowing him better after we finish his book."

"But if you know his songs, why don't you know the meaning of his poems?"

"Because I'm not that smart. With my mom, I could understand what the song lyrics were saying, and I could hear them, and she could explain them to me." Jim grabbed the book of poetry from his knapsack, opened it, and thumbed through the pages. "There are lots of words here, and they're all jumbled up in my head." He pointed to the word "psychology." "I don't know this word. I don't even know how to pronounce it."

"That word's psychology. It means the study of behavior or the mind. Like how people think and how they get to reason the way they do."

"Yeah, but what does that have to do with Jim?"

"I think he's writing about his concerts where he has to understand what's happening with his audience."

Jim shut the book and shook his head. "There are lots of words like that I don't understand."

Sorrie asked Jim more questions, but Jim just let the subject drop. He didn't want to admit there were things he didn't understand about his father. So, instead, Jim began singing one of his father's songs. He ended with words describing going to another place.

"You sang that beautifully, but I'm wondering how your story's going to end," Sorrie said.

"It's a door opening between you and how you see the world. Just remember there is no past, and tomorrow never comes. We're all living between the worlds of life and death."

"Life and death? Is that what this is all about? Do you want to die? You saved me from falling backward and getting killed, and you just want to die?"

Annoyed, Jim said, "You haven't listened to what I've sung." Jim sang the lyrics to another song about someone visiting a theatre to review their life and death. "It's about the pain of life, how people see everyone in their life, and how it's all useless. No one lives a life worth experiencing anymore, and they're only aware of it through pain." Jim grabbed Sorrie's hand and started squeezing.

"That's hurting me," Sorrie said.

Jim let go. "Pain is real, and between the two of us, we got several buckets worth."

* * *

They found an open boxcar near where they'd left the freight yard. The area looked abandoned, but Jim knew where the crews loaded the cars with goods. He found a friendly maintenance hand who told Jim about a string of empty boxcars going west and invited Jim and Sorrie to climb into a car. They hopped aboard and waited for the train to pull out.

After they were safely secured, Sorrie asked, "Why'd he do that?"

"Most people who work on freights are pretty friendly, but let's just say he's a buddy of mine. I know him from other yards."

"Isn't it illegal?"

"You're sure nosy for someone who needs a guide," Jim said. "Nothing we're doing is legal. He's a friend who gives me tips sometimes. Either you help, or you don't. It's just the rules."

"I don't want to help anyone, just myself." Sorrie rested on her knapsack. The boxcar was hot, and Jim could see she was sweating. She fanned herself with a piece of cardboard.

"That might be the right way of looking at things, seeing that some people want to steal whatever you got. They'll even steal a half-eaten bar of candy if they can. So, you're right not to help. But if people go out of their way to help and you don't act in kind, then you don't belong on the road. Or you're just one of those people who helps nobody, in which case, if you're ever in trouble, don't expect anyone to come running. You're asking for a lot of favors for not being able to help."

"Well, I've been paying."

"I've been paying too," Jim said. He leaned back on his knapsack and placed his Boonie hat over his face. The sight of flooded farms raced through his mind. He needed to find out from people who knew what was underwater, and the best place to ask was in a hobo jungle. "You only got a little money left, so it looks like you're running out of things to trade."

"I'll get lucky," Sorrie said, "and I can read, remember that."

They both caught some rest until Jim woke up to find the train holed up in an unfamiliar place. He was sitting by the boxcar door looking into complete darkness when he heard Sorrie stir. She sat up to adjust her clothes and brush her hair. "I can't see where we are. It's so dark," she said, but Jim didn't hear her. He was staring into a black pit. It reminded him of the darkness in his father's lyrics. "What are you thinking about?" She asked.

"Thinking about Jim. I'm always thinking about finding him, of letting him know I'll be there for him. I think about him whenever I'm awake. I wonder what he would think of me if I ever found him."

Sorrie began feeling for her backpack. "When you say that, I don't know whether you're talking about yourself or your dad."

Jim turned away from the boxcar doors and back to Sorrie. "Aren't you the funny one. Of course, I'm talking about my father."

"When can we stop and get something to eat? I'm starving."

"There are some crackers in my coat over in the corner." Jim continued to stare out the opening as Sorrie ripped into the package. Then, without looking at her, Jim asked, "What else do you read? I mean different from coffee table books."

"Novels, biographies, all types of travel books," Sorrie said between bites. "Anything with a title. I read magazines, too. My mother had a great collection of stories and tons of *Life* magazines. I used to stare at travel photos and read the captions. I imagined what it would have been like to live in Paris, New York, or San Francisco." Sorrie closed her eyes. "Paris in the twenties with Hemingway and Gertrude Stein, New York in the sixties with all the beat poets, San Francisco. . . ." Sorrie opened her eyes.

"I bet you traveled lots of places with your family. Like when you had summer vacation and stuff. You traveled to all those places."

"I've never been anywhere." This answer surprised Jim. For all their means, her parents didn't have the good sense to get out and explore.

"I thought you were a rich girl, and you traveled a lot."

"We did travel, but wherever we went, it would be Dad working, Mom watching me like a hawk, and me just staring out the hotel window or her taking me to a museum that I'd visited dozens of times. We never went to the places I wanted to see."

Jim spoke in a monotone as if he was in a trance. "Where did you want to see?"

"She never wanted to visit bookstores or clubs or anyplace she thought we'd be looked down on, but there was this one time when she took an afternoon nap. We were in New York. I snuck out of the hotel and tried to find bookstores I'd read about, but they were gone. It became like a game. We were there for ten days because my father had business meetings, and whenever my mom would lie down, I'd scavenge Manhattan, looking for buildings that no longer existed. I came across a few bookstores, but the insides were tricked-out versions of the local mall. I crept back into the hotel room, and my mother was furious and ordered me to never disappear like that again."

"You let her prevent you from ever going out again?"

Sorrie shook her head. "At least not to bookstores. On my next adventure, I tried to hunt down famous authors' houses or the bars where they gathered, but like the bookstores, some locations weren't there anymore or were rundown—not what I'd envisioned in my hunts. When I got back, the police were there. My mother had called them thinking I was kidnapped."

"You'd go to all that trouble because someone wrote a book?"

"You don't understand. Books take me to places I'm too afraid to go. Sometimes, I'd imagine myself as the characters. Books saved me from going crazy. This is the first time outside my front door in a long time."

"Where do you think you'd like to go?"

"Paris, London, California, maybe. Have you ever been?"

"Sure, Midnight Express. Southern Pacific. I've been up and down the Cali coast with migrants following the harvest to make a little money," Jim said. "Backpacked on the West Coast Trail in Canada. Slept in a girl's purple tent. She was real nice."

"I used to read about people who traveled around the country picking fruit and living in shacks on the farm. I used to imagine myself being there."

Jim laughed. "You? The rich girl pretending to pick crops in a field? If that don't beat all."

"Just because I imagined it doesn't mean I'd want to do it," Sorrie said.

"It's hard work with the sun beating down on you all day, but I did it. I'd make enough to get to the next place. I do anything along the road: clean toilets, pick crops, shovel cow manure. It doesn't matter. It's money."

"Doesn't your foster family in Florida miss you?"

Jim turned from Sorrie and looked at his boots. "They never cared anything for me. They were in it for the money."

Sorrie chewed a cracker and then looked at Jim. "I guess that's why you run."

Jim put his hands behind his head and settled against the boxcar wall. "I don't run. I travel like a free man with the wind at his back."

"And what other free man did you ever know who did that?"

For Jim, there was only one answer: "My father."

5

The Shantytown in the Mountains

THE TRAIN SAT on the tracks for hours, then started moving. All the while, Sorrie prayed aloud that they wouldn't be discovered, and they weren't. The train wound its way around mountains, and Jim was confident in his bearings because of the odor of rock, but at the same time, a choking dryness settled in his throat, making him nauseous. Sorrie took a deep breath and began coughing. Jim asked Sorrie for the bandana he'd given her and coated it with water. He told her to fasten it around her face and then used his hat to cover his mouth and nose to shield him from the tiny dust particles that always seemed to hang in the air of a boxcar.

The passing hills gave off an earthy smell of coal mixed with the scent of burning logs. Jim could tell Sorrie wasn't used to it, and despite the wet cloth, she inched herself closer to the car door to catch some fresh air even though Jim warned her not to get too close to the opening lest she fall out.

The train moved into twilight as it labored around the cold black between two mountains. Jim strained his ears and heard the sounds of excavators and payloaders in the distance. "That sounds like grinding," Sorrie said. "I hope that's not the train breaking down."

Jim tried to reassure her. "That's just equipment taking off the tops of mountains. Sometimes it goes on all night. There's no telling how long. Don't worry about the sound; you're safe with me." He moved from watching Sorrie to watching shadows against the earth, all from the safety of the boxcar. Sorrie gripped her knapsack harder and confessed she didn't like the dark.

Jim didn't mind the dark. He embraced it the way a young boy might hug his favorite blanket. His soul stretched against a billion molecules of imagination, and he felt at home with every part of it. Sorrie told Jim she was afraid to be alone in the dark, and Jim motioned for her to come closer under the protective wing of his black jacket. She hesitated, then brushing off her fear, scampered across the uneven floor and rested her head on his chest. Once the lids of her eyes closed, Jim brushed a wayward strand of hair from her face. The train slowed, and Jim realized some cars were being pulled onto a side track.

There were muffled voices outside, and then the talking trailed off, but the jerking continued until the car lurched to a stop. Jim could hear the hitch being uncoupled. "Damn it," Jim said, "they cut the car."

"I don't know what that means," Sorrie said as she sat up.

Jim hopped out of the car in time to see the train lights turn a corner and disappear into a void.

It was pitch-black now. There was no sound except the tree crickets and night owls and the faint echo of the train's engine in the distance. "I'm afraid," Sorrie said. "Just like that first night in the forest. At least then, there were the stars and the moon, but here there's only blackness like I'm stuck inside a tube and can't get out, and I want to be able to get out. I need to get out," Sorrie insisted.

Jim held up his hand to gesture downward, and Sorrie fell quiet. He was trying to figure out where they were and if they'd have to stay there all night. "Well, we got a few choices: we can stay with the boxcar and hope they hitch it up in the morning, or we can walk a bit and find a tree to sleep against. We may not have to do that if I can figure out our location because I might be able to hook us up with a jungle to settle down in for the night."

Sorrie groaned. "I want to sleep somewhere that's not hard. I'm sore from the ride, and my muscles ache."

Jim looked toward the floor and shook his head. "If you ever want to get to Nebraska, you need to stop thinking like a poor little rich girl and toughen up," Jim said, then turned his attention to the area. "I don't know if I've ever been here. I probably have, but there are so many short lines off the route that it's hard to tell if we're at the entrance to a coal shaft or still on the main line. Let's get out. They won't return for it until the morning, so we have time to explore."

"I don't want to get stuck here, but I also don't want to get lost in a place where we can't find our way out. I remember what you said about people keeping to their own."

"We'll see once I check the compass and railroad atlas," Jim took a paperback from his belongings along with a penlight and tracked the black lines. He tried to remember the codes on the sides of the locomotive but inverted a number until Sorrie set him straight. "If only I found something I recognized," he said as he examined the maps.

The markings looked like spider veins, but it meant a way out. He traced his fingers along several routes, recalling the town where the old man sold them groceries. He studied more lines and names of towns and seemed to know them all, although if the town names were anyplace other than the map, he wouldn't have been able to recognize them. "I think I can get us out of here."

They began to walk, and Jim allowed his eyes to follow the outline of a ridge silhouetted against the moonlight and trees. Some terrain was steep, and he cautioned Sorrie not to wander far because it might mean falling into a gully or a river. He pointed toward a hill, and as they struggled up, he answered her question. "It might be days before we get out, but it's the risk you take when you hop freight. I'm sure I know where we are and that people are nearby."

"I wish I'd taken the train," Sorrie said.

Jim laughed. "You did."

Though dark, Jim was used to walking along tracks and up and down hills at night. He couldn't hear the sound of water, and that reassured him. Then, a few minutes later, Jim smelled the pungent odor of a well-lit fire and heard people's voices. He strained to listen; there was a burst of laughter, then chatter. He took Sorrie's hand, and they moved toward the noise. They navigated to the other side of the hill, and as they maneuvered down the slope, shards of slag came with them, filling Sorrie's sneakers with sharp rocks.

"Ouch!" Sorrie said as she reached down, removed her shoes, and slammed them into the ground. She sat down, emptied them, and put them back on.

Jim hardly noticed and continued to where the fire was.

Sorrie ran to keep up.

"Evening," he said as they approached the group. "My name's Jim; this here's Sorrie. If that's okay, we've been catching out and would like to settle for a while. Mind if we spend some time with you folks? We'll be quiet as field mice and won't take nothing unless it's offered."

An older man in a flannel shirt sat with his back to Jim and said, "I don't know if you're welcome, seeing that we don't fancy to field mice. We're more inclined to have big hollerin' rats visiting this camp."

Everyone started laughing, and Jim recognized the voice before he saw the man. "Church? Is that you?" He said, turning in the direction of the voice.

"Right, you are, Jimmy boy. Come hug your buddy, Church."

Jim let go of Sorrie's hand and opened his arms. They embraced, but as Jim leaned in, the weight of his knapsack threw him off balance, and he stumbled. Sorrie gasped, but Jim quickly regained his footing.

"You already started drinking? Never known you to be one of those mouth suckers who couldn't wait for a brew," Church said. He poked the nearby fire with a long stick.

"Nah, I haven't been drinking; I'm just tired. We've been traveling since dawn." Jim pointed to Sorrie. "This here's Sorrie, my traveling friend. We're headed west toward Nebraska."

A broad smile came over Church's face, and he extended his hand. Sorrie drew back, then tepidly extended her fingers and barely touched Church's palm. Church noticed and pulled back.

"Don't mind, my friend here. She's shy and doesn't trust strangers." Jim said. He sat next to Church and motioned for Sorrie to follow him, placing her between the two. Jim smelled the burning fire and saw Sorrie wince at Church's breath.

Church turned to Sorrie. "Cason Graves is my name, but most just call me Church. I used to live in a converted church, but that was long ago, so here I am, hunkered down in the great state of West Virginia."

Jim interrupted. "Got any food for the offering? We're starving."

"We got hobo stew over in a pot by the lean-to, though there's no meat in it. Not many wanted a cup of vegetables and beans, seeing that we have whiskey. Most around the fire would rather drink than eat—helps us stay warmer that way." Church bumped Sorrie's arm and gave a wink.

Jim strolled over to the lean-to and returned with a cup of steaming vegetables. Sorrie started to rise, but Jim told her to stay where she was as he handed her a spoon and a cup of food.

An older woman sat in the circle and introduced herself as Classy J. There were five around the fire, including Church and the older woman. There was a young man in a wheelchair who sat near the fire, and Church introduced him as Batman. Batman nodded in a drugged haze but didn't speak. The two others introduced themselves as Longshanks and Martha. Longshanks was a thin, bearded man with gray hair, while Martha introduced herself as his wife, to which he said, "But we ain't married."

"Hush now," Martha scolded. She was tall and thin and wore a floral skirt with thick black boots.

Jim leaned into Church. "Have you seen anyone new lately? Maybe a man with curly brown hair who resembles me, but who's older? Anyone come around like that?"

Church looked forlorn. "Jim, boy, every time I see you, you ask the same damn question. I know you're looking for your father, but I haven't seen anybody like that. I'd be the first to get word to you. How do you think he's doing anyway?"

Jim looked up from his stew, licked a portion of the hot drippings from his spoon, and let the warm broth sink into his throat. The stew was salty and thick. "I've been traveling so long that everybody looks like my father. Everyone gives me the same argument that he ain't alive, but I know different. He wrote so much about the road that I know he's out here somewhere."

"Well, at least you're headed toward something. Old Church has been in this place long enough to know none of these bakeheads know where their needle's pointed."

When Church said this, Classy J piped up. "Speak for yourself, old man. And pass that bottle before you fall over and die on top of it." Church handed Classy J the bottle of whiskey. The alcohol made everyone's face glow red.

"Oh hell, I always know where my needle's pointed, just like Mr. Mojo," Jim said.

Classy J looked in Jim's direction. "Well, you better put it to good use than seeing how you're facing the right direction. You come to see old Momma J when you're ready."

"I figured you were looking more for the man with a gun in his hands," Jim said.

"'You got the gunnin', and I ain't runnin', just get me some funnin', and I'll be a-comin','" she said. Everyone laughed, but Jim could see Sorrie didn't get the joke. While the people around the fire were easygoing, Sorrie stood stiff and lost.

Jim leaned over. "Are you okay?" He asked.

"Why are they all so happy?" Sorrie whispered.

"The whiskey just grabbed at 'em. We'll talk about it later. Just act like friends but try not to get too close—for hygiene reasons, you might say." Sorrie squinted her nose and pulled her legs up to her chest.

Just then, a man emerged from a clump of woods. "I thought I saw a familiar face." The man's voice was gruff and irritating. He latched his thumbs onto his pants and kicked an empty bottle of whiskey away from his path. A wiry smile came across his face, and if Jim didn't know any better, he would have thought the man had come out of a movie about the old West. "What brings you this way, Jimmy?"

Jim recognized the man. They'd had run-ins before. He took a few bites of hot potato and carrots and didn't rush his answer. "I got to get home, is all. Besides, what business is it of yours, Dan?"

The man spoke again. "You still believe that crazy story about your pappy being Jim Morrison?" His face betrayed a smirk as he sat directly opposite Jim.

A long, slow silence wove its way through the circle, and the only sound besides the crackling fire was the clinking of someone's ring against the whiskey bottle—that and Jim's slurping. Jim took his time the way a box turtle slows up a column of cars as it lumbers to cross the street. He put down his cup and spoon, wiped his mouth with the back of his hand, and looked at the man making all the noise. "Sure, Dan. You don't have to believe me, though. What's it to you? It's my life, not yours. Besides, from what I hear, you don't have much of a life, so you just got to do what you can to steal someone else's." Jim started laughing, which made everyone smile except Dan, who grimaced.

"No, really. Morrison in your blood, or did your Momma cross the wrong tracks?"

"That's my affair."

"From the looks of it, it seems like an affair of the heart for your Momma. You always did resemble a bastard no matter what daddy made you."

Jim could see that most people around the fire were itching to see him get up and take a swing, but he thought better of it. Fighting Dan would be like fighting a one-ton crocodile, and Jim knew he'd lose. He rubbed his hands together and looked into Dan's eyes. "I don't mind being called a bastard because I know who my daddy is. As for you, it must be hard not knowing if the girl you slept with the night before had the same daddy as you did."

"I know who my daddy is and where he's at. You don't know where your daddy's at unless it's that grave in Paris. You're trying to make up a story because you got confused about your kin, but Jim Morrison took the big adios and crossed the Jordan, but what are you left with? A big nothing. Tell me, if Jim Morrison's your dad, why didn't you ever benefit from it?"

This was a question Jim had long asked his mother, but hearing it from someone else was unnerving. Jim stood up, walked past the fire, and grabbed the top of Dan's shirt. He stood nose to nose, glaring into Dan's brown eyes. Jim raised a pointed finger. "How many times does someone need to tell you to mind your manners and not put your nose into where it's not concerned?"

Dan backed away and raised his palms. "Sure, Jimmy. No problem. Just asking is all," he laughed.

"Well, ask some other question then," Church growled. His brown eyes glared at Dan, and his shoulders stiffened as he sat cross-legged in front of the fire.

Jim let go, and Dan crawled backward to find an out-of-the-way spot on an old wooden crate. While Church wasn't the strongest, he was the most experienced, which gained him more respect.

Church stretched his arms and took a long swig of whiskey. He offered the bottle to Sorrie, and even though Sorrie hated liquor, she took a swig and handed the bottle back to Church. "You want another sip?" He asked.

"I don't drink," she said, then added, "at least not much."

"It'll keep the bedbugs from biting," he insisted.

"No, thank you." Sorrie looked to the side; Jim watched them at a distance.

Sensing her anxiety, Church said, "Oh, he's just making sure I don't steal his girl. He never goes far when he's got a lady on his arm." With that, Church winked, and Sorrie felt uneasy.

While Church was cleaner than most, the dust from the years on the road was layered in the crusted lines on his face and the crazy way his salt and pepper hair shot out in all directions. But there was softness, too. A gentle acceptance of how things were as if the highway had taken all the fight out of him and every drop of existence was a Zen moment with Church accepting in gratitude each inch of calm the universe offered up.

"Is this what you do?" Sorrie asked. "Go from place to place."

"Well, yeah. You can live real cheap—but good."

"How long have you been doing it?"

"Oh, going on twenty-five years, give or take. It's in my bones now. I couldn't stop even if a wildcat from Arizona dragged me away. It's too much a part of me now."

"Why did you stop the argument about Jim's father?"

"Oh, I don't know," Church said unconvincingly.

"It's important for me to know."

Church hesitated as if he didn't want to speak but said, "Take two men on opposite sides of a room. They both ask the same question. Why does one get a laugh and the other a fist? Anyone could've asked that question about Jim's father, and Jim wouldn't have minded—he'd have laughed. But Dan? He's a big mouth and a braggart, which usually gets him a fist. He only asks a question when he can rustle a mean response. I don't appreciate that."

Sorrie accepted this explanation, then asked, "And which of the two are you?"

Church chuckled. "I'm the third man. I sit back and watch the other two."

"But not this time."

"No, not this time," Church said as he shook his head.

There was a moment of uneasy silence as if the universe had paused to breathe. Sorrie spoke first. "What brings you on the road?"

"Probably the same thing that got you here." Church glanced at the fire and then surveyed the dark sky. "I was a history teacher once. I fancied myself a hot shot in those days. I used to teach kids about stuff they weren't interested in learning in the first place. I was a pretty good bull-shit artist and usually kept everyone's eyes because I put on a good show. But one day, I went to work, and no matter how hard I tried, all I got were blank stares. It was as if they were saying, 'Just give us the answers to the test so we can pass' and nothing more." Church picked up a stick and threw it into the fire.

"And that's why you quit teaching?"

"Teaching doesn't always mean the classroom, and learning doesn't always have to come from a book. I'm always teaching and learning, but not the hard way. The fact was that after that day, I realized I wasn't special, no matter how much I cared. Once in a while, I'd see a spark, but not enough to keep me." Church looked into the distance. "At about the same time, my wife died from cancer. I was forty years old. I only had her, my work, and my son. After she left, I found myself staring at the television news and arguing with everyone looking back at me from the screen, even knowing they didn't hear me. I used to get so mad. I had the kind of anger a man has when he realizes no one wants his opinion, but then I reasoned that fighting's another way of distracting yourself from the truth."

"My mother used to say truth was a person's way of looking at things," Sorrie said.

Church snorted. "What's truth? The real truth is you're on your own. You come into this world scared and alone, and no matter how many people are there, when you breathe your last, you'll die scared and alone. It's what happens in between that counts. Are you happy with what you see when you look in the mirror? I knew I wasn't.'"

"But what about your son?"

"By then, he grew past the point where he hung on my every word, so around the time I started hating my life, he started hating me. He had a different view because he was young, and that's as it should be." Church smiled and glanced at Sorrie, ". . . like all young people."

Church threw more sticks into the fire, and as the light from the flames danced off his face, Sorrie realized he was no longer the dirty Santa Claus she'd envisioned but a kind grandfather. Her body relaxed into the moment as a sense of calm washed over her.

Church continued. "But I guess you don't need a father once you know everything. My son took off a few months after my wife died, and I haven't seen him since. After he left, I was dressing for work and decided I couldn't face those kids anymore. But I knew I wasn't useless. I knew I could feel alive again, so I quit my job and sold my house and everything in it. I finally realized it doesn't matter how much stuff you have. Just be honest with yourself, don't hurt anybody, and live like every day's your last. So, whether your life's a dream or not," Church paused, "we all have to have a dream, even if it's not real."

Church took a deep breath, and as Sorrie was about to comment, he continued. "So that's where Jim's dream comes in. He thinks his dad's a rock star. Do I think he's right?" Church shook his head.

Jim heard what Church said and piped up. "Of course, I'm right," he said from afar.

"Right, not right, it's all the same to me," Church yelled back, then added, "Why don't you go count the ants at your feet and leave us alone?"

"I want to know what you're saying about me."

"I'm just saying that you get up every morning with the hope of living out the day, not getting stuffed into someone's version of what your life should look like." Jim gave a thumbs-up but continued to listen. Church turned back to Sorrie. "Living life on my terms might not make me rich, but hell, I never wanted to be rich in the first place."

"But what happened to the money from your house? That's got to count for something."

An awkward silence took over as Sorrie realized she'd asked a rude question, which made Church grimace, but he wasn't afraid to answer. "I had that money over twenty-five years ago. Pissed most of it away. Gave a lot away, too. Enjoyed every bit of it." Church raised a long stick to poke the glowing embers as the burnt logs fell to the side and disintegrated into ashes around the edges of the fire.

"You gave up everything? Kind of like being a leaf that gets carried away by the wind?" Sorrie asked.

Church was intrigued. "That reminds me of the poem, 'A Dream Pang' by Robert Frost. Do you know that poem?"

"It was in a book I found lying around my parent's house. I never memorized it or anything. I just remembered the part about the leaves."

"I hate to disappoint you. Nothing's escaped from my life." Sorrie said she didn't understand, so Church explained. "Wherever I stepped, I owned the dirt underneath. I think I owned every inch of mud from here to San Francisco. Every time my foot hit the earth, I knew I had the whole world beneath me because nothing else could touch it. That dirt was *mine*." Church paused to search his words, then sighed as if speaking had become an effort. He shook his head; his voice was labored, and Sorrie could see he had trouble forming the sentences. "I laid down enough miles of muck and mud until I wound up here. I'll probably die here. After all, nothing lasts forever." Church took a long, slow breath but didn't say anymore as if there was only this moment, and he was busy absorbing himself in it.

Sorrie hesitated, and as her eyes welled up, she asked, "But what will happen to you? Who'll take care of you? Who'll bury you?"

A broad smile covered Church's face. "Whoever's here, I guess. The day I catch the westbound is the day the worms eat me; I'll make a sweet lunch." He chuckled, and in that instant, Sorrie realized she could have been talking to her grandfather.

"I'll bury you," she said.

He turned to Sorrie and shook his head. "First, you got to discover your dream. Then, when you find it, you can come back and bury me. But be reminded, a dream's a lot like that dirt. You have to grab it like southern clay and squeeze it; otherwise, it finds a home with someone else."

Sorrie looked down at the ground. "I think my dream's just to be free," she said. "I've been cooped up inside a house I despised with a mother and a father who just love controlling me. I feel like freedom has been kicking around me for a long time."

"Freedom's a dangerous thing. You wake up every morning with your life on your shoulders. You can live in a fantasy or reality—either way, you still have to eat."

Sorrie didn't want to think about that. Instead, she longed to hop on another train and feel the wind on her face again. "I have a few dreams in my pocket," she said. "I've mapped it all out up here," Sorrie tapped her head and turned to Church. She smiled and asked, "But what about you? What do you still dream about?"

Church hesitated, then laughed. He patted Sorrie's leg. "Now, that's no kinda question for a young girl to be asking an old man like me," he said. Church squinted into the distance. "Looks like your man is walking over to the fire."

"He's not my man," Sorrie said.

"Well, he better be somebody's man before he gets himself burnt up." Sorrie watched while Jim danced close to the fire; she jumped up and hurried over.

* * *

For Jim, it was all about the flame. Get close enough and get burned, or stand on the edge and stay warm with a singe of fire crackling on the tips of your hair. Close enough to be drawn in but far enough away not to light up like a torch. The flame was unpredictable; the trick was getting out alive. Jim was used to living in the moment, looking for the thing he couldn't grab and the person he refused to part with; today, the flame might snap at him; tomorrow, the sky, but there was always one constant: his father circling somewhere in the air around him.

As Jim allowed the tips of the fire to get close enough to warm his legs, he watched from a distance while Church and Sorrie talked. He was glad Sorrie got to speak to other hobos. She was young and needed a boatload of experience before tackling the world. What did his father call it in the poems Sorrie was reading? Was it fear or the way you looked at people? It could be the one thing that draws you into madness.

Jim's mind drifted into the darkness until he saw the light of a train exiting a tunnel, then cars and planes and more speed, the way his father must have traveled—the man on the highway—the dark stranger ready to pounce. He dissolved into his thoughts of finding his father when he felt two hands on his shoulders.

"Gotcha," Sorrie said. "What were you thinking about?"

"Oh, just enjoying the fire and wondering where we'll sleep tonight."

"But not like we're sleeping together."

Jim stopped and watched the flames rise over the black pot that held the stew. "We got to sleep someplace, and why not together?"

"But not in the same sleeping bag." Sorrie's voice trailed off.

Jim seemed annoyed. "Listen, I told you I wasn't in it for sex, but if you want to share a sleeping bag to keep warm, I'd welcome the company, but right now, I'm just trying to find a decent place to flop—one where I won't have worms crawling up my dick." He turned to look at Sorrie. She was happy, and that pleased him. When he met her, tears ran down her face, but now, she smiled. Church must have said all the right things.

"Then you'd better pick a good spot."

"I guess we'll find a place by the willow trees; all the tents and mattresses have been spoken for."

"Did you ask anybody about the trains coming through tomorrow?" Sorrie asked.

"No need," Jim said, walking away from the fire. "I know where we're going."

"But what about the floods?"

Jim sighed. He reminded himself despite everything, he was still a loner and answered to no one. He sauntered over to the clearing without answering Sorrie's question.

* * *

The morning came, and Jim smelled the whiskey on his breath. He walked a few feet away from Sorrie, took out his toothbrush, and put a dollop of paste on it. As he scrubbed, his mouth filled with a salty foam. He spit it out into the dust as his feet covered it with more dust. He was ready for coffee and walked over to Classy J's spot. As he was returning, he saw Sorrie's head look up from her knapsack. She turned in the direction where Jim had been sleeping, but Jim's belongings weren't there. He leaned against a tree trunk, watched as she sprang into motion, and wiggled out of her sleeping bag. She stared down at the imprint from his body, which left an indent in the grass. He caught her mouthing, "Where did he go," from a distance and smiled. It was a shame to leave her, but he knew that one night, she'd shimmy into his sleeping bag, hold onto his shirt, and rest her head against his chest. It was one thing to have sex to make the loneliness disappear, but it was another for an unseasoned girl to fall in love with him. Jim didn't want that.

Jim sauntered over to where Sorrie stood. He was holding a mug of coffee. "I didn't know if you wanted sugar, so I put in three. Too bad we have no cream, and the coffee's only instant, but it will have to do." He handed it to her as she brushed the hair from her face.

"Thanks," she said, taking the hot cup. "I didn't see you. I thought you might have left."

"Maybe you wanted me to leave," Jim said.

"Nothing could be further from the truth. After all, we had a deal. I hired you, remember?" The coffee was hot, and Sorrie wrapped her hands around the mug.

"Yeah, I guess so, but now you got no money, so we only got half a deal," Jim lifted her sleeping bag and began rolling it.

"You don't have to do that," she insisted.

"Well, if you can grow a couple of arms, then maybe, or do you just want to enjoy your coffee? We got to move on if we're going to catch the next train out."

Sorrie gulped down the hot liquid and handed the cup back to Jim. "Do I have time to brush my teeth?"

"Sure," Jim threw the rolled sleeping bag near Sorrie's feet. "Wait here," he said, and a few minutes later, he returned carrying a bucket of warm water. "Get yourself cleaned up and changed and ready to move."

"Where?" Sorrie asked, and Jim pointed to a clump of trees.

"Go back there. I guarantee you no one will look." Then, when Sorrie balked, Jim added, "Listen, it's important to stay clean on the road. Do you want lice and fleas like most of these tramps? Get yourself clean with a fresh set of clothes and some clean socks. We got a long day ahead of us."

While Sorrie washed, Jim charmed Classy J into giving him cheese sandwiches, and Sorrie was grateful when one was offered. A trickle of water fell from the end of her hair into the crannies of the bread as she hungrily attacked it.

"Best quick to eat," Jim said. "We got to get on the road and get the train heading due west out of these mountains, or we'll be stuck here when the clouds roll in. We have a few hops today, so we have to get started early. You're going to need your strength. If we don't catch this first one, we won't catch the string, and we'll spend another night in these hills." Jim hesitated. "Are you going to be up for this?" He asked. "You looked a little slow yesterday."

Without hesitation, Sorrie picked up her gear and looked Jim in the eyes. "I'll be fine," she said, but Jim noticed her eyes moved away, so he turned to see what had attracted her attention.

It was Church in the distance, sitting on a lawn chair. The two approached him, and Jim and Church locked eyes. The glow from the night before was gone, and in its absence was a tired old man.

It was Church who spoke first. "Tell me your plans for getting to Nebraska."

"We'll be heading into what's left of West Virginia, then toward Kentucky. After that, I aim to grab freight clear to North Platte."

"That's many miles between where you are and where you're going. Don't forget all those short hops through the mountains. You might wind up at the end of a coal shaft, having to find your way out in the dark. There are easier routes. You could go south and then up. There aren't as many lines, but they're faster if you want to save time. Plus, you'll avoid most of the flooding."

"Let's say there are certain routes I aim to bypass, if you know what I mean."

Church nodded and didn't debate it. "Yeah, some of 'em holding some pretty mean bulls."

"And other fellas," Jim added.

"I guess you're right. There are better things to do with the day than to start the morning with a difference of opinion. Just don't forget that the area you want to go through was underwater not too long ago. A lot of the farms and some of the towns are gone. If they're still there, I'm pretty sure they look like a soggy mud pit, so be careful. Also, be reminded that the weather could change, especially if you're going through St. Louis."

"I'll remember." Jim winked and Church winked back. They turned to hike out, but Sorrie stopped them. She walked back to Church, who was striking a match to a pipe. He stopped to look up.

"Don't forget, I said I'd bury you," she said.

"I'm not forgetting," Church shot back. "But remember, nothing's permanent, and everything's subject to change. You're welcome to visit again, but I may not be here. Crops need picking, and migrant work is good labor, even for an old stew bum like me."

Sorrie hesitated, and without uttering a word, she bent down and kissed Church on the forehead.

6

Through Coal Country

THE SINGLE LINE going west was deserted, and Jim and Sorrie had to wait until a slow-moving drag train came by; most of the cars held coal, but they found an empty boxcar and hitched on. As soon as they were settled, Jim reached into his knapsack and pulled out a can.

"What's that?" Sorrie asked.

"That's my pee can. I like to keep it when I'm on the road, just in case."

"That's disgusting. You pee in a can?"

Jim smiled. "Nah, I do it like everybody else—in the corner." Jim fingered the jagged edges. "But I better keep the can in case you have to go. We have to get west, so I'm not stopping for any more bathroom breaks, newspaper, or no newspaper."

"I have no intention of peeing—or doing anything else—in a can. Besides, the sharp edges might stab my derrière," Sorrie said.

Jim laughed. "Your what?"

"My derrière; my butt. I'm not putting any part of my body near one of those cans, least of all my backside."

"Still the princess, eh?" Jim said. "I don't have a Golden John stuffed in my bag. Cans aren't just good for the necessities but for lighting fires to keep you warm when it's cold. If the can's wide enough, it can be good to cook over it, but this one's too small," Jim leaned his right hand back and tossed it out the door.

"I thought you were keeping it, just in case."

"You just told me you wouldn't have used it, but you got to be resourceful out here."

"You really like making your own way, don't you?"

"It's the only way: living off the grid," Jim said and smiled.

Sorrie fell silent and then, after a while, asked, "What's a bull?"

"That's the railroad police. They protect the railroad company's property, and they don't care for people like us."

"Then what's a stew bum?"

"That's an old hobo who likes to drink."

"Church said he was just an old stew bum waiting to pick crops."

"Well, he'll say things like that." Jim pulled a cigarette from his shirt pocket and lit it.

"He said he might not be there if we go back."

Jim took a long, slow drag. "He'll be there. He's old and wants to stay near where he was raised. But what makes you think we're going back?"

"Because I promised to bury him."

Jim laughed. "I heard that. It's the stupidest damn thing you could ever promise a guy like him. He'll take a liking to you, and you'll never get rid of him. Just because he's old doesn't mean he won't follow you around the country if he's got the itch," Jim took another drag. He held the cigarette between his teeth as he re-arranged his knapsack to lean against it.

"He's that ornery?"

"He's that ornery."

"Well, then, who's Batman?"

"The kid in the wheelchair? That's Batman," Jim confirmed.

"Yeah, I know, but what's his real name?"

"I don't know. Nobody in the hobo camps uses their full name unless they're stupid. The law's looking for some of those mongrels; either that or they got God-fearing family searching for 'em so they can get reformed." Jim held up a finger and wagged it at Sorrie. "Bring the lost to Jesus Christ all you who sin."

"No, really . . ."

Jim took another drag. "Church is Church. Classy J is Classy J. I'm Jim. I don't know Batman's real name. He's just a kid living on the road like us. He hangs around jungles until he can find someone to help him get a ride out; he's been doing it for a few years."

"What's he doing in a wheelchair?"

"That's not a wheelchair; that's his Batmobile. He's got it supercharged. He got it all souped up with an electric motor that makes it go fast. You could say he got the sports model. He even has it to where it shoots flames like the real Batmobile."

"He's so sad. He didn't even say hello. He looks young for not being able to walk. How does he even get around in the camps? How does he navigate the trails?"

"Sometimes people help him. You have to help those in need. I don't think he catches out much anymore—I usually see him with groups of people on the street in the cities—but he'll find his way to different camps if someone's around who can wheel him over the trails or, if he's got the itch, to use those legs he keeps by his chair."

"Why does he stay in the camps? Why doesn't he just go home?"

"He can't. He fell asleep on the railroad tracks and lost his legs; his family doesn't want him back, so it's like he's married to the road. Don't feel sorry for him. That's what he wants; that's how he gets the ladies." Jim stood up and took his jacket off. "Just cause his two legs don't work doesn't mean he can't grow a third. He does all right."

"But why doesn't he get cleaned up? Realize there's help out there?"

Jim laughed. "He's already got help. Got his parents mailing a check to a flophouse in St. Louis, and someone cashes it and wires him the money. He doesn't need a dealer; he's got all the painkillers he wants for free. He doesn't even need a cooker. Just pop them saviors down, and he turns into the Caped Crusader. He's got paradise on the road with a check, dope, and women. He's with his people. He's got a whole lifetime of endless sky to look forward to. He goes home to his flophouse sometimes, but he likes it on the road better. It's safer. They jumped him last time he was there and dangled him out a third-floor window. Why trade the road for a flophouse where you always wonder if you'll get robbed? I know I wouldn't."

"The people in the camp seemed pretty happy, but I don't know why."

Jim fingered his cigarette and glanced out at the brush and trees. "They're not happy. They're miserable. Not one of those honky-tonkers would live like that if they knew there was a warm bed somewhere and a hot meal waiting for 'em. They hide out because they got nothing else except their tribe."

"Why don't they go to a shelter or something?"

Jim stamped out his cigarette and glared at Sorrie. "If you're so smart, why don't you figure it out? At least they got their freedom."

"You have your freedom, but you're living like a homeless dog who travels the street looking for a place to lay its head."

"My doggie lifestyle's benefiting you, isn't it? I'm getting you to your place of happiness. And don't go saying I'm homeless. I got a place to stay with my Momma if I wanted, but I got to look for my father. I live this way because I have to. I don't think he died in Paris any more than my Momma does. She's been looking, too. What I hate more than being dirty and poor is living in a cage where you dress in a suit and give up your life for money. That's one of the reasons I don't want money, and I don't want to spend another day in one of those shelters."

"It sounds like you've been there."

"Tell me one person living the hobo life who hasn't been down that hole?"

Sorrie glanced at her fingernails and then looked up. "Me," she said.

* * *

Green. It surrounded Jim and Sorrie for miles as they caught one short hop after another; it was the one constant—that and an easy ride—until the fourth train, which coughed and lurched and bumped past bends in the hilly terrain. There were miles and miles of dense brush, emerald grass, jade climbers, shade green, pine needles, pear green, lofty canopies, and a million gold sparkles flashing between the leaves. At one point, clouds descended, and it began to drizzle, making the landscape shimmer in a pallet of glowing silver. The train pivoted around a corner and slowed, then began an agonizing ascent up a mountain pass.

The speed decreased, and their bodies pulled to one side of the car as the train tipped precariously close to the mountain. They shifted to the other side and enjoyed the glow of the rain-soaked gully on the banks below the tracks. In the distance was a river, and Jim pointed out the shingles of wooden shacks below the tree line and talons of smoke rising near the banks. Sorrie told Jim that if she ever had a choice to live anywhere in the world, she would like to be here.

"You can live anywhere now," Jim said. "The world is yours, and you can stop right here."

"I like seeing the smoke rise from the houses and think about how warm and cozy it must be inside," she said.

Jim laughed. "It's probably stills making hooch, and if they got a bad still, they got a lot of alcohol vapor pouring off their equipment." Jim pointed in the distance. "They need a clean water source, so they're probably staying by the river. In other places, it's different. But one bad accident and they'll be meeting their maker."

"What's hooch?" Sorrie asked.

"You know, white whiskey. Moonshine. They usually cook when it's not so obvious, but the moonshiners got to do what they got to do when they can."

Sorrie laughed. "I don't understand. Do you know how to make illegal liquor?"

"Let's just say I got some jailhouse knowledge."

"Have you ever been to jail?"

Jim straightened up and smiled. "That's one experience, little lady, I have *not* had. But I got to know a lot of jaileys on the road, and they clued me in. Some even got arrested for hooch, but locking 'em up doesn't help. They make it in prison out of everything imaginable. Go figure."

"Is that what they are, jaileys?"

"It's just what I call 'em, to distinguish, you might say."

"Distinguish from what?"

"Just other guys who hang around the jungles and bars like fuzz rats that think their shit don't stink. And then there's the lowdown wankers who got nothing better to do than mooch off everyone else."

"I don't understand your language."

"Sometimes I don't know what to call them, so I just make up a name; otherwise, I'm just using words I hear other hobos use, but I'm sure you have your language too, coming from money, so I guess that makes us even."

After a few twists and turns, the scenery changed from green to brown to black, then back to green. Then, digging through his knapsack, Jim asked, "You going to read some more?"

Sorrie took the book from Jim's hand and turned to a page where Jim Morrison talked about cinema and film denigrating into experience or spectacle. Then she read a poem about shamans and séances.

When she was finished, Jim said, "I was at a séance once. It nearly raised the roof of the house I was in. Voices came out of nowhere to scare the living bejesus out of me and everyone else in the room," Jim laughed.

Sorrie looked intrigued. "Where was this?" she asked.

"Some commune out west Momma took us to. She used to drive around the country looking for my father and stopped at places off the road, and this time, we wound up in a commune outside Santa Fe. About thirty people lived there, including kids. They were trying to bring back the spirit of a Wild West bandit they thought was buried on the property. I think they wanted to ask him where he hid his treasure. Pretty weird stuff if you ask me."

"How old were you?"

"Around five. My sister, brother, and I got on there because there was a huge wall, and we could paint it without getting yelled at. We'd wander around the buildings, watching people smoking pot and gardening or fixing outhouses. I remember this one guy who just went around fixing outhouses."

"What about your mother?"

"Momma just took a lot of drugs and hung on the guy she was with. We stayed about a year, and then Momma's romance broke up. That's the way it was with her. First, she dragged us kids across the country, hunting down my father, looking in every bar in a town where she knew he'd had a concert. Then, when she got bored with it, she switched to hunting down some man who told her he liked her. The guys she hooked up with never thought they'd see her again until she arrived at their house. She'd knock on the door at all hours of the day or night, and usually, some girl would answer. The trouble with Momma was that the guys she went with never told her about their girlfriend or wife."

"Are you sure one of those guys wasn't your father?"

"I'm sure," Jim shot back. "She saw my father enough to know, following him around from concert to concert, so she should know. When they said he died, she told me she was all broken up until she realized they weren't telling the truth. She always said he wanted to walk the highways. I think that's why Momma wandered so much."

"Is that how you got to Florida?"

Jim rested on his knapsack and looked into Sorrie's blue eyes. "Maybe," he said. Jim thought to say more but didn't want to reveal all his secrets. So, instead, he closed his eyes, leaned back on his knapsack, and put the Boonie hat over his face. In the darkness, he could hear Sorrie reading a poem about modern life, people as passengers, and all of the backdrops seen from traveling.

Jim had witnessed a lot from car windows, but he'd never encountered someone as smart as Sorrie. Maybe after he found his father, Jim would settle down, look her up, and get something more permanent going, but now was the present. Jim let her voice fade as she recited more poems, and he dozed off. His father's voice filled the void.

What do you see?

"I see junkyard dogs, collapsed swimming pools, blinking red lights, neon signs, strip clubs, long, slow drives with the moon overhead."

What does it tell you?

"It tells me I'm out there."

Where is out there?

"In the downtown, the ghetto, the alleyways watching the whores and drug dealers and hustlers with guns. I see rotten garbage mixed with the smell of Chinese food. My shoes are covered in mud and dog shit."

That's the illusion. The reality is you're between two doors.

Jim started to panic. All he could see was black. "What doors? I'm not where I was. Where am I?"

You're between where you're going and where you've been. You're in the NOW. Are you a movie, or are you real?

"I'm here in the moment. I'm real."

You need to see who you are.

"Who am I? I'm your son, right? I'm your son, right?"

Suddenly, there was a train whistle. Startled, Jim opened his eyes and sat up; the Boonie hat fell from his face. The engine barreled through a short tunnel, momentarily pitching them into darkness. When the light reappeared, Jim found himself clutching his knapsack and sweating. Sorrie looked annoyed. "I hope it was worth it. You missed the last four poems."

* * *

"When are we going to get there?" Sorrie asked as the train moved laboriously up a hill, coughing and belching and moving so slowly that Sorrie suggested they get out and walk.

"Go ahead," Jim said as the train leaned in the opposite direction of where they were sitting. Suddenly, Jim realized the train engineer might be able to see them because of the slant of the cars and hurriedly told Sorrie to hide in a corner.

"I don't understand. He can't see us," she said. "I don't notice any cameras."

"No, but he does have mirrors, and he's trained to spot hobos, so just keep your head down and don't get caught."

Sorrie buried herself in her jacket until the train moved to an even stretch of track. Jim noticed she was sweating by how her clothes clung to her body.

Jim sweated, too. He reached for his canteen, drank a warm mouthful, and offered Sorrie some. The car was stifling, and the heat rising from the friction on the tracks was more than they could bear. Without saying a word, Sorrie stripped from her long pants and shirt to a pair of cargos, a Cami, and her hideous sneakers. Jim scowled.

"What's the matter? Haven't you ever seen a girl change before?" Sorrie asked.

"Yeah, plenty, just not you. What makes you do that now? You never did it before—at least not so obvious."

"I did it before. Don't you remember? Anyway, I've been doing a lot of things I've never done before," Sorrie said as she brushed her hair back and held it in place with a metal clip. "But from what you've said, every girl's your type."

"Yeah, I guess so," Jim laughed, then stood up. "But don't comb your hair like that because it gives my ideas."

A red tint came to Sorrie's cheeks, and Jim could tell she was embarrassed. Sorrie faced Jim full on. "Don't you ever," she said, then changed the subject and asked, "You said we had a few stops to make."

"A few," Jim said, staring out at the sky. He changed his shirt and splashed water down his back. He was painfully thin, and Sorrie gasped when he took his shirt off and revealed his rib bones jutting out. Jim ignored it and splashed water under his arms.

"Are we lost?" Sorrie asked.

"Nah, but our stop's coming soon, so be ready when I tell you."

For Jim, the terrain was familiar. He knew the lines of the mountains and the choking smell of dirt and could even pick out a barking dog in the distance. Was this the freedom his father wrote about in "The Crystal Ship"? The independence his father embraced—like when he hitchhiked from Florida to California before becoming famous? It was just something he heard, and Jim tried retracing his father's route several times without luck. There was no detailed record, and he found himself asking old hobos if they'd ever met his father, convinced he'd run across someone somewhere who would recall something. From camps to shantytowns to $10 hotels to highway roadhouses, Jim asked anyone and everyone who looked old enough to remember. Some just talked about the concerts they'd attended; others said they couldn't remember the strangers from last week, let alone twenty years ago.

He even recalled a conversation with a California musician who mentioned that Jim Morrison wrote his thoughts in notebooks. Was there an account of the trip in these books? The same musician remembered that some notebooks might have been left at an old residence in California, though he doubted they were of any value. So, Jim hitchhiked to a house where his father had lived in Los Angeles, but it didn't exist anymore. Not even the house number. If only he could find the diaries and learn to read better. He knew his mother didn't know the route, but he needed to find someone who did.

He gazed out the door to lose himself in the beauty of the wildflowers bursting out from the underbrush. Then he looked at how the sunlight traveled into the car and radiated off Sorrie's translucent skin.

Jim lingered on how pretty she looked in the light, but then he dismissed it and concentrated on getting to their next destination.

* * *

The train crossed a river and wound into the belly of the mountains. From a distance, Jim noticed the evergreens diminished, and the land was awash in coal slag, and Jim knew it was time to get off.

He told Sorrie not to forget any belongings because they were jumping down soon.

"I don't see where we can jump. There's no place to go in that dusty mess," Sorrie said as she looked outside the car. Instead of the green they had known, the landscape resembled the moon, with craters and gray rocks.

The train wove through a long tunnel, then stopped. As before, Jim took a rag from his knapsack and coated it with water. He handed the cloth to Sorrie, and she didn't have to be told what to do. The tunnel filled with smoke, and they both waited until the train started up again, cleared the tunnel, and abruptly slowed around a bend. "This is our stop. We have to get over to the embankment," Jim said, pointing to a steep ridge.

"Into that?" Sorrie asked, but instead of reaching the ridge, they jumped into a ditch filled with rocks and pebbles.

After landing, Jim pointed into the distance, where a second track broke off from the main line. "We're going that way."

"I don't understand why we got off. We were headed in the right direction."

"Will you let me be the navigator? It's like you want to take charge of everything because you gave me a few bucks, but I'm the one with the smarts to get us out of here, and you have no idea what you're doing."

"I'm not stupid. I can figure things out, and I did hire you, so my opinion counts," Sorrie said.

Jim turned and stared. "We didn't go that way because it's turning north into where the coal mines are, and it doesn't come out again until it's loaded with coal and headed in the opposite direction. It'll be going east again. We have to go west, and while we're at it, let's get something straight. I'm nobody's bitch, so stop telling me you hired me. We're helping each other, nothing more."

They walked along the embankment and waited until a series of closed hoppers lumbered by. The train cars were back-to-back, and the steep incline made the train work hard to bank around the mountain. As it slowed, Jim and Sorrie hopped onto a ladder and then secured a place on the platform at the end. They had no trouble climbing on, but the space was cramped and smelled like oil.

"Hold onto the rails when you stand up," Jim yelled above the braying wheels.

They rode in silence, with Jim leaning against the ladder and waving into the wind to evaporate the sweat from his body. Finally, after several miles, Jim signaled Sorrie to jump off. He stumbled and then landed on his back with her on top of him.

Sorrie immediately sprang to her feet. "Why'd we get off here?"

"I know someone in the area who can help us get a shower and a quick meal before our connection gears up, but we need to hurry because we don't have much time." Jim started toward an embankment. Sorrie slowly followed.

The area was stark. There was no sound, not even a bird or cricket, just the rustling of a thick bed of dried leaves under their feet, which made walking difficult. "You know someone in these woods?" Sorrie said as Jim led her by the arm so she wouldn't lag behind.

"Not too far," he answered. He fished out his canteen and offered it. Sorrie took a swig, handed it back, and then complained about her feet hurting. They stopped so she could take her high tops off. She removed her socks, and a neat row of blisters was on the bottom of one of her feet.

"God, it hurts," Sorrie cried. "It's those demon boots you made me wear. No wonder I liked the sneakers better."

Jim told Sorrie to fish the boots from her knapsack. They were barely used. "These boots are all wrong. You don't want new shoes; you want shoes broken in. And you think you're going to tell me what to do? You need to listen more," Jim said.

"What? When I walked into the thrift store, did you think everything was going to be custom-made for me? You didn't come in, so it's your fault."

Jim jerked back. "Me? I don't know nothing about ladies' clothes. You're the boss of your own gear. It's not my fault you don't know how to dress yourself. I did my best to tell you."

Sorrie flung her sneakers and socks aside and took a pocketknife from her knapsack. "It hurts, it really hurts," she said as she broke the blusters with the tip of the knife. Then, while Jim watched, she extracted a small tube of Bacitracin from her bag, dabbed the blisters, wrapped her feet in a piece of gauze, then put her high tops back on. "I'll be all right."

"I believe the princess will remain on her throne." Even though Jim was annoyed with her earlier comments, he had a newfound respect for her resolve, then explained, "We go a couple hundred feet and over to the road. My friend's house is only a country mile away; it's just a little hop around the corner, so your feet should be okay. My friend may not be home, but the family's used to helping hobos."

"I'm not a hobo."

"You can call yourself whatever the hell you want," Jim said. "If the truth be told, I don't care what you think you are, the same way I don't care what people call me. Hell, a hobo seems like a fitting description. I'd rather be a hobo than a plain old bum. I've been called lots of things, but if it came down to it, I like hobo best because a hobo will work if it's available, but a bum won't. In the world of junkyard dogs, it has some respectability. And it also means I don't have to be tied to anything."

"You need other hobos, though," Sorrie responded. "You need the rails, you need to eat, get clothes. That's being tied to something."

"I don't need the rails. As for food and clothes, hell, I can get those anywhere. Just sneak into rich people's neighborhoods on garbage day, and there's plenty to fish out of those big plastic bins. I wake up every day where I want to or on the way to where I'm going. So don't expect me to say 'yes ma'am' and 'no ma'am' when all I really want to do is be alone to be myself." Jim fixed the latch on his belt and looked up toward the ridge. In the distance was the silhouette of a man dressed in black. The man was tall with his arms by his sides, looking in Jim's direction. His stance was casual, but he didn't move.

"You ever have a job?" Sorrie asked.

Jim turned to Sorrie. "Huh?"

"You ever have a job?" She asked.

Jim turned back to the ridge, but the man was gone. He concentrated on Sorrie's question. "I guess you never got to interview me, so now's your chance."

"Knock it off. I'm serious. Did you ever have a job with a paycheck?"

"I had one or two real jobs, not counting picking crops and cleaning off tables. I pumped gas at some quickie mart until the owner decided I wasn't trustworthy enough to handle cash, even though I was honest and never took anything from him—not even a bag of chips. He let me go after two months." Jim paused to reflect. "I worked cleaning floors and scrubbing out the food court in a bowling alley. I was let go there, too. I couldn't keep the day hours they gave me. I guess I'm not cut out for a regular job."

"I never needed a job," Sorrie said.

"Not even one?" Jim asked.

"I used to volunteer to read to kids at the library but didn't get paid. Momma insisted on signing me up so we could maintain respectability. I always wanted to travel, though."

Jim was only half-listening to Sorrie's response. The outline of the man on the ridge wouldn't leave his mind. "Listen, when you said your parents might send someone after you, did that mean they'd kidnap you?"

"I don't know what they'll do. They might have someone spy on me, but it's more likely they'd try to convince me to come home, and if that didn't work, they'd probably force me into a car or something. I don't think they'd just watch me."

Jim was tempted to tell Sorrie about the man on the ridge but changed his mind. He didn't want to alarm her, but he asked himself if the man wasn't coming for Sorrie, who else would he be coming for?

* * *

They slogged up an incline onto a gravel road. The mud created by the morning rain made walking difficult, and Sorrie kept stumbling over the edge where the street met the land. "I told you to put the boots on," Jim said. He grabbed her arm and kept her steady until she felt safe enough to walk unassisted. "Looks like someone didn't get enough sleep," Jim said.

Sorrie glanced at Jim and sneered. "Are you kidding me? How can anyone sleep soundly on a noisy train?"

"I do it all the time. You have to get used to it, oh, but I forgot. Are you one of those princesses that needs a bunch of mattresses to sleep sound?"

"Why don't you just concentrate on getting me to where I need to be instead of wondering if I'm too soft to take it?" Sorrie scowled.

They turned into a side street and walked a few hundred feet. Despite looking hungry and exhausted, Sorrie seemed invigorated, especially after Jim told her that if everything fell into place, she could count on a hot shower and something to eat.

Jim led them through thick underbrush, and suddenly, a white cottage with a wooden porch and a cobblestone path leading up to the front steps emerged. It was simple and elegant, and in the distance, Jim could see a large garden with stakes of tomatoes and other vegetables in the backyard. "The house is so beautiful. Who lives here?" Sorrie asked.

"It's someone who cares about me but knows better than to tell me what to do."

"Cares how?"

"As an angel would care," Jim said, then signaled Sorrie to keep quiet as he crept around the rear of the house. The asphalt driveway was covered with dried, brown truck tracks, but there was no truck—just a child's three-wheeled scooter and a red and yellow bouncing ball. Sorrie followed as Jim walked up the back steps and gently knocked. "If the old man's home, we got to take off like jackrabbits, but if it's my angel, we'll be invited in."

Sorrie waited on the bottom step and noticed a circle drawn in chalk with an *X* in the middle of it on the door leading to an underground basement. "That's a funny place to draw that," Sorrie said. "What's the blue one for?"

"That's to tell hobos they might get a meal here—and they're right." Jim knocked again, but it was becoming obvious no one was home. He reached above the door and grabbed a key.

The home was small but warm. The wood stove in the kitchen had held a recent fire, but there was only a faint glow of embers inside the glass door. Jim pointed toward the hallway. "Hurry if you want to get a shower," he said.

Jim directed Sorrie past a blue couch in the living room to the hall linen closet, where towels, shampoo, and lemon-scented soap were on the shelves. She quickly entered the bathroom, and Jim could hear the water streaming in the shower. "Won't your friend mind if we're here?" She yelled through the door.

"Not unless she comes back with her old man. Now take your shower and hurry up." While Jim waited his turn, he sat in the kitchen, staring at the linoleum floor. Then, a thought flashed into his mind. He glanced at the backpack she'd left on the chair. She said she had no one, but could he believe her? He'd been conned enough by the best. Maybe that knapsack held an address or two, and he could contact her parents, letting them know where their daughter was—for a fee. Jim glanced at the bathroom door. He could hear the water running; it was time for some exploration.

He reached for the backpack and rustled through it. There were a few pairs of black pants, T-shirts, and pink underwear—items Jim remembered seeing when he first grabbed her knapsack. The boots Jim insisted Sorrie wear were at the bottom, along with an address log and a separate book. He held the book up to the light. "*Mythology.*" Jim tried to sound out the word but couldn't, so he tossed it back and flipped through the address log. There was an entry for someone in Manassas with a last name he couldn't pronounce but no number; Jim saw another entry he guessed was the uncle in Nebraska. The rest of the pages were blank. It looked like she was telling the truth about not having any friends.

Jim heard the water stop. He threw the book inside the backpack, hurried to close it, and arranged the knapsack to look the same as before when he heard a sound behind him.

"It's not in there," Sorrie said.

Jim turned around and saw Sorrie wrapped in a yellow bath towel. "Huh?"

"It's not in there." Sorrie walked over to her bag, placed her dirty clothes inside, and took the knapsack from Jim.

"What?" Jim innocently looked up.

"My money isn't in my knapsack. I took it with me into the bathroom."

They stared at each other while an air of mistrust circled the room and settled into the space between them.

"Here, see," Sorrie said as she extracted the red purse from the pocket of her dirty jeans. She clipped it open. "There's a twenty-dollar bill and nothing more. Go on and look if you don't believe me." She tried to hand it to Jim, but he refused to take it. She put it into her knapsack.

"I wasn't looking for that. I wasn't looking for anything." Jim tried to brush off what had just happened. He hoped she didn't accuse him of being a thief.

"Then what were you doing looking in my things? There's nothing in there that I need to hide from you."

"I was looking for an address book or maybe the phone number of your uncle to tell him we were coming."

"You're a liar and not even a good one. Did you find it? Of course, you did. And what did you find?" Sorrie reached her hand into her knapsack and extracted the log. She tried to hand it to Jim. "See? Here it is. Take it."

"Oh my God, it's just a log. Calm down, would you? It's okay; just put it back in your sack. I don't need to see it."

"Probably because you already saw it," Sorrie said, throwing it back into her knapsack.

Jim tried changing the subject. "Hungry for some food?" He asked. Sorrie didn't answer. Instead, she took her knapsack and inspected her clothes. "Don't worry," Jim reassured her, "I didn't touch anything."

She extracted some underwear, a pair of jeans, and a black T-shirt. Jim could hear her close a bedroom door. When she returned, the smell of bacon hung in the air.

"Since I didn't think you were going to cook for me, I took it upon myself to throw some food on the stove," Jim said, motioning for Sorrie to sit at the table.

"How do I know I can trust your cooking?"

"Don't worry. I'm not going to poison you, and I'm sorry about before."

"Okay, we'll call it even for now," Sorrie said as she relaxed into the kitchen chair against the wall."

"I learned how to cook a long time ago. I had to with Momma gone so much of the time. What's more, I learned to whip up a good-tasting meal with ingredients that got no business being together."

Sorrie seemed intrigued. "Like what?"

Jim scooped the bacon and some fried eggs onto two plates and placed them on the table. Then, sitting down, he said, "Oh, barbeque sauce and oatmeal. Potatoes and radishes, stuff like that."

"You ever eat that?"

"Nah, I never had the pleasure, but I saw a hobo dip cucumber slices into ice cream. He didn't complain. Besides, he hadn't eaten in two days, so anything would've tasted good."

Changing the subject, Sorrie asked, "Will your friend be home soon?"

"Don't know. The wood stove was warm, but that could have been from the night before. She has twelve-hour shifts, and her husband's usually working on the oil rigs in Texas this time of year."

"What does she do?" Sorrie said, reaching for some ketchup to slather on her eggs.

Jim looked up from his plate, surprised that Sorrie would even take an interest. "She's a nurse. That's where I met her. She was working some night shift when I came in all screwed up, and she took care of me in the emergency room."

"Screwed up from what?" Sorrie asked.

"Well, likely too much drink. That's the trouble I get into mostly. Drinking too much and then starting fights. I don't remember half of 'em, but I've been cut enough to know I came out on the losing end that night." Jim put down his fork and lifted the bottom of his shirt to reveal a two-inch gash on his belly. Don't know where I got that, but I think it was the night I met my angel. I was in the hospital for two days."

"I didn't notice that when you changed your shirt in the boxcar."

"It's there, all right. Sometimes I have to drink to calm the tricksies in my head; sometimes, I drink cause I like to drink. I'm not hurting anybody, but this time, it got me into trouble and put me in the hospital for two days."

"Tricksies?" Sorrie asked.

"Just the little thoughts that come in and out of my brain when it's quiet, and they say things I don't like, so I calm them by drinking. It shuts them down. You should try it. It might help you not to ask so many questions."

Sorrie scooped up the rest of her meal and, between bites, asked, "It seemed to me that two days is awfully short to be in the hospital for getting cut in your stomach."

Jim shook his head. "I told you I don't remember the fight, but when the hospital found out I didn't have insurance, they bundled me up and showed me the door so paying customers could take the bed. Maxine saw me leaving and told me whenever I needed a quick shower and a hot meal to come by. So, I've been coming around whenever I get to this part of the country. I hoped she would tell me the fastest train to get to Louisville. She knows the trains pretty well. Lots of hobos come here. That's why she got the X marked on her basement door."

"You're telling me you don't know what train to catch?"

"Timetables change. This is different from a people train with a regular schedule. Some of them go as soon as they're loaded and packed up, or the coal's ready to be hauled, or the crops are in, or the passenger trains aren't running too close together—most trains run on people lines, so if there's an accident, everything has to wait down the line."

They ate the rest of their meal in silence. While Sorrie did the dishes, Jim hopped into the shower but was out quickly. He crept around the corner and spied Sorrie, checking the money in her red purse. She then pulled a brush from her knapsack to untangle her hair. As she formed it into a ponytail, she tiptoed to Jim's sack. Jim knew she'd never get it open. It had been secured with an intricate seaman's knot—a skill he learned from an East Coast fisherman stationed in Montauk.

Suddenly, a voice out of nowhere asked, "Who are you, and what are you doing in my kitchen?"

Sorrie pivoted around to see a woman wearing a nurse's uniform holding a brown bag of groceries. The woman placed the food on the counter.

"I'm Sorrie."

"Damn right, you're sorry. What are you doing here? I've never seen you before, and the only travelers I let into my home are those I know," the woman said as she took the items out of her bag. She put a can of peas on the counter. Then, noticing Jim's knapsack with its intricate knot, a smile came over her face. "Jimmy? Jimmy boy?"

"He's in the bathroom taking a shower," Sorrie said, but Jim wasn't. While he dressed, he'd watched everything unfold from a corner of the hall.

Getting no response, the woman raised her voice. "James? Where are you, James?" She glanced back at Sorrie. "You traveling together?"

There was a hesitation in Sorrie's voice. "I guess so."

"Traveling with Jimmy? Lucky you. What's your name anyway?"

"Sorrie."

"Why do you keep saying that? I'm looking for your name, so we aren't strangers."

Just then, Jim emerged dressed with a folded towel in his hands. "I was standing in the hall. I didn't want to appear indecent to my favorite nurse. Give this homeboy a hug, Maxine." He put the towel on a chair and stretched out his arms. "Meet my girl, Sorrie."

"Don't know why everybody keeps apologizing to old Maxine. I don't think I like it. It makes me feel like I did something wrong." She folded the brown bag and put it under the sink.

"Sorrie, her name is Sorrie," he said as he adjusted his pants.

"Sorrie? How'd you get a name like that?"

"It's what my mom called me," Sorrie sat at the kitchen table.

Maxine eyed Sorrie, then said, "Child, you look about as lost as a hen in a snowstorm."

"I'm not sure what you mean by that." Sorrie glanced in Jim's direction.

"I don't think you do," Maxine said again. She excused herself and went into a bedroom. "Long night, last night. I feel like I've been pushed through a keyhole."

"The top of your stove was lukewarm, but the embers were still glowing when we got here," Jim said.

"That was old Whipjack leaving for the night. He was here before you. He got cleaned up, ate something, then left this morning, or so I supposed." Maxine closed her bedroom door.

Sorrie looked at Jim and whispered. "That woman's crazy."

Jim undid the tangle on his knapsack and shoved his dirty clothes in. "She's a good friend who's going to get us out of here just as soon as she changes."

"I hope you're right," Sorrie said while Jim looked at himself in a wall mirror. Within a few minutes, Maxine emerged in a blue robe and sat on the sofa.

"So why are you here? I haven't seen you in a raccoon's age, and now you're showing up on my door—and bringing company?" Maxine pulled a stick of gum from a pack inside a table drawer. She offered one to Jim, and he took it. Maxine looked at Sorrie. "Gum?" She asked, but Sorrie shook her head no.

"We're here for a meal and advice." Maxine waved her arm but didn't speak. Jim continued. "You know the trains running through. We need the fastest route to Louisville."

Maxine sighed. "Jimmy boy, you been through here a hundred times. You should have the routes tattooed on your ass by now."

"Not since some of the coal mines shut down, and those left decided to take coal out by truck. Everything's different."

"Well, it's sure damn different with all the flooding this year. I've heard stories about problems from Minnesota to Baton Rouge."

"Is there any news to be told?" Jim asked. He was worried. If they couldn't make it to Nebraska, they'd have to find another way, adding days to their trip.

"I think most of it's been cleared out by now—just don't expect those 'green fields of grain' like you're used to. There are still pockets, though."

"I'll have to remember to ask down the line. It's been a while since I've taken the route."

"Where you been anyhow?" Maxine asked, kicking off her shoes and settling comfortably on the sofa.

"You know where I've been: searching in Cali and Florida looking for my father, and in between, I been looking for jobs to earn some money."

"Have any luck?"

"I cleaned toilets and bussed tables in Brooklyn until their regular help returned from vacation. I picked crops in New Jersey, then got a week's worth of work with some boatyard out on Long Island cleaning fish charters. I had an urge to take one of those babies out onto the water and sail clear down to Mexico, but they were too big, and I can't drive a car, let alone a boat. I ran out of money after a job I was told about in Florida didn't pan out, then hitched to Virginia; that's where I met Sorrie."

"When I asked 'any luck,' I meant finding your father."

"No. I been searching bars in towns where The Doors had concerts, hoping someone would recall seeing him. The only person who remembered anything was an old timer in Bakersfield who saw him at a bar sipping whiskey back in 1969, but he hadn't seen him since. I haven't stopped looking yet."

"And what brings you into this godforsaken place?"

Jim responded. "Got to get to Montana is all—with a short hop to Nebraska first."

Maxine accepted this explanation, and Jim explained they had to get through as soon as possible to avoid the flooding. He didn't mention the man on the ridge.

Maxine drew in a mouthful of air and sighed. "Well, I'll have to draw you a map."

"Use my atlas." Jim removed it from his knapsack.

Maxine put her glasses on and began rifling through the pages. "Lots of coal companies went out of business faster than a bell clapper in a goose's ass. Most of 'em are useless anyway because the short runs go around in a big, wide circle to load up the coal and ship it the way the train comes in. I don't know where to begin, but Chicken Wing passed through not too long ago, and he told me about a line going west that hooks up with a real hotshot, which, if my memory serves me correctly, should take you into Louisville and beyond. No need to hurry because you can get to the tracks directly, and you got time. The train leaves closer to ten tonight." Maxine studied the atlas and began scratching something on the page. She examined it further and then wrote a note in the margin. Looking satisfied, she handed the atlas back to Jim. "Just be careful of the weather. Some lines barely made it through, and some stopped altogether, but if the good Lord's willing and the creek don't rise, you should get there in time to catch daylight over the Ohio River."

"Much thanks to a graceful lady," Jim said.

"You want some reefer before you go?"

"I don't do drugs anymore," Jim said.

Maxine snickered, then looked at Sorrie. "You want reefer? One of the hobos left a joint on the kitchen table last week as a thanks, but they know I don't smoke anymore, being a nurse and all. I see enough of those hopheads in the ER as it is." Sorrie shook her head. "Maybe a drink then?" Maxine said as she got up and reached for a bottle of bourbon on a nearby cart, then poured a shot. She held the glass out to Sorrie.

"I don't do drugs—or drink," Sorrie said.

Jim grabbed the glass from Maxine's hand and downed it. "My drink now," he said, then turning to Sorrie, mouthed, "Time to go."

Before saying goodbye, Maxine gave them candy bars and dried fruit. "Any extra room in a knapsack should always have food and water in it," she said as she wrapped her hand around Jim's arm. "Know how I met this guy?" she asked Sorrie.

"Something about a fight?" Sorrie said.

Maxine looked surprised. "No, not a fight. He drank too much. Got drunk and had to have his stomach pumped. Had a gash, too, from falling on a knife. I still like him, though. He's cute as a button, smart as a whip, and deadly as a copperhead, so be warned, he has different faces." She reached over and kissed Jim on the cheek.

"I'm sure you see him a lot coming through," Sorrie said.

"Only when he's hungry and wants to get cleaned up, usually for some girl," Maxine winked.

* * *

They didn't have to wait long for the diesel. Jim knew it would take them clear across Kentucky. Beyond lay the west and an opportunity to split with Sorrie and get where he needed to go.

They had no trouble finding a stacker, which, despite the train's lumbering speed, they still needed to run to catch. They managed to grab hold of the ladder and jump into the bucket where they wouldn't be spotted by passing train crews. It had a solid steel floor and a place to store their knapsacks. Jim warned Sorrie it would be cold, but the car provided an excellent ride. Sorrie leaned on her backpack and played with the stem of a daisy she'd picked. She began by caressing the flower and then stripping it of its petals. "Why did you do it?" She asked out of nowhere.

"Do what?" Jim questioned.

"Go through my things."

"I thought we were done with this?" Jim asked.

"I don't believe you."

"I wasn't sure if you were telling the truth about having nowhere to go. I thought you lied. All I found was a book and a few telephone numbers." Jim waited for Sorrie's reaction, but she didn't look surprised, which annoyed him. "Aren't you going to yell at me or something?" He asked.

"The thing I'm upset about is that you didn't trust what I said. I told you I had no friends; my parents disapproved of anyone I brought home after school. You didn't believe what I said, and that hurts worse of all."

"Aren't you furious at me or nothing? Don't you want to yell and scream at me?" He asked.

Sorrie turned and looked directly at Jim. "Look, I don't think you understand how rich my parents are. It's better for me if there aren't big scenes that will attract people's notice. There's probably people out looking for me right now, so we have to be careful we won't get noticed anywhere we go. It's not above them to take out full-page ads in papers with a big 'Reward' at the top of the page and my face plastered all over it."

Jim's ears perked up. It wouldn't be above him to turn her in and claim the reward, but then he thought of her safety. "You're eighteen, right? They can't touch you."

"You don't know my parents. They'll kidnap me and have me declared insane. That's why I don't want you going through my stuff, and I don't want you to know any more than you need to about me and my life. Keep looking around because I can guarantee someone is chasing us down right now." Sorrie flailed her arms around and accidentally hit the side of the bucket. Her eyes closed, and she bent over as she rubbed her hand.

"Are you okay?" Jim asked.

Sorrie opened her eyes. "It will pass." As the sharp sting subsided, Sorrie went back to her first concern. "We better be looking around corners for the unexpected. I wouldn't put anything past them."

"Come to think of it, I did see someone early this morning standing on the ridgeline when we got off the train. He didn't say anything, and I couldn't get a good look at his face, so maybe that's the guy that's following you."

Sorrie sat up, and Jim noticed she stopped rubbing her hand. "You should have told me. From now on, let me know about anyone you see who looks out of place. We'll have to make a run for it if it's the guy they employed. After all, we're friends, right?"

The honesty of Sorrie's words brought Jim to a standstill; all he could think of were big black letters spelling out the word "Reward." Jim stared into the distance and avoided her look. "I guess we don't have much in common, but you said I worked for you just like that private cop gets hired by your parents, so for now, we better stick together." Jim avoided asking the question about how much Sorrie's parents would pay, but he told himself if someone approached him with a deal, he'd be willing to listen.

* * *

They rode in silence until Jim noticed Sorrie was trembling. "Are you okay?" He asked.

"I've been colder," Sorrie replied, seemingly trying to put up a good front.

Jim invited her to put her head against his chest for warmth.

Sorrie got comfortable and looked up at the stars. "Do you believe in God?"

Jim glanced at the metal floor. There were red drops resembling paint, but Jim didn't want to look closer. "I know when something disturbs the air, so I guess there's stuff I can't rightly see that's been driving me through my whole life. Hell, I been saved so many times from getting killed that God's got to be in the mix somewhere."

Though Sorrie's face was in shadow, Jim heard her voice: "I hate God. If he's there, I just hate him with all my heart."

"Why would you say a thing like that?"

"Because he's not fair."

"For you? Looks like you got the golden end of the stick." Jim said, but Sorrie remained quiet. Jim wrapped an arm around her shoulder and let her drift off. As she did, he cleared the hair from her face. "Don't fear, princess, I'll make sure you're sleeping sound tonight," he sang.

The night sky descended, and Jim surveyed the landscape. It was still coal country. He could hear the *chugga-chugga* of the machinery making soup bowls of the earth. Jim glanced at Sorrie again. No pot marks, no scars, but he could see two tears rolling down her face as she slept. What secrets did she have that she needed to hide? What was she so fearful of in the dark that would make her cry?

* * *

Their trip ended with a rude lurch the next day. The freight yard was massive now, almost too large, with strings of tracks in both directions and several dozen lines.

Before they left the train, they drank some water, ate the dried fruit Maxine had given them, and re-arranged their knapsacks.

They strolled down the ladder, and just about the time their feet hit the earth, Jim spied the bull in a truck by the side of the tracks. He gently motioned for Sorrie to back away. "He'll never get out of the truck," Jim said, "no bulls ever do." They began hurrying as they heard the roar of the vehicle's engine start behind them, and Jim knew they'd been spotted.

Suddenly, the bull yelled, "Hey you!" He put his vehicle into gear and barreled down the yard as the two took off down the tracks. "Hey you," the bull yelled again. The truck wheels got caught in the mud, and the bull pulled over, but he wasn't deterred. He exited the truck and lit out on foot.

Jim and Sorrie dodged railroad ties and stacking racks and almost slammed head-first into a yard hand. Instead, they went past rolling stock and wooden skids, and as they ran faster, so did the bull, which made Jim laugh. It was unusual for a man in his position to take off like that. Most preferred the comfort of their trucks. Either way, no bull ever overtook him. But Sorrie had difficulty with her knapsack and slowed them down just enough to allow the bull to keep pace.

They traveled more than fifty yards, but the bull didn't stop. He was a big man, and Jim pegged him at close to two hundred pounds. Still, he had the agility of an athlete as he dodged pit marks, mud holes, and piles of crushed stone ballast, which made it harder for Sorrie and Jim to get a good lead. They picked up their pace, evading an incoming train lumbering toward a sidetrack as the bull pursued them. They ran until there were only a few lines of track left. Then, the brush grew thicker, and the incline of the terrain got steeper, which caused them to stumble. Finally, Jim spied a long strip of chain-linked fence with a wide gash cut through one of the sections. He pointed Sorrie in the direction of the opening. They barreled toward the gap, and still, the bull drew closer.

Jim grabbed Sorrie's knapsack and tossed it over the fence with his own. He pushed Sorrie through the hole and was about to slip across after her when the bull ran up and caught the belt around Jim's pants.

"Gotcha," the bull yelled, pulling Jim from the opening. He held onto the strap with one hand and tried to grab Jim's arm with the other.

Stumbling and scraping the ground, Jim tried to push the bull away, yelling, "Get off me!" But the bull was solid and quick, and they fought to see who would come out ahead, as Jim's thin frame was losing against the bull's body.

Finally, in one explosive gesture, Jim lifted himself and pushed the bull hard, making the man slip on the wet dirt. His body hit the earth with a heavy thud, and his head crashed against a railroad tie lying in the middle of a dirt pile. Jim shot a worried look toward Sorrie. The bull wasn't moving. Was he dead? Had Jim killed him? They waited and took long, deep breaths.

Scared now, Jim watched Sorrie come through the fence in his direction. He motioned for her to back away, but she was bewildered.

"Should I call for a freight hand?" Sorrie asked. "He looks hurt. Maybe we should get an ambulance."

"We aren't calling nobody for nothing," Jim said. "If you ever want to get to Nebraska, we got to let it be and disappear. Otherwise, it could mean jail." Then, remembering a memory from the past, he said, "Damn, I forgot to get his wallet in his back pocket."

Suddenly, the bull's head came up from the dirt. He was conscious. It looked like he was more surprised at having fallen than anything else. Jim alternated between feeling relieved and anxious. Stunned and flopping like a caught fish, the bull had trouble getting up.

Finally, he struggled to his feet. "Damn kids," he said. "I'll get you sonsabitches."

Jim grabbed Sorrie's arm and pushed her toward the fence, but instead of following, she broke free and ran back. "What the hell?" Jim yelled.

Sorrie hesitated, then reached out toward the bull. But instead of latching onto his arm to help him, she extended her hand and snatched the wallet from his back pocket. The bull felt her arm. He staggered to his feet and realized what she'd done, turned, and tried to run after her, but the mud was too thick, and he stumbled again and fell as Jim and Sorrie ran off into the distance.

They sprinted through a clump of woods. Then, satisfied the bull hadn't followed them, they rested against a tree and inspected the wallet's contents. There was a license and some credit cards, but Jim was only interested in the billfold.

"Nice work," he said as Sorrie counted two hundred dollars. She folded the money and was about to put it into her purse when Jim said, "Hey, at least half that money's mine."

"What makes you say that?"

"Because you would've never gotten out of there if it weren't for me."

"Well, I did all the work running back and such. You could have done the same once he slipped," Sorrie said.

Jim eyed Sorrie. "I was more concerned for *you*," he said.

"Still lying to get what you want, eh?" Sorrie peeled five twenty-dollar bills from the bundle, "Here," she said and handed the money and wallet to Jim. He took it, checked the compartments for anything they might have overlooked, and tossed it into a nearby ditch when he didn't find anything. Sorrie gazed at the money in her hands and the spot where Jim had thrown the wallet. She looked regretful. "It's yours," Jim said. "You earned it. And I have to say that for someone who doesn't want to attract attention, you're sure making a lot of trouble for yourself."

"We can't starve," She said. "We needed the money, right?" Sorrie placed the twenties in her purse, walked over to where the wallet lay in the dirt, and picked it up.

"What the hell are you doing?" Jim asked.

"Be right back," she said as she returned to the rail yard. Jim followed behind, warning her they could get caught and that what she was doing was stupid and insane. The more he talked, the more she quickened her pace until she was back beyond the slit in the fencing, back to where the trains came in.

The bull was nowhere to be seen. Instead, the place looked deserted except for the high-pitched sound of a lone whistle in the distance. Jim was afraid. Would this extra time near the freight yard attract the police? He thought of grabbing her and hauling her away. But she stood there, rubbed the wallet with her shirt to clean off any mud or fingerprints, and walked to a nearby wooden building where she tossed the wallet to where a yard worker might find it.

"That's for you, Toad," Jim heard her say.

7

Kentucky to Indiana

ANOTHER MORNING AFTER a night spent in the woods meant hunger. Hunger meant food, and that meant having to come out of the shadows and look for a place to eat—it was that or scavenge for breakfast in the dumpsters behind the grocery mart, but as Sorrie told Jim, "If we have money, then at least we should eat properly."

Jim had a better idea. "There's a free kitchen not too far from here, and we can get a hot meal if you're not picky about what you eat and who you eat it with. I don't think the people looking for you will suspect you went to a broken-down place like a soup kitchen for food—that's if anyone's looking for you at all."

"What about the wallet? They're bound to find it and come looking for us. Shouldn't we be on our way? If they find us, they'll find me, and I don't want to go back."

"Seeing as how you threw it back into the yard, that's the last place we should be going at this time in the morning. We need to lay low for a few hours and stay out of sight. We'll get there soon enough."

Sorrie agreed and then spent a few minutes fixing her dirty clothes and dabbing on mascara. After examining her face in a mirror, she used fabric from the arm of her shirt to clean her teeth. Then, noticing her unkempt hair, Sorrie picked out a few wayward leaves and twigs from her red strands and brushed the dirt from her pants.

Jim watched with the expression of a man annoyed with what he saw.

"Why are you looking at me that way?" She asked.

"I don't see why you want to get all dolled up when we're just going into a church for something to eat. Besides, you can do that in the bathroom at the church."

"I like to look nice."

"They don't care if you look nice. It's almost better if you look worse; then they think you really need to be there. Besides, I'm hungry."

Sorrie dabbed at her eyelids. "I don't want to look dirty. I want to look presentable. Like I'm somebody important, not just a bookworm hiding in the closet."

"When did you ever hide in the closet?"

"Lots of times. Usually, when my mother wanted me to do something or go somewhere, I didn't want to go."

"Like where?"

"Charity galas, garden parties, gallery openings, anything you could think of so we could get our names in the society column in the local magazines for rich people. I hated those events and those people, so I'd hide in a closet beneath the stairs so she wouldn't find me. There were cartons of books tucked into the corner, and I stayed behind the boxes until she left without me. Reading saved my life."

They walked out of the woods and into the street, but only after Jim surveyed the road to see if anyone was watching. "I never learned to read good, but the teachers kept passing me along. Finally, Momma asked one of the school districts to analyze me, and they said I had something wrong with me to where I couldn't learn," Jim said.

"How could they know that unless they did a bunch of tests?"

"They said I had . . ." Jim thought but couldn't remember the word. "It starts with a 'dis' . . . dis something."

"You mean dyslexia?"

Jim got excited when Sorrie said the word he couldn't remember. "Yeah, that's it: dyslexia. I didn't know what that meant, and Momma didn't either, but they put me in the special education classes."

"What do you mean?"

"Special education. They said they would help me, and they did, and I started to learn, but then we went on the road again."

"Dyslexia's not a disease. It's just a learning disability where people have a hard time reading. The letters get switched up when you read or write them. If you're dyslexic, certain letters probably look like they're backward. Now I understand why you couldn't make sense of the book of poetry."

Jim kicked a pebble down the road. "Damn. All this time, I thought I had some disease or something, and it's been eating away at me. But you're saying it's just some learning thing?"

"I read about it in a book. There are ways to figure out the words. It's nothing to be ashamed of. A lot of dyslexics are pretty smart."

Jim felt a sense of relief. "Poetry or no poetry, I aim to memorize my father's poems like I memorized his songs. So, keep reading to me so I can remember it."

* * *

They were out in the open now, and while Sorrie marveled at the scope and beauty of the city skyline, Jim scanned the horizon for the church. They walked further, and Jim pointed to a group of people taking their places in line outside a basement door. A few minutes later, Jim and Sorrie were making their way to a table, each with a plate of scrambled eggs, home fries, a few strips of bacon, and a roll that Jim said was probably a day old. Sorrie took a bite, and the crust disintegrated in her hands.

"Told you," Jim whispered. He was seated against a wall where he could watch the room and the people coming in. Some faces looked familiar, and he nodded here and there. Still, most had the type of blank stare only a night of heavy drinking could bring: drooping, bloodshot eyes, shaky hands that couldn't hold a plate steady, and the zombie shuffle as if every molecule in their bodies was so heavy that their legs couldn't find the power to lift their shoes off the floor.

"Everyone looks a little scared and deranged," Sorrie said as she popped a piece of bacon into her mouth.

"Whoever's not scared is deranged," Jim said as he leaned back in his chair, scanning the new arrivals waiting for a cop to show up. As he did, the overwhelming smell of coffee hung in the air, as did the stench of wet laundry and human sweat. "But there are families too. Lots of people who are out of work or who can't make the paycheck stretch come here for a meal. There's no shame in it."

A white-bearded priest circled the room, helping to feed those who had trouble feeding themselves. He glanced down at someone every few minutes, spoke a few words, patted a hand, and squeezed a shoulder. When he saw a family, the priest talked with the mother or father and then the children. Jim thought it was all very Christian, but then he reminded himself he didn't need convincing that God existed.

Sorrie sat across from Jim. Between bites, she dabbed her face with a paper napkin. "What are you doing that for?" Jim asked.

"Between the grease and the sweat, the air's a little thick. My face is raunchy, and my mascara's running down my cheeks."

"I think it smells good with bacon and sausage in the air. Coffee, too, and it's free. There's nothing better," Jim said, scooping up some fake eggs.

"If it's so good, why are the eggs bright yellow? I've never seen eggs that color."

"It's fake eggs. Put a little ketchup on it for taste. Anyway, who cares? It fills my belly, which is the important thing. You better scoop it up. I want to get out of town without being seen. I don't need cop problems after yesterday."

"Is that why you're sitting with your back against the wall? To look for someone looking for us."

"You mean you, don't you?"

Sorrie's face got red. "You think he'll come for me?"

Jim looked out at the crowd, wondering if he should be worried. "Could be," he said, surveying each face. The tingling in his nerves matched the excitement in his thoughts. It might be fun to run into the cop looking for Sorrie, but then he thought better of it. They might accuse him of kidnapping her, and that would be a crime that would get him twenty-five years in jail. She might even say she was taken against her will until things settled down, and then she'd run away again.

Jim took a cigarette from his shirt pocket but didn't light it. Instead, the white cylinder dangled from his lips and moved in a seesaw motion as he surveyed the room. Jim spotted a tall man sitting in a corner opposite where Jim was sitting. His face was ruddy, and he looked like he could use a shave. He was trying not to stare at Jim by lowering his head and raising his eyes occasionally. Jim thought of going over to him, but then the priest came over, so Jim had to resist the urge to get up.

"I'm Father Bob," he said.

Jim wondered if that was his name. He'd met plenty of Father Bobs in soup kitchens. The priest reached out and shook their hands.

"How are you two doing today?"

Jim nodded and didn't say anything, but Sorrie couldn't resist.

"We're travelers on the road like Sal and Dean in that book."

"Are those your names? Sal and Dean?"

Jim knew he had to step in. "Those aren't our names, and we kind of like to keep to ourselves, father. So, if you don't mind . . ."

Father Bob shook his head. "I understand. Let's just have a word, and then I'll leave you two alone." He laid his hands on both of their shoulders. "Because you are here '. . . you are no longer foreigners and strangers, but fellow citizens with God's people and also members of his household,' for as Jesus said in Matthew 25 . . ."

Jim sensed the priest would recite half the Bible, so he interrupted him. "Amen," he said. "Thank you, Father."

"Thank you, Father," Sorrie said and crossed herself.

"Thank you, my son and daughter." Father Bob turned to leave but then looked down and saw Jim's cigarette. "There's no smoking in here," he said sternly.

As Jim nodded and said he understood, the priest whispered something and walked away. Jim glanced beyond Sorrie to the stranger in the corner. But the stranger was gone. Jim perused every face but didn't see anyone resembling the man.

Sorrie leaned over the table. "What do you think he said?"

Jim was startled and focused back on the priest. "I think he said 'blessings,' but I'm not sure. It doesn't matter. We need to keep our heads down, so don't go talking to anyone else."

Jim and Sorrie lingered long enough to get a stale Danish and a second cup of coffee. Before leaving, they both freshened up in the bathroom, and Jim held up his right hand and whispered "blessings" before they left. He figured Father Bob must have been onto something with the Almighty because the cops never showed up. Neither did the bull.

* * *

The best way out of town was through the expansive freight yard, but that meant returning to where Sorrie had picked the bull's pocket, so Jim asked if it was okay for them to split the cost of a motel room, reasoning that they would have a better chance of hooking a connection after dark and not being seen. When Sorrie questioned Jim's motives, he insisted, "Look, all I want to do is shower, take a nap, and avoid trouble, okay? Can you try not being suspicious all the time?"

They found a local flophouse, and with the money from the bull, they managed to talk the clerk into letting them have a room for thirty dollars split down the middle.

The space was painted khaki green and smelled like wet paper, but the bathroom was clean and contained plenty of fresh towels. Jim wasted no time jumping in the shower and scrubbing the dirt from his skin while Sorrie stretched out on the queen-sized bed and played with the television remote.

As Jim showered, he could hear Sorrie switching the channels between cartoons and the news. Jim rubbed his rough hands over his body and wondered if the change of scenery might loosen her up a bit—get the crick in her back untied. She was a pain, all right. But he was beginning to like her and how she always had the aroma of lavender.

Jim leaned against the wall with his arms and closed his eyes. He took a deep breath, anticipating the flowery scent of the soap, but he could only smell the pine disinfectant they used to clean the tub. Then he stopped and realized the outside room was quiet. His eyes shot open; was the television still on? Jim turned the water off and listened. He heard the animated voice of a cartoon character through the door, then a *click, click, click,* and a loud scream; she must have found a horror movie. He turned the water back on and scrubbed his arms; as he did, he reminded himself that even though he liked her, Sorrie could be annoying, too. When she started speaking to the priest, she clearly didn't know the first thing about blending into the crowd and not bringing attention to herself. But her thinking of him as a hired hand stuck in his craw, too. He hated being tied to a girl he hadn't rightly known for more than a week.

Jim emerged ten minutes later. He was clean, shaved, and had slicked his hair back. Sorrie lay on the bed with the television remote in her hands. "Your hair looks so neat instead of flying in all directions. You resemble a TV star I once had a crush on," she said.

"Which one?" Jim asked. Beads of water hung on his chest.

Instead of answering, Jim saw Sorrie's eyes focused on the gash on his stomach.

"It isn't anything," Jim said as he looked down. "Maxine was right. I got drunk and fell on a knife." Water ran along the scar and dripped onto the towel. In a different light, it could have resembled blood. "I heard the television screeching. It sounded like there was a murder next door."

"No, just a fight," Sorrie explained. "A couple was arguing; I couldn't hear what they were saying because it was so muffled and annoying, so I turned up the volume to drown them out."

"What was it about? Money?"

"Who knows?" Sorrie said. She scooped up her knapsack, passed the air conditioner, switched it on, and entered the bathroom. Jim positioned himself on the bed, the towel hanging loosely around his genitals. He closed his eyes and thought of the women his father might have liked.

The hot shower and humidity outside had generated a rush of desire. He lifted his chest, extended his shoulders, stretched his arms against the headboard, then curled his backside along the pillow's contours and sucked in his stomach, which expanded his chest and filled his lungs with air.

As he closed his eyes, he saw his father onstage. Steaming sexuality as his father twisted into a chameleon-like pose, collapsing onstage, singing into a microphone, not caring what anyone thought. It was all performance. Jim felt it seep into his skin, electrifying his nerve endings.

"Here I am, world," he said. He closed his eyes and tried to concentrate on the sensual voices of the women he'd liked, but all he heard was the hum of the air conditioner and high heels on a bare floor in the room next door. Every few seconds, Jim listened to a *click-clack, click-clack,* as if the woman was running out of the room. Once the noise stopped, Jim took a deep breath and noticed Sorrie's scent on the pillow. Jim brought it up to his nose and breathed deeply as the flowery smell of lavender filled his nostrils. Then, moving back, he opened his eyes and tossed it onto the bed. The pleasant mood he was in soured. She would be more likable if she treated him like the man he was. Not a servant.

Sorrie finished quickly. Jim readied himself to greet her as she unlocked the bathroom door. When she threw it open, Jim was there, naked and lying on the bed.

"Oh, oh my God," she said, turning away.

"What? You've never seen a man before?" Jim said innocently. "You've seen me change my clothes. So, it's not like you never noticed."

"Please put some clothes on," Sorrie said from behind the half-opened door.

"I forgot my pants. Can you hand them to me? They're over on the chair," he said.

"I'll go back into the bathroom until you're dressed. I'm an Emily, if you didn't know."

"What's an Emily?" Jim was intrigued as he covered himself with the towel again. "Are you like two personalities or something?"

Sorrie hid behind the bathroom door and clicked the lock shut. "I really need you to get dressed. I consider myself an Emily, and I can't have sex with you," she said through the door.

"Did you think that that was on my mind?"

"Yes, of course, that's what I thought."

"I'm just messing with you, but if you want to, we can get dirty right now," Jim said. He extended his arm to grab onto his pants on the chair, but he wasn't close enough.

Behind the locked door came an almost inaudible voice; it was low, like a child admitting to a wrong. "I'm an Emily, like the virgin Emily Dickinson. I've never had sex."

Jim fell silent. "You never what?" He asked.

"I've never had sex. I've never been with a man," Sorrie said as the weight of her body against the door made the hinges squeak. Jim stopped reaching for his pants. Was this true? Was this girl who had been traveling with him, hopping freight, getting dirty, changing her clothes in front of him, a virgin?

"I've never even been on a date," Sorrie said. "My parents would never allow it."

"But what do you do when you like someone," Jim asked, "and they want to take you to a movie or a park?"

"I've never had that experience. Most of the men I know I know from books."

"And you never met a man you wanted to be with?"

"I wanted to be an Emily, a virgin. I wasn't one to throw myself at any guy who just came along. I wanted to wait until I'm ready."

Jim got out of bed and put on his pants and a shirt. "I would think that anyone who decided to live in a closet would be afraid to go out into the world like you did, but on the other hand, it takes a lot of guts to light out on the road without thinking about what might happen."

"I had to get away."

"You decided to leave home and hook up with me tramping around the country? How'd you know you could trust me to get you through, seeing as how you're not used to people." Once he was dressed, Jim laid back on the bed.

"Because I looked into your eyes."

"*You what?*"

"That day on the bench when you gave me back my money. I looked into your eyes and decided you were honest, and I thought that someone who could be honest couldn't hurt me, and you admitted it, too."

The idea was so absurd that Jim couldn't help but laugh. "Just looking into my eyes? I can tell you you'd be ripe for the picking by some biscuit shooter if you told that to anyone else."

"And when you agreed that I could give you some money for you getting me to Nebraska, I thought I wouldn't have a problem."

"What did you think we would do with all the time we spent together? Did it ever occur to you that maybe we'd hook up sometime?"

Sorrie exited the bathroom, slumped against the wall, and held the towel in her hands. She gazed down at it. "I looked at it like I was your boss. We had a contract. Don't you remember?"

"I do, but you know the way now, and we both have enough money. In the beginning, we could help each other. But remember that I don't have road buddies, and no one owns me. I travel alone because I like to be by myself."

"I like being by myself, too."

"I needed enough money to get me to Nebraska, and you were the golden ticket. I grew up poor, sister, with nothing. You were my best shot." Jim felt like a man who'd lost a fight with a nasty dog. "Look, original agreement. I'm only doing you a favor for a few meals to see you get safe to where you're going . . . and the book."

Sorrie walked over and sat on the edge of the bed. "That's so pathetic. If you don't care about me, why do you care if I'm safe?"

Jim was at a loss. He searched his thoughts to come up with an answer. "Because maybe I felt sorry for you," Jim blurted out. "Maybe it's time you admitted that I might know more about what we're doing than you do. I know what happens to girls like you on the road because I've seen it happen. I was trying to protect you and get something out of it for myself." An awkward pause crept in, and Jim could hear Sorrie crying. "What's the matter? Hey, I didn't mean to make you cry."

"I just wasn't thinking that way," she said. "I mean, I don't do that kind of thing." She began crying harder.

A lump formed in Jim's throat. "Well, I didn't mean anything by it. I just thought maybe a little relaxation. I mean, we've been traveling together for a few days now, and I thought you'd be comfortable with me."

Through her sobs, Sorrie blurted out, "Not like that, not like that."

Jim came over and sat beside her. He rubbed her back and took her hands. "You're the only man I've ever talked to like a friend. You seemed nice, and I guess I got comfortable with that and let my guard down." Jim guided Sorrie to the bed, but the sight of her crying took all his passion away, and he didn't force her to touch or even kiss him, so she let herself be guided. After rolling into a fetal position, she grasped her knapsack, held it tight against her chest, then closed her eyes.

Jim walked to the other side of the bed and lay down. This was a hell of a way to spend a steamy afternoon. In thinking about it, Jim concluded that his first order of business was getting to Montana, reward or no reward.

In the distance were high-pitched whistles of the freight yard, and Jim closed his eyes, imagining the chugga-chugga of the train cars rolling along the tracks. That old standby—his one true love—was calling. Best to go back to what he knew rather than trying to learn how to play angel.

The thought crossed his mind to go while she was asleep, but the heaviness on his bones made him close his eyes; he was tired. The recent drama and his dissipating energy created an exhaustion that painted his skin with a coat of fatigue. He focused his mind and saw the meandering Mississippi and the miles and miles of rolling prairie and railroad tracks set out in front of him. He'd be in Big Sky country in just a few short days, his dad's book in his sack and a smile on his face. That was all he needed except for one more thing: finding his father.

As he drifted off to sleep, all Jim could think about were Montana's towering mountains and fast-moving rivers and how getting his father's stuff was the gateway to every possibility in the world.

* * *

A train whistle woke him. It was dark now, and Jim looked at the clock on the wooden nightstand beside the bed. *Nine o'clock.* It was time to wake Sorrie and head over to the freight yard. He rubbed his eyes and looked over to where she was sleeping. Her skin and red hair radiated in the moonlight, and her mouth curved into a frown.

"Who are you?" Jim whispered, then he noticed a dried tear on her cheek.

Looking at her, Jim suddenly felt like a blind dog, not knowing what direction to take or where to go. He told himself it was better to stick to the original plan, but the devil on his shoulder whispered louder: *Forget the reward, if there even is one. Leave her. Put her on a train heading west while you go north.*

No sooner had the voice come and gone when Sorrie's eyes opened.

"Time to catch a train," Jim said, then smiled.

* * *

The streets were deserted, but they passed a closed burger joint with a full dumpster, where they found a few packages of cooked fries hidden in a bag. After they chowed down, they were energized enough to hoof it through some backstreets to the freight yard. Jim appeared fun and upbeat, considering their argument. Sorrie didn't know what he was planning and acted like everything was okay. Jim tried to make their conversation pleasant until after he got away. Besides, it wasn't the first time he'd walked out on a girl.

With no yard police in sight, they scanned the scenery. The metal line in front of them had so many cars on the tracks that Jim didn't know where to begin.

"How are we ever going to find out what train we need to catch in the dark?" Sorrie asked.

"Instinct," Jim said. "It's all a matter of details: what you smell and hear, the markings on the trains, the tracks they're on, what you feel in your gut. I've been here lots of times. Jim said.

Tracks were covered with rows of cars—some lines were hundreds of feet long. Jim examined the switching and then had an idea. He walked up to a yard hand and asked what track the train to Lincoln, Nebraska, was on and what time it left. Jim and the man spoke, and as the conversation ended, Jim returned to Sorrie and motioned to a yellow car a few feet away.

"That's the one. It'll be moving out shortly."

"Is this the one the man said because I thought he pointed to a different car?" Sorrie asked.

Jim reassured her it was the train they wanted. It was a grain car with a wide trim and a solid porch, and he took her hand and helped her up until she was sitting on the platform. Sorrie rested her back against the flat steel wall.

"This is the one he said to take," Jim said. He looked around for anyone who may have followed them and then up at the moonlit sky. A cool breeze curled around the trains and ran along Jim's skin, and for a minute, it reminded him of the air conditioning in the motel room. He glanced at the light coming off the moon. He'd get a good ride, but not on this train. All he needed was to convince Sorrie to stay where she was. He'd even forgo any extra money for a chance to take a different route.

"This is the one we want. You stay here, and I'll be along in a minute. I forgot to ask the yard hand something."

"How will we ride on this? We're exposed. Won't we fall off?"

"I'll explain it all when I get back."

"Why don't I believe you?" Sorrie asked.

Jim took off his leather jacket. "Here, you know I can't ride without this," he said as he handed it to her.

"Come back soon," Sorrie covered her legs with the jacket.

Jim walked away. All that book learning and she never noticed he had another jacket in his bag?

He shuffled along the tracks and looked down to where he spied a dollar bill on the ground. Smugly, Jim grabbed it and put it in his pocket. "Must be my lucky day," he mumbled under his breath. Jim leaned against a car and lit a cigarette. As he watched the smoke dissipate into the air and felt a deep warmness in his throat, he looked from side to side. No sign of Sorrie or the yard hand. They must have gotten there during a crew change, which made things even easier for him. He inhaled deeply and looked into the distance, where he thought he spotted someone. He couldn't make out their features—they were just a lone nobody standing between the tracks staring in Jim's direction. Jim looked away. If this was the man Sorrie's parents sent to find her, he didn't want them to see him. Instead, he concentrated on the echoes of the sights and sounds surrounding him: traffic from a nearby highway, muffled voices that seemed to come from all directions, and the flicker of a lightbulb about to flame out. Jim finished his cigarette, dropped it to the ground, and crushed it into the dirt. He figured Sorrie was trying to find out where he was, so he needed to be on his way.

Jim hopped over a series of coupled cars—something he told Sorrie never to do—and walked to a train he knew was headed west. Jim wanted to make like a cannonball and get as far away from Louisville as possible. He stopped to adjust his knapsack and then looked down the line of cars.

He found an open boxcar and grabbed the handle to hoist himself up and into the safety of the darkness as he made one final scan of the yard. Nothing. Not even the stranger he thought he saw. *Free again.* He had money in his pocket and air in his lungs. Maybe he'd even find a lady of the evening along the way. The thought made him smile. He adjusted his knapsack, and just as the engine whistle roared and the cars jerked forward, Jim heard a voice.

"Why did you do it?"

Jim turned around. There, in the corner behind him, was Sorrie. Large streaks of mascara tears painted her face black. "Was it because I wouldn't sleep with you? Is that it?"

Jim was stunned. It was as if a ghost had sprung up through the floorboards. For a moment, Jim's anger took hold, and he thought of grabbing her and throwing her out of the car but stopped himself. "What are you doing here?" He asked.

"I have to get to Nebraska," she said, "and you promised to take me."

"You need to find someone who can care for you, and that's not me."

"I need to go with you."

Jim's anger welled up. "What makes me so special? There are plenty of guys who'd take you along for some money. Hell, girls, too. There are plenty of girls on the road. Why me?"

Sorrie looked bewildered. She searched for an answer. "I don't know. A feeling inside tells me you're the one who has to take me, and just as much as you take care of me, I need to take care of you."

Something in the determination of her voice made Jim relent. He was torn now. She was smart and sassy and stood up to him, but she seemed to need someone—and all that talk about freedom was just bullshit. She was still that same little girl hiding in a closet surrounded by books.

"Why are you scared all the time? You act tough, but you're just a scared little rich girl inside."

Sorrie's eyes were defiant and stern. "They just try to control every-thing. I try to fight back, but they just try more control, and more con-trol, and more control. They're destroying my life. When I was home, my escape was my books. But here, I only have one thing, and that's you. Why? Why did you leave me there? Why won't you help me?"

A knot in Jim's throat prevented him from answering. He wanted to say it wasn't personal; he traveled alone, but he knew she'd never under-stand where that urge came from. He tried to verbalize his thoughts, but the words wrapped around his vocal cords, choking him into silence. His breathing became like a brick against his throat until his lungs filled with air again, and his voice relaxed. "I don't know," he whispered. "You want freedom, and so do I, but my freedom has to be on my terms. I can't concentrate on looking for my father if I have to . . ." His voice trailed off.

Sorrie was skeptical. "You know. You can tell me."

Though they were only a few feet apart, the chasm that separated them was an ocean deep. Jim answered. "All my life, I've been carrying people—my mother, brother, sister—even my foster family and all the kids they got. I just got sick of carrying people. I've been traveling alone for eight years, and I had no need for a wife, a girlfriend, or anything like that. I'm just out there looking for my father."

"How about if you just get me to Nebraska?" Sorrie asked.

Jim nodded his head but remained silent.

8

Indiana to St. Louis

I T WAS THE bright light of the day that awoke them. Sorrie raised her head from the cold, metal floor as the early morning sun shot laser beams through the middle of the car. Jim was already awake.

Sorrie sat up and poked her head out. "There's a muddy river down there," she said. "Is that where we're going?"

"Might be," Jim said. "We can't go around fifty cars. But we'll find a way as soon as I can get my bearings."

Sorrie stretched her legs and was about to lie back down when a sound pierced through the silence. Jim stiffened, and Sorrie crawled over to where he was seated. It was the sound of dogs—not entirely clear at first—but coming closer. Suddenly, the barking was outside the closed side of the car. Jim caught the faint whiff of cigar smoke along with muffled conversation. As footsteps on the pebbled dirt grew louder, so did fear.

It was the bull.

He was on the other side of the car along with someone else—and the dogs. Trying to muffle her voice, Sorrie said in the tiniest of whispers, "Jim, it's the railroad police!" She grasped the edges of his shirt and whispered again.

Jim nodded, then lowered his hand for her to be still as they waited for the bull to act. The smoke from the cigar snaked its way into Jim's nostrils, and he repressed an urge to sneeze. They heard the voices of two men above the barking dogs. Jim squinted to see them through a tiny split in the metal wall: an old hand with a white linen suit, burly and big with suspenders holding up his gut, a mushy cigar between his lips; the other, a scrawny tenderfoot, lapping at the big man's ankles, squeaky voice and thin, like a mouse trailing behind the body of a giant rat confident in the world it was controlling.

"Yeah, well, one thing I can't stand is the destruction of railroad property," Mouse said.

A man with a smoky voice countered, "Isn't that right? Time to look inside some cars to see if we got any stowaways." The dogs continued barking wildly, and Smoky shook the door hatch.

"You ain't getting that door open," Mouse said. "You need a strong hook and lift truck to move that heavy load."

Smoky laughed. "I know that. Do you think I'm stupid or something? Used to be I could open these sliders with my two front teeth, a wish, and a prayer. Not anymore. Made of steel now, not wood."

"Couldn't get those open; you need a couple of men to move that weight. Best talk to the engineer about getting these cars onto the platform to see what's piled up in 'em."

Jim didn't move. He sat like a statue, one arm wrapped around Sorrie's shoulders, the other around the strap in his knapsack just in case they had to run for it. The men's voices melted into the distance, but the dogs kept close, barking, whooping, and jumping against the outside, the nails of their paws scratching against the metal. Noticing the dogs' interest, the men came back.

"Maybe a dead raccoon in that one to have old Hitchcock go wild like that. Either that or we got a bindle stiff—hell, maybe a dead one—because I don't hear any sounds. Better to check the other side." Smoky said.

Panicked, Sorrie whispered, "Jim, we've got to run before the *dogs* find us."

"Wait," Jim cautioned. He'd been in this situation dozens of times and always managed to see it through. The thought didn't give him comfort, though. Jail was jail, no matter what town he had the misfortune to wake up in.

They listened as Mouse said, "Now, if you want to get to the other side of this car, you'll have to walk around fifty other cars—either that or jump over a coupling—and you know you don't want to do that. Puts a squeeze on your balls."

Smoky laughed. "Don't want to do that. Melinda would be upset. She made me promise not to hurt old Mel 'cause she has a fancy to having more kids," and as both men laughed, the dogs continued to claw against the side of the car.

"We should let the dogs loose. They'd sure find out who was hiding on the other side."

"Yeah, but then they'd run after the nearest rabbit. These are prized hunting dogs, and I wouldn't want to explain to Ned how we lost 'em on a hunch."

The dogs began wailing. "Shut up," Mouse said. "You'll be getting your breakfast once the cars get moved."

"Just have the engineer pull it into the yard, and we'll start taking her apart to see what she's hiding," the man in the white suit said.

"That isn't up to you. That's the engineer's decision."

"Let's go talk to him then," the big man said, and as Sorrie and Jim listened, the footsteps grew fainter against the pebbles. The barking dogs went with the men. Jim waited until he could hear only the low hum of the train engine.

"What are we going to do?" Sorrie asked.

"We're going the only route we have," Jim said as he strapped his knapsack to his back and pointed toward the ditch.

"Out there?"

"Out there." The cars began moving, and the train gained traction. Jim and Sorrie jumped to the ground while the train cars rolled down the tracks and into an unloading dock in the distance. Sorrie looked relieved, and Jim shrugged off his sleepiness. He said nothing but began walking along the side of the river. His feet were fast and solid as if every foot of earth he walked on was his and his alone.

Sorrie followed behind, asking Jim to slow down so she could gain her balance. Suddenly, they heard a sound in the distance as two dogs began barking and running toward them.

"Get them!" Smoky yelled.

The dogs moved faster and faster, and Jim and Sorrie had to quicken their pace, but the dogs wouldn't stop. They kept running in their direction. Even with a good lead, Sorrie found it hard to keep pace and stumbled at one point, almost sailing into the gully along the riverbed. Mouse and Smoky were less agile, preferring to let the dogs do the work while they sauntered far behind.

Finally, Sorrie could run no more. She stopped, bent over, and tried to catch her breath.

"What are you doing?" Jim asked from several feet away. "If they get their teeth into us, we're going to get arrested. You have to come now."

But Sorrie couldn't come; she stood immobile with her head down, clutching around her rib cage. "Just let me find my breath."

Suddenly, the dogs were upon her. They caught up to her and then slowed, but instead of acting aggressively, they circled her and sniffed at her pants, shoes, and dangling hair.

"It's okay, boys," she said, holding one hand to her middle and extending the second to pet the dogs.

"Have you lost your mind?" Jim yelled.

"They're not snapping at me or anything." Sorrie stood up and took one long, slow breath. She began coughing and cleared her lungs. The dogs were still circling her, their tails wagging and their mouths panting with their tongues hanging out.

From a distance, Jim could hear the Mouse calling to the dogs.

Sorrie opened her canteen and poured some water into her cupped hand. The dogs lapped at the water as the Mouse whistled into the air. "It's okay, buddy. You can go with him," Sorrie said, and with that, the dogs emptied Sorrie's hand of water and took off back to the freight yard. Sorrie began walking toward Jim.

"How the hell did you pull that off?" Jim asked.

"I guess they needed a friend—like me," Sorrie answered. She shook her hand, and a few drops sailed into the air.

When they were safely at a distance, Sorrie asked if she could pee. "Go ahead," was all Jim said, and as she found a place in the tall grass, Jim turned his back and surveyed the landscape. "We need to catch up, clean up, and get a decent change of clothes." Jim lit a cigarette and started walking toward a road. Sorrie emerged from the weeds and ran to catch up.

"Why don't you ever wait for me?" Sorrie asked.

Jim weighed his words for a minute, then spoke. "I go at my own pace. I'm not used to having someone on the road with me. You're helping with my father's book, but sometimes a man needs more than companionship."

"Oh, we're back to that, are we?"

"Okay, I won't ask again. Let's make this as pleasant as possible for everyone involved." Jim walked up the embankment and across some empty tracks; Sorrie followed. He hadn't told her to get lost because he owed her a lot. But that wasn't something he wanted to discuss.

They found a public restroom in a red brick building near the sports field. Sorrie washed up and changed clothes quickly, but Jim took his time bathing himself with a hand towel drenched in hot water and strong soap. Jim spied her standing outside and made her wait twenty minutes for him to shave and change, then emerged with new clothes and the scent of mint.

"Welcome to the new Jim," he said. Sorrie looked skeptical.

After walking a few blocks, they found a general store where they bought coffee and rolls. Soon, they were perched on the top of a fencepost looking down at the river. Then, finally, Sorrie asked the question she'd been afraid to ask all morning. "Why did you leave me last night? Why did I have to run after you?"

Jim shrugged. How would he pour out his soul and explain that being able to do what he wanted to do when he wanted to do it was his way of living? "You tell me something first," he said. "You tell me how you knew what car I was in and how you got there so quickly."

"I saw the freight hand point to it when you talked to him, remember?"

"Yeah, but how'd you get there before me?"

"The freight hand showed me a shortcut, and I gave him five dollars."

Jim laughed. "Lousy Judas."

"But why did you do it?"

"I keep telling you, but I don't think you get it. My father's the only one I care about. That's something you should get used to. My head's filled with his words and songs. It takes up all the space in my brain, and there's no room for anyone else. I'm a loner like he was. I never cared much about anything but being his son, so why should I care about you?"

"That's not something I expected to hear," Sorrie said. "But why should you care about me? My parents only care because they wanted to control me, which I guess is one of the worst kinds of love you can show a person." Sorrie hopped down, walked around a patch of weeds, and up a road. Jim followed closely behind. She stopped to rub her ribs and take a swig of water, then continued to balance her body on the path.

"Is that why you're a virgin?" Jim asked.

"That's not why."

"Well?" Jim pressed the point as he stumbled along the path. The rising humidity of the day made him sweat so much that it affected his vision as the moisture on his brow formed salty droplets that kept stinging his eyes. He stopped briefly, dabbed his face with his shirt, and continued. "So why are you still a virgin?"

"I guess I never had the opportunity. And the further I got from it, the more I wanted to keep it. It's the only thing that belonged to me— like you being alone. I was lonely a lot, too, but I hated it. So, I vowed never to be alone again after I got out of there," she said.

"I thought you had a lot of things. You were rich, right?"

"It's the worst kind of rich: loving things and never realizing that being rich doesn't mean owning stuff."

"Is that why you read so much?"

"Yeah, maybe. You could say the only lovers I had were men in books."

"These are your favorite stories?"

"No, my favorite stories came from fairy tales. There's the one where a bathtub keeps moving around the house. I thought that was funny. And there was one about a little girl who asked all the animals in the forest if they would play with her, and they refused, so she just went by a tree, and before you knew it, all the creatures came to ask if she wanted to play, which showed me that if you really want something, don't ask for it, and it will come to you. So maybe I should stop asking you to take me, and maybe you'll want to."

They sat down on a curb in the shade.

"So where are we anyway?"

"We're hopping the next train out," Jim said, "It shouldn't be too long, maybe a few. . . ." Jim looked across the street at a large, overgrown field. The sun's reflection off a jagged piece of metal caught his eye, interrupting his thought. "What's over there?" Jim asked as he ran across the street.

"It looks like a carnival," Sorrie said. Jim hopped the white picket fence surrounding the grounds and discovered nothing was moving; there were no people. The site was abandoned.

Sorrie followed Jim, who was sauntering through the outskirts of the park.

"Looks like this was left to rot long ago," Jim stared at the fixtures in the distance. "I've never been to an amusement park." He stepped through the tall reeds but stopped when his feet hit a soggy rubber mat surrounding a rusty slide sinking into the earth. The soggy mess was near an asphalt parking lot, which framed half a dozen buildings and metal trailers. The site was just a boneyard now, and Jim's sudden joy gave way to distress. "You'd think there was at least one working ride," he said. He touched a faded mural of two smiling clowns. "Where did all the people go?"

"I guess no one comes here when you have rides that don't work."

"It can't be that old." Jim ran his hand across the glass casing of a fortune-telling machine. Inside was the figure of a woman wearing a glittering gold mask. The mask was ripped, but her deep purple eyes seemed alive. Her right hand was suspended over a white orb. "You think it still works?" Jim asked.

Sorrie examined the frame. "No."

"How can you tell? It may work. Maybe it'll read my fortune. Maybe it will tell me if I'll ever meet my father."

"Not without electricity," Sorrie said as she held up the plug from the back.

"Okay, then I'll tell my own fortune." Jim closed his eyes. "Now, I'm going to count down from ten, and I'll tell you what I see." Jim rattled off the numbers and then opened his eyes. "I saw my father smiling at me. He's laughing, telling me to keep traveling through life to get to the other side of it. He's telling me not to fly too close to the sun."

"Kind of like Icarus," Sorrie said.

"Who?"

"Icarus. It's a Greek myth. Icarus tried to escape Crete and made a pair of wings from wax, and even though he was warned not to, he flew too close to the sun, and the wings melted."

"What happened to him?"

"He wound up drowning in the sea."

Jim stared off into the distance but said nothing. Instead, he focused his eyes on the horizon. At the far end of the carnival were go-carts scattered along a cracked asphalt track. "Want to go for a ride?" He bolted into the distance, sat in a blue car, and tried to move it with his legs, only to discover it was frozen. He tried several more cars until he sat in a lime green go-kart stuck in the rubber bumpers lining the track's curves. "Guess this one's not working either, but I don't see why not. The metal's strong. There's no rot. I've never been on these rides. I don't understand why it's not working."

Sorrie sat down on the hood of the car. "No electricity," she said.

"My first time to an amusement park, and it's not all that amusing." Jim took a moment, then reached his hand toward the rubber bumpers and picked a few wildflowers growing through the cracks. "Bouquet, boss lady, oh, I mean princess?" he asked, extending his hand. When she didn't take the flowers, Jim threw them onto the road and lifted himself out of the car. Next, he walked over to where a child's blue bicycle lay in the dirt and tried to set it upright, but rainwater had collected inside the rusting metal fender and splashed onto his boots. With one quick motion, Jim hurled the broken bike across the field. "I liked these boots," he said.

They walked around the grounds and discovered more twisted metal and skeletons of rides neither Jim nor Sorrie could figure out. They soon stumbled onto a hotdog sign and faded red ticket booth among some vacant trailers lining the parking lot. "Maybe we can just sleep in one of these tonight," Jim poked through the open doors and saw a wooden desk and a metal floor with papers scattered all over it. "Nah," Jim changed his mind. "With that type of floor, it's just as well to sleep in a boxcar and to get somewhere."

Sorrie reached into the opening and picked up one of the papers. "It's a bill for plastic cups." She raised her head. "Let's get out of here."

"What's the matter?" Jim asked. "Don't you want to explore? I never saw half this stuff. Tell you what. I'll take a short tour instead." Jim bolted from the trailer and began running between the trailers.

As he moved haphazardly through the mounds of trash and machinery, Sorrie hurried behind him, trying to keep up with his frenetic pace. Jim pushed a mechanical ride sign to the ground and threw a wire garbage container into the air. He spied a silver Venetian mask and put it on. "This is my new face," he said. "Like it?"

"I'd rather see the real Jim."

"There is no real Jim," he said through the slit of the mouth, and then noticing that Sorrie didn't respond, he removed the mask and stared at her. "He died."

Unamused, Sorrie walked away. "I wish everything didn't have to end with you acting like a jerk."

"Oh, I'm sorry," Jim said. "Did I offend you? Did I insult you? Did I upset your princess outlook on life?"

"No, you didn't," Sorrie said unconvincingly.

Jim waved his arms in the air. "Look at where you are. You're surrounded by filth and dirt and decayed metal." He walked on the wet pavement, and the heavy click-clack of his boots resonated against the trailers.

Sorrie leaned against a faded clown statue. "My parents took me to places like this. I loved the roller coasters best. The feelings of wind in my hair, throwing my arms up but never knowing if I'd fly out and soar into the clouds. It was all a big adventure for me. That was one of the only times my parents couldn't control me—when I was in the air like that. I was free."

Jim slumped against a signpost that read, "*Amusements here, you've come to the right place.*" He crossed his arms against his chest and started back toward the freight yard. "To me, it's just garbage."

9

Places In Between

Not long after they'd left the amusement park, they found themselves in an open boxcar headed to St. Louis.

Though the noise of the tracks made it difficult to talk, Sorrie returned to her original questions: "What train did we take yesterday? Where are we headed?"

"We rode through Indiana, but I wanted to catch a hot shot out of Chicago headed to Montana. You changed that plan."

"What did you think I would do when I saw you weren't coming back?"

"The trick was to make you *think* I was coming back," Jim shouted above the engines. "Besides, the train you were on was taking you straight to Nebraska. You would've been there by now if you hadn't followed me. You'd be safe with the people you're looking for, not some raggedy bum like me. So now we got to go down and around."

"Will you promise not to do it again?"

"I can't promise anything."

"Why?"

"Because I do whatever I feel like whenever the urge hits me."

"That's a deceitful thing to say."

"Would you rather I lied?"

* * *

They rode on into the late afternoon light without speaking. The sun radiated off vast patches of brown dirt and mud. At times, they'd pass fields of corn and soybeans as the train wound through streets and towns and villages filled with people walking around, stumbling from bars, riding motorcycles, and kissing on park benches. Kids threw rocks and insults in one town—not at Jim or Sorrie—but at the rumbling train as if its beastly presence cut too much into the quiet countryside and vacant fields.

After a while, Sorrie's eyes got heavy, and she tilted her head back to sleep. It was Jim who interrupted her stillness. "What would you have done if you stayed on the train?" He asked.

"I don't know. I'd have gone to the next town and found someone to take me the rest of the way."

"It wouldn't have been good if you stopped. The only things you'll see on that line are thieves and users. Besides, there's no next town short of Grand Island, Nebraska, on that route. If those crooks knew your parents were looking for you, they'd have turned you in faster than you could have gotten away."

"I don't know what I would have done. Besides, I haven't seen anyone, and you said you only saw the man on the ridge, which could have been anyone."

Jim didn't want to tell her about the man by the tracks, so he said, "No."

"If you thought I would have gotten into trouble, why did you let me stay there? You said I would have made it to Nebraska in one breath, then told me I would have been turned in. Make up your mind."

Jim thought about what Sorrie said. In his heart, he was sure she would've made it, but his anger at being caught in a deception got the best of him. His voice grew soft. "I believe you would have made it. Anyone who got in your way would have been tangling with a wildcat, so I take back what I said."

"Are you apologizing?" Sorrie asked.

Jim spit out the open boxcar and rested his head against the wall. "Maybe."

Sorrie settled back next to him. "You think I don't know who you are, but I see who you are."

"And who's that?"

"You're just a guy. A lost and lonely guy thinking you're controlling your destiny, but you aren't because you're looking for something in the shadows. The problem is you don't know what it is. You're so stuck in darkness that it's hard for you to see what the shadows are." Sorrie rolled over and looked at Jim. "And I think you like me more than you let on."

Jim examined her words. He wasn't lost, he wasn't lonely, and he didn't live in darkness. The rails, his father, the book, and a thousand nights of starry skies were there. But maybe he did like her underneath; perhaps that was why he kept her around. "I ain't saying anything about liking you, but I lived the life I wanted to, and if I'm lost and lonely, it's because I want to be. I make no apologies for it. I took you along because I felt sorry for you. I'm a gentleman like my dad."

"A gentleman wouldn't have pretended I was going one way when I was going another. A gentleman wouldn't have left me on one train knowing he'd be hopping another."

"Yeah, well, I already apologized for that, but have I stolen your stuff?"

"It's not for lack of trying," Sorrie said, then she spit out the same door Jim had.

"And that's another thing. I noticed you changed. You're acting more like a man than a girl, and I don't like that."

"How's a girl supposed to act?"

"She does girl things, you know. She asks for help and doesn't act like she's better than everyone—like how you disrespected my friends in the hobo camp."

Sorrie was bewildered. "What did I do? I thought I was nice to them—especially Church. I thought I was very respectful."

"It was in the way you looked at them and moved away from them. I could tell how your mouth puckered up, and your eyes got small—like they weren't people. My father always preached that love for someone is letting them be who they are. You should learn to love the people in the camps by appreciating them for who they are and stop thinking you're better than everyone."

"The only thing I see is that if you can't read, then where did you suddenly get all this information about your father?"

"My mother used to tell me things," he said. "But look, I'm just trying to tell you to stop thinking you're better than everyone."

Sorrie laughed. "We've been riding one filthy train after another, peeing in ditches, eating food out of garbage bins, hanging around with people who have fleas and lice, and God knows what else, and you're upset because you think I'm being too much of a princess?"

"None of my girlfriends treated people differently the way you do."

"I thought you said you didn't need a girl for anything but sex."

Jim pulled back. "It depends on who the girl is. There was this girl I remember. She was smart like you."

"Where did you meet her?"

"I met her in eighth grade, at least on the days I decided to go. I called her the Queen of Angels. I didn't know her real name; I'm not good that way. So that's just what I named her."

"What did she look like?"

Jim's voice softened. "She looked like you, only with real red hair, not that fake color you got. She was gentle and sweet, like a little sparrow in my hand."

"How did you come to know her?"

Jim shrugged. "I didn't know her in *that way*; she was just a girl in school. She had pretty eyes and a soft voice. I fell in love with her from across the room. It was science class—the only class I attended regularly because she was there. She always had the right answers to the questions. Trouble was I never got to meet her."

"I thought you said she was your girlfriend?" Sorrie asked.

"She was in my mind but from across the room. She used to stare at me and do stupid things with her hair. She winked at me once, and I could tell she liked me."

"You never asked her out?"

Jim stared down at the metal floor. "It was the eighth grade; besides, I never had the chance. She died."

"Oh, that's awful," Sorrie said.

"Yeah, well, one day she wasn't in class, and the kids were whispering, saying she died. No one told me how; those kids never spoke to me anyway. I just knew that one day she was there, and the next day she was gone," he said.

"You must have taken it hard."

"Let's just say that was the last time I went to class," Jim said. "Like my father sang about being alive and being dead. We all got to die sometime, right? Death is always the end, so I guess it was her time. But I see her face, talk to her sometimes, see her blue eyes from across the room."

"You'd like to go back there, wouldn't you?" Sorrie asked.

Jim rested his head on the wall of the car. Sorrie asked questions he didn't want to answer. "I like it here just fine. Thinking about that stuff is like spitting into the rain. I'm just one of those guys where fate decides for you." Jim felt uncomfortable and shifted his position away from Sorrie. "Tell you what, let's just get you to where you're going, and then we'll say farewell."

* * *

At a distance, the silhouette of the freight yard outside St. Louis looked like a big, bold chunk of iron diesel factory and smelled the same. The choking stench of fuel made Sorrie gag but sent Jim into a wonderland of black and red hoppers, coal cars, silvery oil tankers, and unused blood-colored cabooses resembling the poem about the senses Sorrie had read in *The Lords and the New Creatures*. The verses affected Jim so deeply that he made Sorrie repeat them again and again. When he wasn't sure if he could still remember it, he asked her to point to the words until they were committed to memory. Ever since he'd heard it, he'd been looking for something to link it to. Today was the day.

It was late in the afternoon, and Jim was feeling restless. He told Sorrie he wanted nothing more than to hop a car to take him out, but there were only a few in sight and none he could consider. "If time in a freight yard waiting for a decent ride was the hobo's enemy, not seeing anything is a nightmare," he told her, then explained that they'd have to spend the night at another tramp camp—and there was only one nearby—one that scared Jim more than sleeping in the yard.

He'd been there before, and anytime he showed up, trouble seemed to find him—whether it was the cranky old broad who insisted on money for booze or the two brothers who traveled in and out of his life at different stops along the line. But there was a good reason to go: a beautiful, long-legged, musk-smelling lady named Rehab who spent a good deal of time in the camp. Jim smiled as memories bubbled up. The last time he was there, so was she, and that led to a month's worth of dreams no man would ever discuss with a woman, least of all a princess.

He glanced in Sorrie's direction, but she didn't notice him. His focus shifted to the glowing orange sunset and how it reflected off the oil tankers as they traveled into the future. He stiffened his back. "Stop daydreaming," he said as he poked her arm.

"Which one are we taking?" She asked.

"We're staying here tonight with some friends."

"But why?"

"Because the train we're taking isn't going until seven o'clock in the morning."

"Why can't we hop one tonight? I don't want to stay in another camp. I want to get on with it."

"The one we're hopping tomorrow is going to be something special, so don't worry," Jim reassured her. "You'll be grateful we waited. 'Sides, they're all we got because there's just air between the cattle stocks of St. Louis and the Great Plains clear to the Boulder line. It's about surviving with your back in tow and some insurance in your pocket."

"I don't know what insurance you're carrying, but I haven't seen any of it," she said.

"We're not dead yet, are we?" Jim replied. She didn't know Jim was fixed on a woman, some whiskey, and a relaxed night. He pointed the way up a small hill, which led to a gravel path and thick underbrush until they were in a forest of trees. "Where are we going?" Sorrie asked.

"Just the local camp. I got some friends there, and there'll be a good meal waiting and maybe a song or two, plus something smooth to drink if the man I think is there is there."

"Now you're talking in riddles."

Jim stopped and pointed at Sorrie. "Listen, you got to walk softly into camp. Let me go first because you never knew who might greet you."

The woods surrounding the camp were dense and filled with the honey scent of summersweet, which clashed with the underbrush smell of wet leaves. As they neared the camp, he motioned for Sorrie to be silent.

The last of the afternoon sun twinkled between the shades of gray leaves and moss. Jim saw Sorrie shut her eyes. "What the hell are you doing?" Jim asked.

"Trying to catch the warmth of the sun's rays. I'm cold."

Jim grabbed Sorrie's arm and steered her toward an opening. "We'll be there soon," Jim said. "But I need you to be quiet."

"Another night at another camp? The thought of having to fall asleep on hard, cold dirt brings tears to my eyes." Sorrie sniffled and wiped her nose with the arm of her shirt.

"Just go along. Don't forget to be respectful. These people aren't idiots; they notice when a stranger doesn't like them."

"Yeah, yeah, yeah," Sorrie groaned.

Jim smirked. "Things getting tough all of a sudden? Where's the man in you?"

"Where's the man in *you*?" Sorrie countered as she took a drink of water. "What's got you all nervous?"

"About a year ago, I kind of got into an argument with two brothers, and after that, things didn't go so well in this particular location, you might say." Jim took the canteen from Sorrie's hands and downed a few gulps. He would have preferred whiskey.

"'Kind of'?"

"Just a little fight, is all. I wound up stabbing one of 'em."

"You did *what*?"

Jim stopped again. "Look, it's got nothing to do with you. They got loud, did stupid things, and made some threats; I got scared and stabbed one of them."

"Where did you stab him?" Sorrie asked.

"I think I stabbed him in the leg." Jim's voice trailed off as he tried to recall the incident. "I'm not sure. I just know I hurt him."

"Why did you stab him?" Jim remained silent. Sorrie repeated her question.

"Look, it was a fight. The brothers threatened me and tried to steal my sack. I been back since and haven't seen them, but it doesn't hurt to be on the lookout." Jim tried to reassure himself. It was a long time ago, in hobo years. They were probably way beyond this place by now—maybe even dead. The odds of them being in this camp were small to none, but his nerves stood on end all the same.

"And these are your friends? You said you wanted to see your friends."

"Not the brothers exactly, but there are more people. And they'll be good company tonight." As they neared the camp, Jim stopped walking and tilted his head as if someone was whispering in his ear. After a few minutes, the tension dissipated, and he seemed like the old Jim: confident, joyful, and reckless. Jim began walking toward the camp with the assurance of a man ready to take on the world. He was, after all, Jim Morrison's son; his blood was that of the lizard king, and he wasn't afraid of anything.

* * *

As they approached, Jim turned to Sorrie. "Let me go in first. This way, it will be me if anyone has to fight."

Sorrie nodded in agreement. They walked cautiously, and Jim reached out and took her hand. From a distance, Jim saw a circle of people, some holding cans of beer, standing around what looked to be a barbeque made from a rusty oil drum. Jim smelled the charcoal of a well-lit fire, and it reassured him.

"You wait here. If there's a fight, hang back until I yell for you," Jim said as he parted the bushes, approached the crowd, and said hello. Some of them recognized him, and he smiled and gave hugs all around. After a minute, Jim excused himself and ran back to where Sorrie was peering through the brush. "Come on, it's safe."

The crowd ranged from young to old, clean to dirty, and neat to unkempt. Jim counted twelve, including some men and women bikers dressed in leather. Jim introduced Sorrie, and everyone told her their names, including a tall, thin boy in a brown hoodie named Dweeb.

Jim scanned the camp. In the distance were cardboard boxes resting against a few makeshift lean-tos made of green tarps and brown Army blankets. Under one of the tarps was a bench with a mattress on top. A few more lean-tos were visible under trees and in dugouts. There was also a dilapidated school bus in the distance.

The heat of the day was dissipating but left a lingering humidity that made even those who looked clean smell rancid, partly because many wore flannel shirts and heavy jackets. "Don't they get hot in those clothes?" Sorrie asked as she changed into a light shirt.

"Some of 'em don't care. Those bums get just as hot as you do, but they got butterflies upstairs, if you know what I mean. I wouldn't get too close; some don't smell good, but remember to treat them nice unless they give you a reason not to."

"I remember Church told me something about not being afraid and owning each step of dirt under my feet."

Jim spoke from experience: "It doesn't hurt to be a little afraid—especially in this crowd."

"Maybe so, but it gives me courage."

"Looks like you got a nice party going on," Jim said to the crowd as he glanced at the hotdogs and chicken on the open grill. "Some of that meat for us?"

"Maybe it is, and maybe it ain't," a bearded man sitting in a lawn chair said. "Depends on what you got to trade. Nothing's free here, you know that." He smiled and revealed only a few teeth.

"Nothing free, Junkman? That isn't part of the hobo creed—the rule is to help a fellow hobo if you can, and we're much in need. We're willing to work for it. Anything we can do?"

"Oh, I don't know, Jimmy. I'll dig up something. Help yourself to a hotdog and maybe a sausage or two. Cap over there got some pretzels. We could share—not much, though."

"I got a few candy bars and maybe a dollar for the fund."

Junkman's ears perked up. "Now you're talking," he said. "I'll take the dollar for the fund, especially since we've seen different people passing through. The Mississippi floods have been driving people every which way. It's been hard to keep up." Junkman pointed to a fragile old woman whose pale skin was red and speckled from too much sun. "Miss Jewel here can make you a dish."

"Two dishes," Jim corrected him.

"Well, that'll mean two dollars for the fund. We like to give stuff away, but hard times are hard times, Jimmy." Junkman turned to Miss Jewel. "You think that's a fair trade?" The old woman nodded, and Junkman looked back at Jim. "Miss Jewel says it's okay."

Jim dipped into his pocket, pulled out two crumpled dollar bills, and handed over the money. "For the fund," Jim said.

"For the fund." Junkman reached into a satchel and pulled out a brown Army toiletry bag.

"Hey, let me see if they real," a woman named Mercy said. She was much older than the rest, with deep pot marks and wrinkles on her pecan-colored skin. As she walked over to examine the bills, she had a gait in her step that made her five-foot frame look even smaller.

"Nothing doing. I'll never see them bills again if I let you get your babos on 'em. They belong to the fund now," Junkman said as he gently folded the bills and placed them in the bag.

"You got more, Jimmy?" Mercy asked.

"Not for you, Miss Mercy. That's all I could steal from the man in the train yard, honest to God."

"Not even a dime or a quarter?"

"Not even that." Jim collected two plates of sausage, a hotdog, and salty pretzels. Someone opened a bottle of apple wine, and almost everyone took a slug, which loosened the mood and made Jim forget about the brothers.

"Where you folks come from?" Mercy asked.

"We started in Virginia and are headed to Nebraska," Sorrie said.

"Nebraska, eh? I was through Nebraska maybe a thousand times, crisscrossing the country. That's a beautiful state. Miles and miles of corn and wheat and the smell of wildflowers fresh in the morning with a nice hot cup of Pear's Gourmet in your hands. Wind in your hair and the hours and days it sometimes took to find a town bigger than a quarter. And riding that Union Pacific freight from state line to state line."

Sorrie was surprised. "You ride the rails?" She asked.

Mercy laughed. "Oh hell, I been riding these rails since the 1930s. I had no schooling and had never seen a man I couldn't whoop in a fair fight. But you young people got it easy nowadays. Back in the day, we rode the rails with steam engines. Ain't nothing harder than trying to hitch a ride on some cantankerous Ol' Girl, but off we'd go with that smoke comin' at us from the front. I know many a hobo fell off a car because the smoke caught 'em and burned their lungs."

"Except me," a man called Cap said.

"Na, you don't count. Besides, we married." Mercy laughed, and her dentures fell out of her mouth as she did. She shoved them back in and continued laughing until they slipped again, and each time they did, she repeated her actions and laughed some more.

Jim wondered if Mercy ever stopped laughing long enough to get new teeth.

"Why do you ride the rails?" Sorrie asked.

"Because that's all I got, and I got used to it early. During the Great Depression, my poppa said we didn't have money to feed all thirteen, so my two brothers and I got tossed. We were old enough to find jobs by then, poppa figured. I was fifteen. Poppa was a sharecropper, and Mississippi hadn't no money then. Like there is ever."

"What did you and your two brothers do then?"

"Oh, that's obvious," Mercy said as Sorrie drew back. "We went looking for work. Sometimes, we picked fruit; other times, I did laundry for some rich white woman who needed house help. Sometimes, we'd just con someone into giving us something to eat by telling 'em we were orphans and had no job, which wasn't that far from the truth. We were the end back then." Mercy poked a stick into the ground. "But then my younger brother Thomas—one of the brothers I was traveling with—fell under a train car in Pennsylvania. God rest his soul. Me and my other brother, Addie, just left him there under the car because a big, fat railroad dick was chasing us—that evil white man with the gun in his hands. Lord, have mercy. We just had to leave Thomas there all twisted up under that coal car cause we had to run. They woulda lynched us if we slowed down. The last sight of Thomas I ever saw was him getting kicked in the head by that white man. He was all twisted up there, and that man had to kick him in the head. Lord, forgive me."

Mercy looked up at the sky as tears came to her eyes. "Oh Lordy Lord, Lordy Lord." She was crying now. Jim sat, unemotional; he'd heard the story dozens of times. Sorrie extended her hand to the old woman, and Mercy took it, but only for an instant until she pulled away. "It wasn't much fun for a while after that out there in the darkness, hitching onto trains. It was just Addie and me until he got whooped real bad for not letting a white man go in the door ahead of him at a local store. He spent a week in the colored section of the hospital, and when he was healed enough, we found a way to make it back to Mississippi. The hardest thing was explaining to my Poppa about Thomas. He was all torn up after that."

Sorrie squirmed in her seat. "Did you ever hop the rails again?"

Mercy waved her hand through the air as if shooing away invisible flies. "After that, it was easy. Poppa told me every day I reminded him of Thomas, so when the guilt finally got to be too much—like a pressure cooker about to pop with all that steam coming out—I just up and left. I tried to stay out of his way and worked in the fields, but every time his eyes lit on mine, I could see the tears come, and I knew I had to leave. Momma slipped me some twenty dollar bills she'd been saving for whenever I got hitched, and that was the last time I saw any of 'em, though I heard years later Addie and my other brother, French, got killed in the war."

"What war?" Sorrie asked.

"The second war, of course. Girl, ain't you got no history?" Mercy asked, then, without waiting for a reply, continued. "They with Jesus, alongside Thomas."

"How'd you meet Cap?" Sorrie asked.

Mercy looked at her thin fingers and palms. "That's for another time, child. You best head to your man and find a place to bunk tonight." Then Mercy got up and walked into a nearby clump of trees. She emerged a few minutes later, adjusted the denim slacks she was wearing, and bedded down on the park bench that held the mattress. Jim noticed Sorrie eyeing the horizon. "We'll bed down in a little while," he assured her, then walked over to where Dweeb was sitting. Jim gestured for her to sit on the dirt ground, and as she did, Dweeb extracted a joint from his shirt pocket. He lit it and took a long, slow drag. "You want some?" he squeaked as he held his breath.

"I don't do drugs," Sorrie said.

"Well, I do drugs," Jim said as he grabbed the joint.

"Better living through chemistry, right dude?" Dweeb laughed as he coughed from the toke he'd just inhaled.

Sorrie turned to Jim. "You told me you didn't do drugs."

"I lied," Jim said as he took short puffs from the joint.

The two men lingered until all that was left was a little blunt that burned the tips of Dweeb's fingers when he handled it. Dweeb took a paperclip from his pocket, squeezed it onto the stub, and inhaled a few more times until it was ashes. "Guess that's the end of that."

"Say listen," Jim began. "You see a tall man with curly hair wearing a leather jacket come through lately?"

"I see a lot of people coming in and out of camp when I'm here. So, you're going to have to be more specific." Dweeb looked at Jim.

"Kinda tall guy. Looks like me?"

"There was a guy not too long ago. It was only a week or so ago. He walked in—no Harley, no nothing—and asked if certain bars were still open. It seems he'd been here in early sixty-nine. I told him I didn't know anything about it. He was older. He talked real slow. He spent some time talking to Junkman, but in the morning, he was gone. I couldn't even tell you where he bedded down. Kinda creepy, though. He kept talking about wandering the highway."

"Did he give a name? Say what highway he was traveling or where he was headed?" Jim had had plenty of close calls like this and never had any luck tracking the man down after following up.

"We just called him the 'Stranger.' You might want to check with Junkman. He'll tell you."

Jim made a mental note to speak to Junkman, then turned back to Dweeb. "What about the brothers?"

"Brothers?"

"The brothers. The twins. They look the same with dark hair and matching T-shirts and all. They always wear the same thing."

"Oh, the brothers. One has a limp."

"Yeah, I gave it to him. Stabbed him in the thigh when they tried to steal my stuff," Jim said proudly.

Dweeb extracted a plastic bag from his shirt and a packet of papers and began rolling another joint. "I haven't seen those two going on a year, and I been passing through this place a lot. The last time I saw them was on the streets of Seattle, going on maybe six months now. The guy with the limp was begging for money."

Jim sighed and relaxed into the moment. His stress lessened; he decided to change the subject. "You hear from Rehab?"

"Don't see her around much," Dweeb answered. "She hasn't been here in a while either."

"Who's Rehab?" Sorrie asked.

"She's just a girl we know," Jim smirked. He turned to Dweeb and asked, "When did you see her last? Seems like every time I come this way, she's here, and I was hoping to see her."

Dweeb got serious and put his hand on Jim's shoulder. "I think you're out of luck, James. She rode out months ago with some biker dude on his way to New Orleans for Mardi Gras. They were going to the coast after that."

A wave of despair washed over Jim—first, the Stranger he missed by days and then another night without sex; he knew he had no chance of scoring with Sorrie. Perhaps Dweeb was mistaken. "You sure you haven't seen her? I mean, she's always hanging around here. She coming back?" Jim asked.

"Don't think so, James. She was in love." With that, Dweeb burst out laughing.

"Why is she called Rehab?" Sorrie asked.

"Let's just say every man she ever went with needed a rehab after they spent a night with her, and I'm being polite," Dweeb said.

"I don't understand."

Jim leaned in. He smelled like pot and cigarettes. "Well, she's the kind of girl that's so hot she makes men crazy with lust."

"That's disgusting."

"I know," Jim acknowledged. "You want to be like a man, so you got to understand what it's like to think like one. I'm hornier than a two-peckered goat."

Tears came to Sorrie's eyes. "I'm sorry if I'm a disappointment."

"No matter," Jim said. "It's just as well. I'm tired and can see you're tired, so let's just call it a day. Morning comes early, and we got to be in the yard before seven." Jim stumbled to his feet and extended his hand. He helped Sorrie up and led her from camp through a clump of brush near a clearing under an oak tree. They settled on the soft, thick moss, climbed into their sleeping bags, and rested silently until Jim asked, "You asleep?"

"Not yet," Sorrie answered. Jim could see her eyes were fixed on the stars.

He pointed upward. "See all those stars? Some Indian tribes believe the stars are crystals, and others think they're cornmeal scattered across the sky."

"I'm more interested in the moon," Sorrie said. "It's billions of years old."

Jim was impressed with Sorrie's smarts but didn't want her to know that. "My father once compared the moon to a woman's face. Like your face," he said.

Sorrie turned to Jim. "Not my face."

"No, he didn't compare the moon to your face, but I do," Jim whispered, turning to Sorrie. The pale color of her skin reflected the moon's glow and turned iridescent in the light of the beams. He saw the outline of her large eyes and full lips. She resembled a porcelain doll in the window of a toy store.

"You look pretty in the moonlight," he said. The chill in the air drew him closer, and Sorrie didn't resist. He grabbed a thin brown blanket and covered both sleeping bags with it. The covering warmed enough to cut the breeze but didn't shield them from the dampness. He reached out and cradled her in the soft earth. Sorrie stiffened and gently pulled back. "Why won't you let me kiss you?" Jim asked.

Sorrie hesitated. "Because I'm afraid of what might happen next," she whispered.

"What if nothing happens? What if I just kissed you, then nothing else happened?" He said.

"Then I would let you kiss me." Jim leaned closer as the flesh of their lips caressed each other's cheeks. Jim extended his body and felt the warmth of her breasts between the fabric of the bags. Beads of sweat formed on her forehead, and he could feel her heavy breath on his face. Jim leaned in closer, and their lips touched ever so slightly before Sorrie backed away. The evening was over. "That's all I'm comfortable with," she said.

The night Jim had hoped for slipped away. There weren't going to be any mugs of dark beer or music or round-bottomed girls with big breasts and red lipstick. Instead, there was just a stout little princess with the gentlest kiss he'd ever felt. He closed his eyes and drifted off into sleep with the thought of finding the Stranger Dweeb spoke about.

10

The Fight

THE MORNING FOUND Jim sitting next to Junkman, asking about the Stranger. "I see him every so often. He drops in a couple times a year, but he never shares any information; he just says he's a wanderer like everyone else."

"Any idea about where he comes from or how old he is? I mean, does he say what he does?" Jim was intrigued and wanted to get as much information as possible.

Junkman examined his thoughts. "I think he just said that he didn't want to be part of this civilization anymore. That he had dropped out and didn't want to struggle anymore—and that's not unusual with this crowd. He didn't say much more than that, but he did say he'd be wandering the highways if anyone came looking for him."

"Did he say what highway?" Jim fidgeted so much that the chair he was sitting in vibrated back and forth, and at one point, Jim had to check himself to be sure he wouldn't fall over.

"I think he said he enjoyed the desert highways the most. I didn't ask any more questions because he seemed anxious to be on his way." Jim got up from the chair with a yearning to get back on the road. His father was out there, and he needed to find him.

Seven o'clock found Jim and Sorrie sitting back at the freight yard, waiting for the auto rack Jim had promised the night before. It would be the Cadillac of train hops except for one thing: the train wasn't there. Time passed, and Jim kept looking at his watch: *7:30, 8, 8:45,* and by *9:15,* Jim was anxious. Where the hell was the car? It's too damn late now; the bull will be making his rounds, the crews will be changing, and they'll be stuck there like yesterday's rocks. Then Jim noticed something he'd never seen before. He'd become so accustomed to the rhythm of the yard that when there was no activity, it was as if his mind couldn't register it. Suddenly, he realized there was no noise, no clanging of steel, no hissing of brakes, no banging of cars, no humps, no sounds of shoes on pebbles, no men with clipboards, nothing. They'd been sitting near the edge of the tracks for two hours, waiting for something to happen, but nothing was moving. Nothing was being sorted: not the tank cars, not the closed hoppers, not the flatbeds; *nothing was moving; nothing was getting out.*

With dozens of tracks, both outbound and inbound, every car in the yard seemed frozen. And there was silence—no separating cars according to destination, no maintenance crews, nothing.

Jim wondered if there was an accident on the tracks holding everything up. He arose and brushed the dirt from his pants. "You wait here," he told Sorrie, then walked to where a yard worker was smoking a cigarette. He came back a few minutes later. "Grab your stuff," he said.

"What's going on? When are we leaving?" Sorrie asked.

"We aren't. Worker slowdown," Jim bent over to pick up his pack.

"What does that mean?" She asked.

"It means nothing's going out today. The freight workers decided to slow everything down over some contract thing."

Sorrie was bewildered. "What do we do now?" She got to her feet and grabbed her knapsack.

"Well, unless you're prepared to walk a couple hundred miles, it means going back to camp." Jim gathered up his gear.

The thought of returning to the same camp both troubled and delighted Jim. After all, Rehab might show up—but so too might the brothers. He and Sorrie could try hitching out, but that could scatter them to the wind—and it would be hard to tell what parts of the Midwest were still covered in floodwaters. Freight was faster, easier, and, in most places, was still running.

* * *

"What're you doing here?" Cap asked when he saw Jim and Sorrie come through the brush.

"Missed our train," Jim said.

"You just couldn't resist another night of excitement." Cap laughed. He was turning over some hotdogs on the barbeque. "Nothing like a Weiner Fest and some beer for breakfast."

Jim dropped his knapsack on the dirt and sat in a lawn chair, and as he did, he caught the scent of bacon. He followed the smell until he came upon the old school bus. "Anybody home?" He asked.

"Who the hell are you?" said a familiar voice. It was Mercy. "Why Jimmy, what you doing here? Thought you were fixin' to leave on the rack this morning. Why aren't you halfway to K.C.?"

"Worker slowdown."

"Don't ever try to speed those men up when they're determined to slow down," Mercy said.

Jim decided that instead of being annoyed by her comments, he could lighten his mood by turning on the charm. "Mercy, please have Mercy. We're starving. You got some food to help us out?" Jim asked as he waved to Sorrie, who was standing behind him.

"Half the camp's starving. Nothing in life is free, Jimmy."

"Though it's against my better judgment, I can rustle up a little contribution if you like," Jim looked at Sorrie.

"Last night, you only had two dollars." Mercy eyed them suspiciously. Her deep brown eyes squinted, and the wrinkles around her nose deepened while her mouth turned downward.

"I know I can trust you," Jim said. "We got a little more and can slip you some extra Washingtons, but you got to promise not to tell anybody because that's our traveling money."

Mercy's eyes got wider. She waved a spatula, and a few drops of grease fell onto the floor. "In that case, come on in, bring your girlfriend, and close the door behind you," Mercy went back to her cooking. "I got a Coleman here that'll cook anything. Cook enough food to keep us going but less than y'all can eat. I got a soft spot for y'all but nothing for those others. They vipers." Mercy got a mean look on her face. "Believe me, I know."

"You cook on this little stove?" Sorrie asked.

"Oh honey, I been doing it this way long before you was knee-high to a grasshopper. I just open the windows and let the flavor tumble out. I don't mean to poison myself with no gas now."

"You got some breakfast then?" Jim asked.

"Three-dollar contribution will get y'all a few slices of bacon, some toast, and two eggs a piece. I got no hoecake or possum pie if you're looking for it. Got coffee, just black with no extras. And by the way," Mercy whispered, "don't tell Cap about our little swap."

"Deal," Jim said.

After breakfast, Jim and Sorrie searched for a local gas station a few miles away to wash up. The attendant was no older than a high school kid and said very little; he just asked if they'd come on foot or by car. He seemed irritated when Sorrie told him they had walked but reluctantly handed over the keys to the restrooms. He then returned to his perch on a metal chair near the pumps. Before they left, Jim asked if the attendant had seen a man traveling on foot with curly hair and a leather jacket, to which the attendant said, "no."

They returned to camp wearing less dirt and carrying a few sodas. The place had come alive with activity. What had once resembled a sleepy hobo stop now looked like a jamboree with motorcycle riders, music from a boom box, and cold beers stored in a Styrofoam cooler. A few more people showed up, including a Harley-riding couple named Sam and Sandy, who told Jim they got directions to the camp from a fellow Harley hog.

They seemed to think there'd be a wise old man perched on a Zafu cushion who whispered the secrets of the universe, but instead, they settled for the Junkman: a tall, white-bearded, self-described hippie who walked hunched over with a cane. He owed his disability, he said, to a Harley accident in Colorado where, after a six-pack and a joint, he went sailing off a cliff. "Got hooked on a rainbow of pain pills, but weren't the accident's fault; that was from Vietnam. Lucky to be alive after the combat I saw, "Junkman added that he still smoked pot daily and rode a Harley whenever someone was brave enough to loan him one.

Sam spit into the dirt. "I ain't that brave," he said. "Love my hog better than a woman. But I'll tell you what, I'll offer you a ride around camp as a thank you for giving me back road directions to the West Coast. It's the least I could do." Sam looked sincere, but Junkman declined, so Sam extended the offer to anyone in the group. All said no until Jim volunteered Sorrie. She didn't want to do it, but Junkman yelled, "Nonsense!" and showed her how to mount the back of the bike. "No woman turns down a ride on a Harley, least of all a pretty girl like you," he said. Jim was delighted.

Sam got the Harley talking with a few loud roars, then shot like a cannon from the clearing between two trees and around in a circular motion up and down the surrounding dirt and gravel. The Harley spat, fired and made like a wild horse, and Sorrie held on for dear life. Jim watched as the wind whipped her red hair into a tornado, and the sun lit her eyes. She didn't seem afraid but smiled so broadly that Jim thought her face might crack. The currents of air and the morning sun made her spirit lighter as if her soul was floating on a path only someone with no fear could travel. For the first time in their journey, she looked like a free woman: no cares, no burdens, living in the moment with a shining glow.

The biker rode in circles as Sorrie laughed and laughed until she stopped laughing and settled into a feeling of calm. She rested her head against Sam, which made Jim jealous. He wondered how long the ride was going to last. When Sam finally stopped the bike, Sorrie high-fived the biker as he went to join the others. She turned around in circles, and Jim saw her waving to him. He sat under a tree and waved back. Then, she walked toward Jim with a newfound lightness, her arms spread out at the sky, her face giddy. "That made me dizzy," she said. But her light mood didn't last. As soon as she reached Jim, she folded her arms across her chest, and Jim sensed the heaviness return as though concrete had been poured into Sorrie's legs. Jim looked at her and smiled; she smiled back, and then the laughter receded the way water funnels down the insides of a whirlpool. He was both relieved and annoyed. His mood shifted from happiness to indifference.

"Have fun?" He asked while exhaling cigarette smoke.

"Don't you ever not smoke?" Sorrie said as she sat beside him.

"I guess you could say sometimes I do. But I like to smoke; it helps ease the tension if you know what I mean." In the distance, Sam was extending the helmet to Junkman, asking if he'd like to reconsider.

Sorrie turned back to Jim. "Aren't you afraid of dying of lung cancer?"

"I'm not afraid of anything, least of all dying. If I died today, I'd be ready. My only regret would be not finding my father." Jim was anxious to get on the road and follow Junkman's leads, but he knew better than to rush, not knowing the deserts the Stranger was referring to. Traveling by train was faster than foot; if he played his cards right, he could spot the Stranger from a boxcar heading west. "I'm ready to fall into that long sleep any time the universe is ready to take me."

Sorrie changed the subject. "I'll be glad when we leave here." She picked up a rock and flung it into the distance.

"With the slowdown, very little will be heading out. There's also flooding in Nebraska. The railroad bridges might be closed. We'll have better hope tomorrow. Besides, it looks like you were having a lot of fun."

"I was enjoying myself, but that's not going to help me get to Nebraska just like it's not going to help you get to Montana. Can't anyone see to getting us out of here?"

Jim laughed. The crowd could have had luxury sedans lined up, but Jim didn't trust any of them to drive without attracting the cops. "Sure. I'll call the chauffeur and ask 'em to take us door-to-door. Will that be all, madam?"

"You know what I mean."

"Nothing going out of the freight yard means nothing coming in any place down the line. It's like a stack of dominoes. If you can't push one, the rest don't fall, so even if we did get to the nearest working yard, we'd still have to wait somewhere along the way, and this is as good a place as any. You never know what the next camp will look like—or who'll be there. So, we'll stay here one more night and hope for the best." Jim was confident that after the first night, they'd get through a second night without seeing the brothers. It also gave him another opportunity to see if Rehab showed up, especially with bikers coming into camp.

"And what if it doesn't get better? What if they slow down again tomorrow?"

Jim stood up and threw what was left of his burning cigarette onto the ground. "Better hope things change by tomorrow; otherwise," Jim stamped his cigarette out, then looked at Sorrie, "we may have to hitch our way to Nebraska."

After a few hours and some sobering up with food, the camp members decided to visit the local tavern. Some hopped motorcycles, but most chose to walk the two miles to town, sober or not. Only Miss Jewel stayed behind.

When they arrived, the outside resembled an abandoned building. Still, as soon as Jim entered the dark, cavernous space, he smelled the odors of stale beer and dust, and he knew it was like being home. Junkman slapped hands with the bar owner while Jim walked toward the back where the game area was; Sorrie followed. Sitting at a back table, he turned toward the others in the room but didn't recognize any of the faces except those who'd come with him; his father wasn't there. He tilted the chair to lean against the wall and fingered a cigarette.

Mercy sat next to him, complaining she wasn't used to walking long distances and that arthritis in her legs ached as bad as a hurt tooth. But Jim had other worries on his mind—Sorrie might not be allowed to stay if they proofed her—either that or she might get hauled in by the cops, who might send her back to her parents. But Mercy reassured him. "Don't worry, sugar, nobody in these parts going to mess with old Mercy. If I say Sorrie's twenty-one, then honey, she twenty-one."

"It's okay. I won't be drinking," Sorrie said, "so there's no need to worry."

To the bartender—a middle-aged man with a horseshoe mustache—the group's arrival was unexpected but not surprising. Sorrie, Jim, and Mercy decided to get up and walk to where he was polishing glasses behind the bar. Half the group filled the available barstools, but that didn't stop the ones who couldn't get seats from bellying up to order a glass of tap beer. Mercy insisted Sorrie sit on a stool next to her. With only a few locals in attendance, the group made themselves at home by taking over the pool table and the two pinball machines against the wall.

The bartender asked Sorrie if she wanted a glass of beer, to which she replied, "No, but if you have a glass of water, I'll take that."

"Water's free," the man behind the counter said as he grabbed a beer glass and ran it under the faucet. "You aren't from around here," he observed.

"Virginia," Sorrie said, "But I don't think many of us are from around here."

"Oh, I know most of these guys. They come in every so often. I sometimes have to throw 'em out, but not today. It's early, and business is slow."

Some bikers hovered near the pinball machines while Jim excused himself from the bar to scan the jukebox selections. It played a Hank Williams song, and Jim sang along with the lyrics until the tune faded into silence, and another country song began. Jim scanned the selections for a Doors song. He fed a few quarters into the slot, and a few minutes later, the room was filled with a heavy drumbeat. Jim froze in position and then took over the middle of the room in an explosion of dance. His movements were fluid and spontaneous as if rubber bands had replaced every bone in his body. Then, with a quick jerk, he was rigid, cement-like, not moving but electric in his stillness. Lost in a trance now as the images of his father guided his movements, Jim turned his head, and seeing Sorrie across the room, he danced toward her.

Everyone watched as he leaped into the air, landed on his heels, twirled around, and began hopping on one foot. At one point, he turned his back to the bar and glanced over his shoulder like a Flamenco dancer. His movement alternated between frenetic, stylish, and animalistic, but it was all Jim. He slid up to Sorrie and put his hands on the back of her barstool. "Don't you recognize 'L.A. Woman'? Can you hear how the guitar mimics my father's voice? It's like they're talking to each other," Jim said, swaying his hips forward and back and bringing his lips near hers. Then, closing his eyes, he began rocking back and forth, nuzzling his face against her neck. He tasted and smelled the saltiness in her sweat.

"Stop," Sorrie whispered.

But Jim didn't stop. Instead, he moved his hips dangerously close to Sorrie's thighs and snaked his body along an invisible current of air. He started to sing, and with the last syllable of the verse, he opened his eyes and began rubbing against her. There was the smell of perfume on her body as sweat began trickling down his face and soaking his black T-shirt. Jim pressed against her; their flesh separated by a few swaths of clothing. Sorrie's muscles tightened up and grew stiff against Jim as he retreated deeper and deeper into the song while whispering the lyrics in her ear.

"Jim, stop," she said as he leaned closer. "You're pushing me off the chair." In the distance, the others played pinball, chatted, and lined up to down tequila shots. Only Cap and the bartender noticed Jim nuzzling against Sorrie. The bartender didn't seem interested, but when Jim's eyes met Cap's, Cap looked stern, like a principal about to scold a wayward student. Jim didn't care. Cap needed to mind his own business; Jim leaned closer. "Jim, you need to stop. You need to stop *right now*," Sorrie said. After a few seconds, she firmly pushed him away.

He opened his eyes. The spell was broken, his private moment escaped into the past, and reality returned. Eyeing Sorrie's glass of water, he said, "I am so sorry, Sorrie." He smirked. "Sorry, Sorrie." He let out a cackle, then straightened up and got serious. "Tell me, don't you ever think about sex?"

"Not like you do, that's for sure," Sorrie said.

Jim decided to change the subject. "Say, you got some money for beer?"

"Why do you need beer in the middle of the day? Besides, you got half the money from the bull. Why don't you use your own?"

"Because you promised to pay, remember?"

"I think you have more than I do."

Jim fingered his pockets. "I must have left it in camp, so be a good girl and give Jimmy some money for beer cause we both know who stole the wallet from the bull." His brown eyes penetrated hers; he felt expressionless, dead.

Sorrie reached into her pants and took out her change purse. She peeled a $20 bill from the bundle, crumpled it into a little ball, and waved it in the air, daring him to reach for it. Their faces came dangerously close while Sorrie shook her arm, then moved it away just as Jim's hand came up to grab it. She stopped, lowered her hand, and opened her palm to reveal a green clump, then she whispered, "And we know who tried going through my stuff." Then, as Jim took the bill, she added, "Or maybe just try to kill me for it. I just want you to know I'm not afraid of you."

Jim was unperturbed. "I'd keep a few of those handy," he said as he put a cigarette to his lips. "We'll probably be here a while, and after all, I do work for you, right? I need to get paid, right?" To Jim, it was all a joke. He knew he was nobody's servant, but staying together might come in useful money-wise.

As Jim slapped the bill on the counter and told the bartender to line 'em up, Cap stood beside Sorrie. A Patsy Cline song crooned from the jukebox, and Cap wrapped an arm around Sorrie's shoulders. "Are you okay?" he asked. Jim glared at him. "I mean, Jim's got a reputation for treating his girls harshly, if you know what I mean."

Jim leaned over and took a brew from the bartender. "Wasn't nothing," he said to Cap. "You've seen worse."

Tears began to form in Sorrie's eyes. "I'm okay. Jim just got a little anxious."

Cap laughed. "That's a smart word for it."

Sorrie emitted a nervous laugh. "I'm glad you came over before." Her voice trailed off.

"Before what?" Jim took a sip of beer.

"Oh, nothing," Cap said, "You just go back to drinking your beer and stop harassing this little lady."

"Nothing happening in this corner, Cap. You don't have to worry about me."

"Don't matter, Jimmy, and for the record, I ain't worried about you, but you got a nice girl here that you might want to treat better."

"Why is it that everyone's telling me how to treat Sorrie, but nobody's telling her how to treat me?"

Cap surveyed the crowd. "No matter, Jim. Sip your beer and enjoy the music while it lasts. To tell the truth, I don't think we'll be staying much longer."

But Cap turned out to be wrong. The partying continued for hours until people ran out of money or became too drunk to walk straight. Finally, Mercy gathered everyone together to return to camp, but only after Jim stopped at a store for a couple of cold six-packs and cigarettes, paid for with another $20 Sorrie peeled from her wallet. Sorrie used the occasion to buy some ham and cheese and chided Jim for wasting their money. "Service fee," was all Jim said before he stumbled back to camp. It was getting late now, and Miss Jewel had set a fire in the barbeque pit and was cooking a pot of meatless chili. Sorrie sat on a large rock to eat her cold cuts while Jim followed closely behind.

"What's the matter? Don't want to share?" Cap yelled at them.

"Just want to be alone, is all," Jim yelled back as he sat beside Sorrie away from the crowd. He drank a beer with his right hand and held onto an unopened can in his left.

"Why do you drink?" Sorrie asked.

"Other than because I want to?" He answered as he let out a loud burp.

"Why do you like getting all messed up and out of control? I don't understand that. Whenever there was a holiday, my parents would throw a big party, and half the crowd would get sloshed before the dinner toast, and I could never figure out why." Sorrie began rolling slices of ham and biting into them.

"Did you ever think that maybe I'm an alcoholic?" Jim asked.

"Yeah, but we've been traveling for a couple of days, and I never saw you drink like this."

Jim guzzled what was left of the first beer, crushed the can, let out a long, slow burp, and then snapped open the top of the second. "Maybe you don't know me very well," he said.

"I know you."

"What do you know about me?" then Jim remembered what Sorrie had told him. "Yeah, yeah, I'm a lost little boy, and on and on."

"Do you know you talk in your sleep about your father, and sometimes you repeat parts of the poems I read to you? I know you want your freedom, but inside, you wonder if you'll ever settle down to a normal life because you can't ride the rails and live like a bum forever. Your father would have never approved."

"I think you got it all wrong. My father would have definitely approved seeing me walking against a desert sky with cracks of lightening in the background and a storm coming up over the horizon while I catch a red ball going south." Jim guzzled more beer. "I'm not afraid of anything, least of all you. But let me ask *you* a question. Ever wonder why you wake up with so much sand in your eyes?"

"I don't know. Maybe it's allergies."

"It's because you cry in your sleep. Why do you suppose that is?"

"I don't know. I guess I have an eye thing."

"What if I told you your tears were like blood?"

"It's not blood."

"I know, but what if I told you your tears ran like blood? Running like a man's blood when he gets cut up in a fight or shot in a war."

Sorrie gazed into Jim's eyes. "You're forgetting that women bleed too, and not just that way, but real blood from all the hurt they've seen, usually from the way men treat them," she said.

Jim stared at her for a moment. "You never been with a man, so how can they hurt you? How much hurt have you seen living with satin sheets and someone to deliver breakfast in bed?"

"I never had satin sheets, and no one ever brought me breakfast. It wasn't like that for me. I grew up just as lonely as you did. And for the record, you hurt me plenty in some of the things you said and did, and don't act all innocent like you don't know what I'm talking about. I've tried to be nice to you, but you don't respect me, at least not that I can see."

Jim stood up. "You got to earn respect in my book. You got to show your loyalty." Jim straightened his shirt and picked up the rest of his beers. "Right now, I think I need better company. You can stay here if you want, but I think it's time to get some exercise in my legs and go over to where the party is."

Jim walked toward the crowd around the barbeque. He smelled the charcoal of a seasoned fire and walked toward where there was an empty chair to sit in. What little sympathy Jim had for Sorrie dissipated in proportion to the number of beers he drank. After six, all reason flew away, and Jim was left listening to Junkman talk about his experiences in Vietnam: "And then we went into one village where the ARVNs were questioning some captured Charlie, and they didn't take no shit from those bastards. They did what we couldn't do but were thinking. They just took those sons-of-bitches up in the helicopter about a hundred feet, and if they wouldn't talk or tell 'em where the enemy was hiding, hell, they'd just push 'em out the chopper, and they'd land like a bug on a windshield—splat on the ground, and that would get everybody talking."

Just then, Sam jumped in. "Hey, Junkman. I hear you have some great stories about being in Vietnam, even though you weren't there. Somebody told me you were stateside cleaning latrines at Fort Hood."

"Let me get a hold of the son-of-a-bitch who says that," Junkman replied.

The crowd around the fire laughed, except Jim, who was half listening, half nodding off. He held onto a small piece of sobriety to keep his mind in the game, but the beer kept winning, taking him into a dark place filled with fire-breathing dragons and voices yelling his name. He drifted back and forth from the darkness of sleep to the glow of the fire. He tried to position his body so he wouldn't fall into the dirt if he passed out. He could see Junkman laughing, but he couldn't make out why. Hell, they were all laughing, except him. He didn't understand the joke. Maybe it was him they were laughing at. Had he lost his pants? He reached for his belt, and it was there around his thin waist. Had he wetted himself? No, his pants were dry. "Sonsabitches," he whispered. A wave of dizziness washed over him. Being buzzed was one thing; being flat-out drunk was torture. It came on so fast, and he missed all the fun: just staring at light and shadow. Even if Rehab showed up, Jim doubted he could get down to business.

His eyes grew heavier. He stood up and squinted to see what patch of grass he wanted to pass out on when a hurling shadow entered his sight and hit him BAM on his left jaw. He spun around with the force of the blow. Then his legs came out from underneath him, and he landed on his knees.

"Who in the hell hit me?" Jim slurred as he stumbled, only to be clocked again on the other side. He raised his hand to his face, felt the inside of his mouth, then moved his tongue around to see if he'd lost a tooth.

"That's for me, you bastard, and the other's for my brother, who you put in the hospital for three weeks."

Jim looked up and recognized the face of the man he had fought. "Casey? Is that you?"

"Damn right, it's me. Now get up, you bastard, so I can kill you while you're still standing. Or do you want to die with your face in the mud like the gutter rat coward you are?" Jim focused his eyes. The man called Casey stood about 5'6" but looked to weigh over two hundred pounds. His stringy blond hair and matted beard told Jim he hadn't had a proper bath in days. In fact, Jim could sense the pungent odor of urine from almost five feet away. The rest of the camp stood by, waiting to see what would happen next.

Jim tried to focus by wiping his face and then his eyes. He felt stickiness on his hand and glanced down; he was wiping his face with blood. He didn't even need to see it; he caught the scent of iron in the air. "What the hell did you do that for?" Jim asked as he stumbled, trying to center his line of gravity so he wouldn't fall again. He was sobering up fast. Casey clinched his fist and was about to bring it down hard on Jim's face when Jim said, "What the hell did I ever do to you? You were the one who tried to rob me. I was defending myself, is all."

"My brother can't walk right because of you. You think you're better than the rest of us having a famous father, but you know what I think? I think you're a bullshit artist. You're just a washed-up trailer trash grifter making everybody believe you're so bad when you aren't nothing. 'Oh, my dad, oh my dad.' Jim Morrison was never your father. He died in Paris, like they said. So, now I'm going to kill you because I hate listening to your sad stories and because of what you did to my brother."

From deep inside his fabric, Jim found the rage he'd been avoiding all day. With one quick burst of adrenaline, he went after Casey, grabbing him around his thick middle and wrestling him to the ground. Casey held onto Jim by his shirt and began smashing his fist into Jim's face, creating more gashes and blood. He grabbed Jim's hair and stood him up, preparing for another punch. Jim fought back but didn't have the physical strength to free himself from Casey's grip. Casey tightened his hand around the top of Jim's T-shirt, twisting it and making it hard for Jim to breathe. He pulled Jim's face within a few inches of his own. "The next one's going be the last time you see daylight, and then I won't have to listen to any more putrid stories. This one's for my brother, you lying bastard. Prepare to suffer."

Casey stiffened up as Jim felt Casey's breath on his face. Fist at the ready, Casey geared up to slam down the hammer when suddenly a banshee cry came from nowhere, and Jim saw Sorrie fly through the air and pounce on Casey's back.

Sorrie wasted no time wrapping her fingers and nails around Casey's eyes, trying to pull them out. Casey let go of Jim and tried peeling her fingers from his face, but she was too strong as she dug her nails around his eye sockets. Casey gripped her hands and managed to get them off his face, but then Sorrie wrapped her arms around his neck and gnawed at his left ear, biting down hard. He became a spinning dervish as she struggled to stay on his back. When she couldn't coil her hands around his face again, she clutched his neck, squeezed his Adam's apple, and grabbed hold of his legs with the edge of her boot. In a frenzied panic, he tried protecting the area around his throat. Still, Sorrie tightened her hands around his eyes again. He spun faster and faster to throw her off, but Sorrie was too powerful. She held on, screaming into the air that she would rip out his eyes so he'd never be able to fight Jim again while Jim tried to sober up and realize what was happening.

"Get her off me!" Casey yelled as Sorrie clawed at his face. He held his lids tight, and when Sorrie saw she wasn't doing the necessary damage, she grabbed his nose and tried to bend it enough to break it. Casey continued to spin, but she hung on, determined to hurt him. "Get her off me." He yelled as he whirled around, spitting and spinning.

Jim found his legs and stood up. "If I get her off you, will you leave me alone?" He asked.

"I will! I will!" He screamed.

Jim suddenly seemed to be having fun watching Sorrie savage this little man. "Well, now, do you promise?" Jim asked politely.

"I promise! I promise!"

"Say pretty please."

"What?"

"Say pretty please," Jim said as he watched Sorrie pound her heels into the back of Casey's legs.

"Okay, okay! You win! Pretty please!" And with that, Sorrie flew off Casey's back, not so much by what Jim said, but because Casey stopped spinning and bent his body over so she couldn't hold on any longer. She landed in a clump of brush a few feet away while Casey collapsed into the dirt.

Jim knelt beside Casey. "Come on and get up, mofo. Who's the bastard now?"

Sandy rushed over to help Sorrie. Jim watched as she brushed herself off and touched the inside of her lip; there were drops of blood trickling from a cut. Sorrie tried to wipe her hands on her shirt, but it was filthy. She rolled the inside of the shirt bottom around her hand and dabbed her face.

Jim went back to staring at Casey. "Who's the bastard now?" Jim asked.

It was Cap who intervened. "Jim, stop. Let the man get up. Nothing can come of this."

"The hell so," Jim said. "This little piece of shit tried to kill me."

"Then call it square. Let the man clean up and get yourself fixed, too, so you can be gone by first light." Cap reached out his hand. It held a white rag. "Do it now," Cap insisted, "before the cops show up. We don't want them threatening to shut down the camp again." And Jim knew he was right. The fussing and fighting with Casey and his brother a year ago drew the cops, and Jim had a hell of a time getting back in.

He labored to his feet and glanced at Cap. "You're right. But I'm letting him go because I don't want to cause anyone trouble. You got to remember that I'm a lover, not a fighter."

"You're right, Jimmy," Cap agreed. "Now let the man be so he can think about what he did."

Casey stood up and brushed himself off. Jim stopped in front of him. "We square on everything?"

"Maybe so, Jimmy, but this isn't over," Casey said as he wiped his face and walked toward the stream running along the camp. "This isn't over," Casey said again as he turned and walked away.

"You almost came within an inch of your sorry-ass life if it weren't for your girlfriend over there," Cap said.

"She's not my girlfriend."

"Well, I'd think more about that because she just saved your life." Jim realized Cap was right. He'd done very little to defend himself—he was too drunk to care—and it wasn't like anyone was coming to his aide; he was used to telling himself that a man needs to fight his own battles, but Sorrie rescued him. Even after he abandoned her, ignored her, and pushed himself on her, she cared enough to prove her loyalty. The phrase kept reverberating in his mind. *She saved your life.* Almost sober, he walked over to where she was bent down, spitting blood.

"Looks like I cut my tongue," she said.

"Looks like you saved my life," he said.

Sorrie looked up. "Well, someone had to. You didn't want to save it, and I still need your help."

Jim realized she was right. Maybe he was expecting it at some point; perhaps he was so tired of looking for his father that catching the westbound to the boneyard in the sky was the only option, and the one way he knew how to do it was to lie down and let someone else do the beating. "I guess you're right," he said. "Why should anybody care about me—including me—when no one ever cared my entire life?"

"I care about you."

"After the way I treated you?"

Sorrie cut him off. "It's about time we started caring about each other. Like family, you know? I mean, I look around here, and they have a family. It's something I always wanted."

"Something I always wanted, too," Jim said. Just then, Jim took Sorrie's arm and helped her stand up. There was a drop of blood at the corner of her lip, and Jim took the white rag Cap had given him and dabbed her face.

"You don't have to do that," Sorrie said, gently brushing his hand away.

"Yeah, I do," Jim said as they started for the stream. "But one thing I don't understand. Why did you go after him? It wasn't your fight. Hell, a girl like you shouldn't be fighting anyway. I mean, you were some crazy fool."

"Like I said. We've been traveling together, so it's like we're family. Besides, this time, it was better to act like a man." Sorrie dipped the end of her shirt into the stream and cleaned her face and arms. Jim did the same and noticed Casey off in the distance, lying against a tree with his eyes closed.

"Yeah, but you never acted that hard before."

"Let's just say the more time I spend with you, the harder I get inside."

* * *

The excitement and partying from the day before didn't do much to quell Jim's hunger. He awoke to his stomach growling and the new day blanketing his eyelids. The sun was high. He looked into the morning rays, and when he did, he felt a different kind of hunger—the kind that only a man who's been chained for a long time knows, the type of impatience that has a man's feet constantly twitching, even in his sleep. He couldn't wait to light out and hop the auto rack, especially since Casey was still somewhere in the camp. The nervousness in his bones fueled a drive to move on, and he knew it was time to go.

Jim lifted himself and felt pain, not only from the beer but the beating as well. But he had no time to lose. "Sorrie, Sorrie, we got to get up. We got to get the train; otherwise, we'll have to hitch."

Sorrie, still asleep, turned to the other side, and Jim repeated his plea. He rose and felt a sharp pain on the side of his face. Was his jaw broken? He hadn't thought much about it last night, but today was different: almost every muscle and bone ached. He reached into Sorrie's knapsack to look for her small compact mirror. It was there—along with her red change purse. He fingered it and saw it glisten in the sun. She had enough to get through, but so did he, he reminded himself. Then Cap's words rushed back: *She saved your life.* Jim let go of the purse and grabbed the compact instead.

When he saw his reflection, all he could say was, "Oh, damn," as his fingers followed the red streaks from his jawline down his neck past his black T-shirt. He fingered around his face and shoulders, trying to feel for any broken bones, and then told himself that if his jaw was broken, he'd be in a lot worse pain than he already was. He tried to use his spit to wipe the streaks from his face, but he didn't have any. The beers from the night before had given him dry mouth, and he needed to get to the creek for some cold, clear water to wash up. He looked again at Sorrie, who was still dozing. *She saved your life.* Must not let her see me like this, he thought, and he rushed to wash up and change clothes. As he removed his shirt and scrubbed under his arms, he noticed Casey wasn't under the tree. Alarmed, he scanned the woods but didn't see him. He needed to get Sorrie up.

When Sorrie moved from twilight to wakefulness, she glanced at her open knapsack and then at her wallet next to the compact. "We got to get moving," Jim said, extending a ham sandwich he'd bought from Mercy. He was clean and fresh with new clothes.

Why were you in my knapsack again?" She said.

"Don't panic. I didn't take anything. I wanted to borrow your mirror to look at my face, that's all. You can eat your breakfast, but make it quick."

"Water first," she whispered.

Jim handed her a canteen of cold water. The day was turning hot and humid, and the dew lingered. Sorrie poured water into a washcloth and ran it over her arms and neck, then tucked it back into a pocket of her sack. She flung the bag aside as she grabbed for the sandwich. "What time is it?"

"Time for us to leave." After Jim told her it was seven, she sprang from the ground and began putting on her clothes. Holding the sandwich between her teeth, she alternated between eating and getting dressed.

They were about to hike on the trail when Casey emerged from behind a tree and stood in their way. Jim hesitated to move past; Sorrie stiffened up. Jim addressed Casey first: "You okay?"

Casey shuffled his feet, and dust rose into the air. "Just a little sore. Your girlfriend's got quite a temper."

Jim let the comment pass. "Listen, let's let it go. We don't have to be friends, but I don't want to fight."

Casey hesitated and stroked his chin. "We'll leave it for another time," he extended his hand, and Jim shook it.

"Another time," Jim said as he and Sorrie exited the camp.

They left in high spirits like drops making whoopee in a barrel of rain. But before they left, they stopped to say goodbye to Cap.

"As the caretaker of this camp, I've seen my share of young bucks ready to take on the world only to be slapped down hard by circumstances or luck—and wasn't everyone who landed here unlucky?" Cap addressed Jim directly. "When I first saw you all those years ago, you walked in at your own speed wearing an old newsboy cap and a pair of ripped jeans with empty pockets and a tight belly screaming for food. You were about the sorriest sight imaginable. About the only thing sorrier was a man who had to crawl in because he had no legs. And I saw plenty of those, but now you got a traveling companion, and if I were you, I'd keep to her side." Cap made the sign of the cross against his chest. Jim thanked him for his advice and told him they'd be on their way. No sense arguing with experience.

11

The Auto Rack

WHEN THEY GOT to the yard, Jim strolled up to the first freight worker he saw to ask about the trains leaving that morning. It was a bold move, but in Jim's mind, they needed to head west as soon as possible. The best news was that the slowdown was over, the rivers going toward Nebraska had receded, and the trains were running again, but the freight hand had seen them. He let them know it: "Just because you got the urge don't mean you got the license to hop this freight. I'll be calling the bull directly if I see you again."

They waited in the bushes until the worker was out of sight, and then Jim snuck over to a bi-level auto rack and climbed the metal skeleton. Sorrie followed closely behind. Jim fished for the keys to a blue-colored Cadillac El Dorado in its front wheel well and found them taped to the inside of the fender. Opening the driver's side door, Jim quietly placed their knapsacks in the backseat, then instructed Sorrie to crawl over to the passenger's side, making sure not to touch the brakes or the horn.

She had trouble navigating the middle console as she crept across the bucket seats. She caught her pant leg on the transmission stick but managed to free it before Jim crawled in behind her. She shimmied to the passenger's side and then sat up, only to have Jim's hand yank her back down. "Keep your head down," he whispered as he gently clicked the door closed. He raised his head high enough to peer out the window.

The train hadn't left the yard yet, so there was still a danger that the bull would spot them, especially when autos were involved.

"What do we do now?" Sorrie whispered.

"We just wait," Jim said as he rolled to his side.

And wait, they did. Instead of pulling out at eight, the train stood for over an hour. The sun heated the interior, and the air filled with steam from their bodies. Jim cracked the door open to let the breeze in and cool down the interior.

"I'm so hot," Sorrie said, "and my legs are cramped. What's going on?"

"I don't know," Jim said. "I hope they don't cut us."

"What do you mean?"

"When a train has too many cars—especially heavy ones like this—there's a chance the yard might cut the line in half. We're up toward the front, but you never know. We're lucky to be getting an open rack. Most are closed now."

"I don't understand why they would switch."

Jim laughed. "Probably because of guys like me."

Time took over, and every so often, Jim thought he heard voices outside the car, but they faded quickly into the distance.

"What's taking so long?" Sorrie said.

"Don't know, but if you're thinking of getting off, you can forget it. This rattler's going to blast off; I just know it." As Jim finished the sentence, the morning air was cut in half with the weight of two short bursts of the train horn that Jim thought might shatter the windows. Then, they felt a jerk as the cars began moving. "See, I told you," Jim said as he adjusted his posture. The train sputtered around a bend, and Jim looked behind him to see strings of cars being separated onto different tracks. "Lots of trains going out this morning. They must have had a huge backup," he said.

Not long after, the train cut through a swath of St. Louis and over a rickety bridge. He'd been on this route dozens of times and knew this part, but he still couldn't get used to the feeling that the bridge would collapse into the swollen river below. He took Sorrie's hand. This might be that time, but Jim reasoned they wouldn't let dozens of cars be washed into the rushing water. The train hesitated and made an agonizing, snaillike pass. They heard the creaking of brakes and steel and rivets bending under them. The train stopped, then lurched, then finally picked up speed.

When they were moving at a steady pace, Jim opened his eyes. "Time to have a little fun," he said as he inserted the key into the ignition and started the car.

"Can you do that?" Sorrie asked.

"I already did," Jim answered. He reached for the radio, tuned it to a rock station, then turned on the air conditioning and sat up straight as the cold air began circulating inside the car.

"Time for breakfast number two." Jim reached back for his knapsack and pulled out a handful of soft cheese slices wrapped in cellophane and a bag of peanuts.

"Where'd you get the food?" Sorrie asked as Jim handed her a slice.

"Mercy gave it to me. She thought we looked unhealthy." Jim gingerly opened the nuts and emptied half the bag into Sorrie's hand. "Don't spill it, and don't make a mess in the car. We need to leave it the way we found it."

"Why are you so concerned about a car you broke into?"

"It's like this," Jim said between mouthfuls, "If hobos leave a big mess in a diamond like this, the owners of the yards will make it harder to get a ride—any ride. In fact, if I were the bull, I'd be thinking of hiring my cousin or brother to come down and help get rid of Wandering Willies like me. So, I like to be polite and keep things the way I found 'em, like I wasn't even there."

"But you'll use the gas in the car so we can listen to the radio," Sorrie laughed.

"Oh, that's nothing. They'll think someone forgot to fill the tank. The guys on the other end will say a few choice words over that." Jim took a bite of cheese. It was soggy and soft from the heat and turned his palms yellow. After he scarfed it down, he wiped his hands on a white handkerchief he had near.

"For someone who likes to travel on the road, you sure keep yourself tidy," Sorrie said. "Just like when we were in that town where we went to the supermarket."

"You learn fast to keep things neat; otherwise, you lose focus. So, you got to be on guard, knowing where everything is."

"You don't trust anything or anybody, do you?"

Jim laughed. "Why should I? I've been kicked from here to hell and back all my life, so I grew hard. Do you think Casey was the first one to ever beat the tar outta me? Hell, that started with my foster family," then Jim corrected himself. "No, actually, it started with my mom."

"What kind of a person is your mom?"

"She's just a person," Jim said. "She got me and my brother and sister all filled with ideas. She was really smart. We learned about music and history and traveled to different places. But she got the disease now, you know?"

"What kind of disease?"

"You know, like someone who took too many drugs and drank too much booze. My mom's not right in the head."

"You never told me your mom drank."

"She did lots of things I never talked about. But now I've got to go see her. She has some things from my dad that she wants to give me before she passes on. She's still nuts but smart, not like me."

"I think you're smart," Sorrie said as she popped the last of her food into her mouth.

"You're the first one who ever told me that or listened to me. The first one I ever kept with me steady. My Momma never listened to me. She was too busy doing drugs or searching out some man she could latch onto who would give her money."

"How'd you come to live in Florida then?"

"Oh, she tried to leave us in a supermarket and got in trouble with the law, so we were taken away. My brother and sister went to live with their pop in Montana, but I got put in foster care. The people I lived with only cared about the monthly check coming in. They never minded that I didn't go to school; they just thought I was crazy for not being able to sit still, which was okay because I was a loner, right? I never really cared about other people much, and besides, in the end, when all the cards were laid on the table, I just wanted to be left alone."

"I feel so wrong for asking," Sorrie said.

"Don't be," Jim said as he turned to Sorrie and gazed into her blue eyes. Their bodies drew closer as he took her face into the cradle of his hands and slowly kissed her, allowing the moment to linger. She pulled her lips away from his, but Jim could tell she still felt his breath on her cheek. She smelled like salty peanuts, but her lips were plush like a velvety blanket.

"That was better than the last time," he said. "Can I kiss you again?"

Sorrie hesitated. "Yes," she whispered, and their lips drew together. They parted, but the sentiment of the moment lingered as he kissed her again. Finally, she disengaged and sat back; the moment was over.

Jim froze, eyes closed, letting his lips hold the memory. He threw his hands into the air and looked at Sorrie. "I guess that's all, folks," he said, then reached for the dial on the radio. "How come we been listening to this damn radio for a half hour, but they haven't played any of my father's songs? They say they're the Voice of Rock. I say they're more like the Voice of a Crock. If I had a phone, I'd just call 'em up and tell 'em what I wanted to listen to."

"They go by a playlist," Sorrie said.

"I don't understand."

"They go by a playlist of songs selected for them, probably by a program director who works for the corporation that owns the station. You can't just call up and request a song; chances are all the songs are strung together on tape anyway."

"I'll be damned," Jim said. "I learned something today. A playlist, eh?" Jim thought for a minute. "Well, who says I need to call up and request anything? I'll just sing my own song." Jim began singing about nodding to unconsciousness. He turned to Sorrie and started serenading her, making up his own words as he went along. Sorrie began laughing, "Stop it, stop it," then, as Jim got closer, Sorrie put her hand against his face, "Stop, you're making me blush." Jim leaned in closer but got pushed away. "Whoosh, you have to do something about your breath. You stink," Sorrie said. Jim stopped singing, and they laughed as the train inched closer to Nebraska.

* * *

By the time the train slowed and stopped halfway into the next freight yard, the battery in the El Dorado had gone dead, and with it, the air conditioning and radio. Jim reasoned the car must have run out of gas midway through, but they were dozing and didn't notice until the sun's heat made it too hot and clammy to sleep. Jim cleared the window of the fog from their breath and looked out. The train had stopped on a bridge, so there was no safe way to exit unless they wanted to take a chance on the dirty water below.

"Where are we?" Sorrie said, rubbing her eyes.

"Must be west of Kansas City, but I'm not sure how far west," Jim said as he gazed out the window. "I don't recognize this view."

"Can't I open the door and look?" Sorrie asked. Jim grabbed her arm when she started to move the lever.

"I wouldn't do that," he said, "not unless you want to swim in some nasty-looking water." And when Sorrie looked down, she agreed.

They waited in the heat while Jim pointed to the distant buildings. Then, finally, the train sputtered over the bridge and into a massive yard filled with hundreds of cars. As the train slowed, he surveyed the land-scape through the Cadillac's window. He wasn't afraid of the bull because they were already here, and what could the bull do except chase them off? Of course, a beating might be in order if he got caught, but Sorrie was with him, and a bull would think twice before raising his stick to a girl—especially one who looked as young as Sorrie.

Jim noticed some trains sank into a dip in the middle of the yard while some that were newly coupled moved with slack between the cars. Still, others had crews standing by, ready to receive the engineer's orders. Jim silently motioned for Sorrie to sneak around the other side of the Cadillac and serve as a lookout. At the same time, Jim determined the best place to climb off. The train slowed enough for Jim to note a soft patch of earth next to the tracks, and it was where, after grabbing their knapsacks, he guided Sorrie down the ladder and onto a slight embank-ment near some brush. The train stopped, and they walked off the trailer; it started again, and Jim waved his hand as the train passed and then guided Sorrie down the embankment to a safe stretch of road. It was then that they heard a familiar voice behind them.

"Hi," the voice said.

Jim recognized it and turned toward the person who said it. "What the hell are you doing here?"

"Nice to see you, too," Dweeb said. He parked his hands in his pocket. "'I was gonna wait in camp, Jimmy. Honest, but then I said to myself, 'Weeb, where you think Jimmy boy's going with that girl?' So, I said, 'he's going west,' then I thought, 'Weeb, if you were going someplace other than the nowhere places you come from, where would you be going? And then I just about fell on my ass thinking of where I should be going, and sure enough, it was west, the same place as you." Dweeb took his hands out of his pockets and pointed them at Jim.

"There are no vacancies," Jim said. "You weren't invited."

"Funny, cause I asked myself the same question, and the way I figured it, the train's free for all who can hop it, so it just so happened I was riding in the same direction as you. In fact, it's interesting to see what kind of car you got, Jim, cause I rode in a Buick Roadmaster with a tinted window and a long, lean backseat that gave me one hell of a nap."

"Must have been a used car," Jim said, "but that still doesn't measure up cause we got a fully loaded Caddy."

"Well, that's a good car, but for padding the ear, my flop was the better of the two."

"Looking at you would have me believing that any more questions about your ride would have you sailing back to the starting gate because you act like you didn't believe what you just said," Jim remarked.

"Come to think of it, I don't believe what you just said," Dweeb countered.

Sorrie decided to change the subject. "Can we stop and get something to eat? I'm starving." It was now the afternoon, and her stomach had been growling since the morning.

"I'm flat broke," Dweeb said.

"Well, we got a little," Jim said, "but nothing for you. Maybe we can let you lick the plates."

"Glad I tagged along then," Dweeb said, smiling.

The small coffee shop near the freight yard had an old-style Coke emblem in the window and a sign over the door reading, "Breakfast,

Lunch, Late Night Snacks," though the hours only listed six in the morning to five in the afternoon. The faded black and white sign over the entrance said, "Fleur-de-lis," which Jim pronounced as "flour-d-lisp."

The main area had dark wooden tables with different colored metal chairs and checkered tablecloths. A few construction workers sat reading papers in a darkened corner. One silver-haired man made a passing glance, but no one bothered to pay any attention to the group as they sat down, except for a middle-aged waitress who got off a stool near the cash register to take their orders. She brought some glasses of water but no menus.

"What'll you kids have?" She asked between snaps of gum.

"Can we get some menus?" Jim asked. The waitress looked annoyed and went behind the counter. Jim whispered to Dweeb, "We don't have much money, so you're on your own."

"Come on, Jimmy, you know I'm broke."

"I didn't ask you to come with me, did I?"

"No, but next camp, I'll rustle up a collection and pay you back."

"To hell you will. You don't have friends."

"Maybe not even take that long," Dweeb reassured him. "You know I got the sympathy vote with the old ladies."

"Maybe if you take a bath and get some new clothes. You smell awful."

"Tell you what," Dweeb continued, "Bet I could steal a pie or two from the bakery truck."

"Where are you going to find a bakery truck in the time it takes to get on a train? Besides, it's the afternoon."

"Oh, I'll find one. Good one, too. You just wait and watch." Dweeb paused a moment, then went into a story about the day he turned fourteen and how he hijacked a bakery truck full of bread and muffins. The cops chased him clear across town, and he would have gotten away with the heist, but he turned a corner on two wheels, and the back door of the truck flew open, and skids of baked goods sailed onto the street, making the police cars swerve to avoid the mess. "Made a hell of a fix. I got put into the crazy house for that," he said. "But it shows you I'm the all-time bakery-stealing champ, so just pick your pie, Jimmy." Dweeb held his hands and smirked. "Since I'm here, maybe you could front me a few bucks until we get to camp or something. I'll pay you back, Jimmy, I promise."

"We aren't going to a camp anywhere in these parts. We're going through."

"Better yet, then. I know you like to keep yourself clean, so I can show you a nice piece of water to get a good bath before the next cannonball whistles down the pike. Won't be for a few hours yet. You know that as well as I do."

"I also know every local bathing hole in the area; besides, we're parked right next to a big one just down the block." Jim looked at Sorrie, who peered into her red purse. She held up three fingers.

Jim looked back at Dweeb. "Listen, if you promise not to bother me for the rest of the day, Sorrie can front you three singles to get something. But you better start looking for change on the street as soon as we leave this dump, get me?"

Dweeb peered into Jim's dark eyes. "Well, hell yeah, Jimmy, that's easy. That's a lot of food for this skinny body. I'd be mighty grateful."

"Maybe we better make it two," Jim said, but Sorrie shook her head. "Okay, three. But remember, with you, nothing's free."

The waitress returned with menus, but they didn't bother to look at them. Instead, Sorrie asked for a chicken sandwich while Jim got scrambled eggs and a side of hash browns. Dweeb asked for "anything you got under three dollars," and the waitress returned with a grilled cheese sandwich, a side of potato salad, plus a cherry coke. "Got me plenty," Dweeb said when he saw it.

After eating, the trio lingered over coffee, even after the waitress removed their plates and presented them with the bill. She fidgeted with it, and Jim could tell she was anxious for them to leave.

"Where are we going next?" Dweeb asked.

"We aren't going any place," Jim said. "Sorrie and I are going to wash up a stone's throw down the road, and you're going to go away."

"But Jimmy, how will I get the money to pay you back? Besides, we come so far together," Dweeb said. He couldn't keep still. He was like a live wire randomly bouncing along the street.

"You don't even know where we're going."

"Don't much matter. I just wanted some company, is all. That camp was getting to be too much of everything."

"Like what?" Sorrie asked.

Dweeb looked in her direction. "Too much booze, too much noise, too much having to be alone and lonely." Dweeb lowered his head and then looked at Jim. "Hey, listen. While we're on the subject, can you tell me why you didn't bother to take the hop from Chicago to K.C.? It would've saved you the stop in Indiana."

Sorrie eyed Jim. "You mean we didn't have to go to that camp? We could have gone right through? Why didn't you tell me that?"

Jim stared at Dweeb but spoke to Sorrie. "In case you've forgotten, we had to backtrack a bit, or don't you remember? But to answer your question, there's flooding along the direct route, especially in Illinois," he explained. "Lots has to do with the type of car, some has to do with the type of schedule, and still most has to do with the weather we run into along the way." Jim was afraid to mention Rehab, but Dweeb knew the truth.

"'Most has to do with the weather,'" Dweeb repeated as he nodded his head and looked at Sorrie.

"Yeah," Jim agreed, "the weather . . . and the company, especially at this table." Dweeb swallowed hard.

"I don't see much harm in him tagging along. He doesn't seem like he'd get in the way," Sorrie said.

"He already cost us three bucks," Jim reminded her.

"Well, it's my portion of the money, and I don't mind having him tag along for a ride or two."

Jim reached into his pants, counted two twenty-dollar bills, and handed them to Sorrie. "Now it's our money, and be warned, he's not as trouble-free as he looks."

"You're probably right, but he's one more body around to be sure you don't abandon me in some freight yard. Besides, he's funny with his scarecrow looks and high-pitched laugh. The only trouble is that talking to him is like having a conversation with a tornado." Sorrie turned to Dweeb. "So, you go to school at all?"

"I told you not to do that," Jim said.

"Do what?"

"Encourage him, ask him questions. He'll just lie, you know." Jim reached into his pocket and extracted a cigarette.

"Yeah, I went to school."

"Tell her about the scholarship," Jim said.

"The what?"

"You know, the scholarship." Jim lit a cigarette and watched Sorrie's reaction to Dweeb's story.

"Oh, that," Dweeb looked at Sorrie. "I won a scholarship to college."

Jim leaned in. "Full scholarship," he said as he released a puff of smoke.

"Full scholarship," Dweeb repeated, "from a big school."

"Really? Which school?" Sorrie asked.

"Stanford, or was it Brown? Don't remember, but yeah, really," Dweeb shrugged.

"Tell her why they took it away," Jim said as he rolled up his sleeves.

"Why'd they take it away?" Sorrie asked.

"I'm embarrassed," Dweeb said, then at Jim's prodding, explained, "It was because of the cat."

"The cat?"

"Yeah, the cat. I didn't like a kid in school—he kept stealing my computer codes—so I found a dead cat in the middle of the road and hung it in his locker. He was upset," Dweeb said without emotion. "You should have seen his face when he opened the locker." Dweeb shrugged. "They suspended me for five days, and the college found out and didn't consider me moral enough to take classes. But. of course, I wouldn't have gone anyway. I can't sit in those lectures for that long."

"Yeah, but you're brilliant," Sorrie said.

"Smart *and* dumb," Jim interjected.

"Well, they took it away, and my parents got upset." Dweeb turned to Sorrie. "You know, you're kind of pretty. I like your eyes. I bet you're real smart, too."

"Thanks," Sorrie said. There was silence, and the awkwardness didn't escape Jim's notice.

Jim interrupted. "Time to leave," he said.

* * *

"How far is this clearing?" Sorrie asked as they walked down a gravel road.

"Not too far," Jim said.

"I don't want to spend another night in a dirty camp with crazy people whose breath smells bad."

Jim studied the dirt path. "Sorry, princess, will it be the country estate this evening?"

"Just a place where the air doesn't smell like stale beer and burnt wood."

"We'll be hopping another train in a few hours. We're only going there to clean up. It's not a camp, just a stream; there might be people."

But there weren't any. Instead, the stream had filled to the shoreline, and the water traveled fast down the bed it had cut. Jim warned them to be careful because the current was strong, and the water had oily patches.

The trio stayed close to shore and scrubbed their bodies and clothes and the metal utensils in their knapsacks. Sorrie complained about the slipperiness of the algae on the rocks and the questionable color of the water. Dweeb stripped down to nothing, but before he took a dip, he said, "So you want to know why I left home?"

"Wasn't it because of the cat?"

"That's why I didn't go to college. The reason I left home was because of the underwear."

"The underwear?"

"Yeah, I got really drunk one night, and I'd forgotten my house keys, so I crept inside what I thought was my bedroom and fell asleep. I even had to break the window to get in. The next morning, I woke up at the neighbor's house. They were on vacation, so I stumbled back into my bedroom, but the neighbors found out."

"How did they find out?"

"Because I left my underwear on the floor in their daughter's bedroom. The neighbors returned it to my parents a few days later. I didn't even realize it was missing."

"How did they know it was yours?"

"It wasn't hard to figure out with all those imprints of spaceships and aliens. My parents got mad and told me I could either wear the underwear on my head for three days or get out. So, I left. Left the underwear behind, too." With that, Dweeb belly-flopped into the water and swam a few feet, then the robust current forced him upstream. The water churned around his body and rose a few inches before Jim realized they might get caught in the rushing water. It was increasing fast.

"He's so crazy," Sorrie told Jim. Jim realized she didn't know what was happening.

"Dweeb," Jim called, "come back. The water's getting higher. You need to come back to where we are. We need to go." He said it with a sense of urgency, but Dweeb splashed in the distance.

"What's going on?" Sorrie asked. She had a panicked look when she glanced at the swirling water.

"Get out of the water, "Jim warned her. "Throw something on, then just take everything and wait by the road."

"What's happening?" She said as the water reached her stomach. Jim extended his hand and helped her to shore. "Get about thirty feet away from the water. Don't worry about him. I'll grab him." Jim was tempted to leave Dweeb where he was but knew enough about water to sense the situation was dangerous. "Dweeb, come back to shore, man. We're gonna leave soon. Something is happening with the water, and we want you to be safe."

"I'll be okay, Jimmy. Don't worry about Dweeb." Jim could see him several feet in the distance. He could also see the water was inching up past Dweeb's chest and feared for both of them; he didn't want to drown saving someone he hardly cared about.

"Dweeb, Dweeb," Jim yelled. He made his way through the muck and grime of the swiftly flowing current and searched out where he saw Dweeb disappear under the water. Jim was frantic now. The stream was rising, and he was having trouble maintaining his balance. He anchored himself with one hand against a tree and searched under the murky water with his other hand to feel for an arm or a head or, God forbid, a body.

But there was nothing. Jim figured he'd have to get Dweeb to shore—no easy feat given the way the water rushed past—but he needed to save himself, too; otherwise, there'd be no Nebraska, no Montana, and no Jim. He let go of the tree, slogged through the muddiness of the shore-line, and found solid ground. Jim spotted something in the distance and sloshed toward it. It was Dweeb faced down in the mud along the shore's edge. Jim grabbed him and hauled him away from the water. He felt like dead weight, and Jim searched his memory for how to perform mouth-to-mouth resuscitation, but just as he was about to pinch Dweeb's nose, Dweeb opened his eyes. "Fooled you," he said.

* * *

After they were safely on the road and Sorrie heard the story, she asked, "How could you hold your face underwater for that long?"

"Oh, I can hold a lot of water, sometimes all at once," Dweeb answered. They resumed walking. Jim was pissed but tried to keep his anger inside. If he had shown it, he'd have pummeled Dweeb and thrown him back in the stream. "So, did you know that it's impossible for you to lick your own elbow?" Dweeb asked.

Jim began walking faster, leaving Dweeb and Sorrie behind. Dweeb noticed. "No, wait," Dweeb said. "Did you know that the first toilet on television was seen on *Leave it to Beaver*? And that women hiccup less than men?"

Jim's anger subsided, and irritation took over. "Now, how the hell do you know that?"

"Well, one time, me and my friend . . ." Dweeb's voice trailed off. He turned to someone not there and asked, "You think I should tell 'em about that one? No? I guess you're right. Okay, just skip that one," Dweeb said. "But did you know that a snail can sleep for up to three years?"

"Where in the hell did you get that?" Jim asked.

"Oh, I read those papers they have at the newsstand. You know, the ones with pictures of UFOs on the cover. Sometimes, people just tell me things."

"And you believe them?" Jim asked.

Dweeb didn't answer but said instead, "Hey, Jimmy, you should smile more and not look at me that way. After all, it takes seventeen muscles to smile but over forty to look mean."

* * *

Their clothes were filthy from the dirty muck of the creek water. The trio walked a few miles to a commercial district with several storefronts and businesses. Jim sought the nearest Laundromat to clean their clothes and use the bathroom. The one he picked had a few people doing their laundry and an old Asian woman sitting at a back counter. For the most part, they were alone. Jim led Sorrie and Dweeb to a corner where the others couldn't see them. "Listen, I'm going to throw my clothes into that machine at the end, and you guys can follow with your clothes. I don't want to spend any money, so once you put your clothes in, you need to act like you're talking and block me from the lady in the back."

"What are you going to do?" Sorrie asked.

Jim extracted a thin piece of wire from his knapsack. "You won't like it, so it's best to keep what I'm doing to myself. Just know that you need to distract her because if we get caught, she'll probably call the cops."

Dweeb handed Jim the clothes in his knapsack. "I know just what I'm gonna do." Not waiting for Sorrie, Dweeb walked over to the wooden counter and began engaging the woman in conversation. Jim couldn't hear them, but the lady momentarily turned away from the direction where Jim was standing. Jim and Sorrie put their and Dweeb's clothes into the machine, and Jim fed a quarter into the coin slot. The amount due read seventy-five, but instead of depositing more quarters, Jim slipped the wire into the opening and jiggled it until the display read zero. The machine started, and Jim pressed the "regular" cycle.

"That's great, but what will we use for detergent?"

Jim casually went over to an unattended basket in front of a machine that held someone's clothes. Careful not to have anyone see him, he took the liquid detergent from inside the bin, opened it, dumped a good measure into the soap fill of the machine he was using, and returned the container to the basket.

Sorrie sat at one of the plastic chairs beside their machine. "You think of everything, don't you?"

"You got to learn to survive out here, princess. No one will give you much of anything, least of all stuff to keep you clean." Jim glanced over. The Asian woman tried to wave Dweeb away, but he kept talking. The two other people who were there when they first arrived had gone. Jim surveyed the aisle. Several dryers had completed their cycles, and the laundry sat in the cylinder, waiting for their owners to return. Jim crept along the dryer row and glanced into the tumblers. There were blue jeans and T-shirts, underwear, and socks in several.

When their clothes were finished washing, Jim put them into a few bottom dryers and started the machine using the same method he had for the washers. He also took the opportunity to extract socks, shirts, and a few pairs of jeans from the other dryers, then quickly shoved these clothes into his knapsack. Just then, he noticed the Asian woman eyeing him from a distance. "What do you think you're doing?" She asked, pointing her hand as she shuffled down to where Jim was standing.

"What are you talking about?" Jim asked.

"You take the basket used for another person and leave it in the middle of the floor. Do you want to make someone hurt? And no running. I saw you last time. You ran up and down like a crazy person and made people scared."

Jim hadn't been in this laundry before and had never seen the woman, but he was glad she wasn't yelling at him for stealing clothes. As nicely as he could, he said, "Thank you, Ma'am. Thanks for the advice. I won't act crazy, I promise."

The woman turned, and Jim thought she would return to her perch. He was wrong. "And another thing. I think you got the wrong dryer when you took something out."

"No, it was mine. I had a few dry things, so I took them out. I left some other stuff in. Honest."

"He's telling the truth," Sorrie said. "Here, let me show you where our dryers are." Sorrie walked over to the two dryers they were using, next to the one Jim had stolen the clothes from. "These two are ours. See? The cycle is almost over. We'll be gone in a few minutes."

The woman acted befuddled, as if she needed to remember what she initially saw. Finally, she shook her head and shuffled back to the counter.

Once their gear was separated and packed, they used the washroom to clean up, then walked into town until they found a supermarket dumpster. Dweeb pulled out a few wrapped pastries, a dozen unopened granola bars, and a container of lettuce. He stuffed everything into a plastic bag. They came to a clearing with a large oak tree, dropped their gear, and sat down.

"How did you find this place?" Sorrie asked Jim.

"Exploring the side roads. Like my dad used to talk about wandering the landscape and all that."

"How do you know he said that?"

"Oh, I saw some interviews on television and stuff my Mom told me."

Dweeb pulled out a joint and lit it. "My dad didn't ever explore anything. He always stuck to the main road, if you know what I mean."

"Well then, how did he get so off track with you, 40 Watt?" Jim said.

Dweeb thought a moment. "I guess you could say he was stiff. He kept his mouth shut, walked straight, and drank two martinis before dinner."

"And you were the result?"

"Nah, my genes are from my mom's side, where everybody's crazy. They eat duck on Easter right after they shoot it. Yep, they're the guns, goose, and boat crowd. As a matter of fact, I used to go with my grandfather to all these duck-calling competitions. He was terrific. Want to hear?" Dweeb cupped his hands and made a trilling sound. He stopped, adjusted his hands, and grunted in short, tonal bursts. "That's a hen sitting on a dead moose."

"Who's calling, the moose?" Sorrie asked.

"Sounds more like the moose's farts," Jim laughed.

"You have to let the rhythm of it roll off your tongue," Dweeb said, then tried to show Sorrie what he meant. "Chukka, chukka, tikka, tikka, blow. Want to hear more calls?" Sorrie shook her head, and Dweeb launched into a series of cackling calls and shouts and noises to demonstrate different scenarios: the duck sitting in water, the duck circling back, the duck mating call, the duck danger call. Jim and Sorrie were transfixed, and the more weed Dweeb smoked, the louder he shouted until Jim had to tell him to hold it down. Dweeb stopped what he was doing and handed what was left of the joint to Sorrie.

She refused to take it. "I never do that stuff."

Dweeb handed the joint to Jim, who also refused. "I never do that stuff either," he said.

"Wait a minute. I saw you do drugs," Sorrie said.

"Yeah, but I'm not interested today," Jim admitted. "I did it as a shock factor to mess with you."

"You're mean," Sorrie said, leaning down to brush some twigs off her clothes.

"I know. I don't do drugs because I saw how sick it made my Mom."

"How did drugs make her sick?"

"They made her a little crazy, like I told you," Jim looked toward the sky. "Going on maybe six now, almost time to leave." Jim glanced down and saw a bug crawling on his knapsack. He gently picked it up and deposited it on the tree. "She had more beatings, near-death trips, and starvation diets than anyone I ever knew."

"Like me, maybe?" Dweeb asked.

"I shouldn't even be talking to you. You know what you remind me of? Kids who took acid when we visited those communes out west."

"You mean like your Mom?"

"I mean the little ones, maybe eight or nine. Their parents used to feed it to 'em all the time. They'd go crazy like you, and after a while, there was no sense in giving 'em drugs because they acted crazy without it, just like you do when you don't have any."

"Oh, I'm much worse," Dweeb said, "I was raised by straight people."

"I think about those kids every once in a while and wonder whatever happened to them," Jim said.

"I think they're programming computers now," Dweeb answered.

"Yeah, well, you *would* say that. You were raised with money, and there's nothing worse than growing up with parents who think they're better than the rest of us, especially when kids have no homes to go to."

Sorrie interrupted. "Excuse me?"

Jim turned to Sorrie but pointed to Dweeb, who was off looking at some wildflowers. "You got to be careful. Whenever there's a girl involved, he puts on a 'poor me' face. I've seen him different, really smart and sane. He comes from rich people—like you. He goes back and forth with 'em, so it's not like he stays on the road much. He comes out to play, gets pumped up on drugs, then goes home, and they stick 'em in a detox. I think he comes out worse after they lock 'em up. Some people can't be caged up like that."

"Like you?" Sorrie asked. Jim saw her eyes staring into his, then turned back to where Dweeb was picking flowers. He gathered a bouquet and headed back to where Jim and Sorrie were.

"Do you think we should rescue him?" Sorrie asked.

"What he says isn't real. It's all about perception. My dad's music taught me that," Jim said.

"But you have a home too," Sorrie said, "in Montana with your Mom."

"Yeah, but this time, I'm going there for the letters and photos she has."

"Well, it's not like you have friends," Dweeb said, staring at the flowers.

Suddenly Jim stood up and grabbed Dweeb by the collar. "Listen, I don't like friends. Friends make you do things you don't want to do. As for you, you better get used to the fact that I'm probably the only person you can trust out here. You're just damn lucky I haven't left you by the side of the road, especially after that stunt you pulled where you acted dead in the water. Somebody else would've tossed you down a grain chute for that number."

"If I were you, I'd be more scared about me leaving you," Sorrie shot back at Jim.

Jim relaxed his hand on Dweeb's shirt and thought for a moment. "Sounds like a fair trade. Let's see who wins."

* * *

The day grew old as the darkening sky told Jim it was time to leave. But the darkness wasn't due to the setting sun. It was the type of darkness that came with storms. The sudden sound of wind rustling through the trees made Jim pause. If the rivers rose, it might be time to catch a freight and continue west. However, hopping onto a moving train with rain pouring down would be difficult, if not impossible, especially for a girl like Sorrie. Lying under a tall oak wasn't an option because that would be a prime target for a lightning strike. Jim rousted Sorrie and Dweeb and hustled them back to the yard before the thunder started. As luck would have it, a freight train heading west was ready to leave.

They settled into the back of a boxcar, rested against the metal wall, and waited for the car to move. Despite his energy, Dweeb sat still, and Jim would have too, except for a nervous tic running through the muscles of his left leg. "Stop," he told his body, but his leg didn't stop. Instead, it kept jerking back and forth. Pain shot up the side, and his calf started involuntarily banging against the car's floor. He tried to hold his leg down with his hands or wrap it under his other leg, but the tic persisted as if his body was betraying the essence of what he thought he was: still and silent and stone. Finally, he gripped the side of his leg and forced it down, straightening it against the cold of the metal to get it to stop. In the distance, the passing clouds covered what was left of the setting sun. The dying light cast Jim's shadow across the wooden floor, and Jim noticed the fidgeting, even in the figure of the shadow. Jim was worried; he'd never experienced anything like that before.

12

Missouri

DESPITE JIM'S PLANS, Dweeb didn't leave. They were on their way to K.C., and Dweeb was traveling with them no matter what Jim said. One comfort was Sorrie's ability to read *The Lords and the New Creatures* under the moon's light until Dweeb started to ask questions. She'd read a line, and Dweeb would ask, "What's the hive?" or "What are they filming?" only to be told to shut up by Jim, who then told Sorrie to keep reading.

Dweeb interrupted five or six times before Sorrie closed the book and went to the opposite end of the boxcar. "See what you did, you idiot?" Jim said as he biffed Dweeb on the forehead, and Dweeb shrugged.

Sorrie curled into a ball and wrapped herself in a sweater against the coolness of the night. "What was your first train ride?" Sorrie asked Dweeb; Jim groaned.

"Oh, me and my friends did it for a laugh when we were about thirteen. Before that, we just threw tomatoes at trains, even the ones with passengers. One day, we forgot about the tomatoes and decided to get on board, but some drunken hobo pushed us off. I cracked a rib, but I was lucky. My friend Donnie got a broken skull and spent six months in the hospital. He never acted right after that, and even today, he bobs his head and slurs his speech," Dweeb's voice was a flat, dry monotone.

Jim lay back and positioned his Boonie hat over his face. "Sorrie, you got to be crazy listening to that boy. He makes so much stuff up that you won't know what to save and what to throw away."

"I don't care about that," Sorrie said. "Maybe someday I'll write a book about all this and put you in it."

Jim laughed as he leaned against his backpack. "That'll be the day."

They rode on for miles. At times, Jim opened his eyes to see Sorrie wide awake, watching the horizon as it alternately filled and disposed of cornfields and tall grass, glowing in the dark until the light crept over the horizon. Suddenly, the world came alive again, with farm trucks and backyards stripped of everything because of the floods. And sometimes, there'd be glimpses of children running in the sodden fields and farmers looking at their farm equipment or women hanging white sheets on clotheslines. Sorrie turned to Jim. "What day is it?"

"I don't rightly know," Jim shrugged. "Can't see many churchgoers, and the farmers are in the fields, so it's probably not Sunday."

"To tell the truth, I don't care what day it is. I used to care about those things, just like I used to care about a mother waking up and telling me what to wear for the day," Sorrie said. "Right now, Life is timeless, and you know what?"

"What?"

"For the first time, I feel free like you."

* * *

The following railyard looked like an endless line of train cars snaking through the horizon and beyond. There were pens and boxcars and numerous lines of metal rails, so Sorrie had to rely on Jim to tell her where to step and what direction to go in because Dweeb didn't know either, which amused Sorrie and annoyed Jim. "All these years, what? Five maybe? And you got no nose for the road?" Jim said to Dweeb. He surveyed the railroad cars and side markings and signal colors.

It was all a line of different painted ribbons to Sorrie, and she said so, but to Jim, it was gold. "So many routes going west and so little time," he said, looking over the massive freights in the distance.

Jim spotted another hobo down the tracks and asked if he knew the lines going to North Platte. The hobo seemed amused and started the conversation with, "Well, if you cake eaters don't bug off wanting to hitch the ride of your lives your first couple of times out . . ." as if Jim was green and Dweeb and Sorrie were hangers-on. Jim contributed to the hobo's attitude because he thought if he acted dumb, the hobo might give him the information he wanted, but that wasn't the case. "What's your price?" The hobo asked as he opened his mouth to reveal blackened teeth.

Jim painted a grin on his face and took the hobo by the arm. "You know the Hobo Creed, don't you? You're not supposed to take advantage of someone in a weaker position, especially another hobo. But I'll tell you what: How about you get to live without being all bloodied up? That's my price." With that, the hobo did more than point out the best cars. He tried to give Jim a lesson on the different types of signals and how to read train lines, but mostly, he prattled on and on about picking the right car. Jim nodded in agreement and mumbled, "speed it up," not amused that the old badger couldn't recognize a fellow boxcar bum like him. Jim nodded his head until the correct information came up: what track, which was the fastest, the easiest, and the earliest—and a bonus if they were going in a straight line. "Oh, that one," the hobo offered, pointing to a sidetrack, and the trio was off.

Once Jim was sure of the train, he began hunting for cars. Though being in a well-guarded freight yard like this was dangerous, Jim felt confident the bull wasn't near. But instead, Sorrie showed concern. "We're out in the open now; won't they find us and kick us out?"

"Nah," Jim said. "That'd mean the bull has to come out of the bunk house, and he won't if it's raining."

"I go with Sorrie, " Dweeb said. "I'm a little nervous being out here."

"You're always nervous. It's the one thing we can rely on," Jim checked more cars. He found a boxcar and then surveyed the best way to climb aboard. Suddenly, he was astonished when he heard the car let out a hiss as the air brakes kicked in, meaning it was prepped to leave.

"We got to go," he said to the others. "*We got to go now.*" The train began humming, pitched forward, stopped momentarily, and then rocked back and forth as if it was about to light out in one quick burst of energy. Jim climbed in the boxcar and reached for Sorrie's hand. She grabbed Jim and, in one swoop, hoisted herself into the car.

Dweeb realized what was happening and began to run. His lean legs and clumsy arms made it difficult for him to coordinate his gait, and he had trouble balancing himself against the unevenness of the track bed, but he managed to hold on. Jim and Sorrie grabbed his thin arms and whipped him into the darkness as the train started moving.

They tried to make themselves comfortable, but as soon as they did, they discovered they weren't alone. In the corner of the car were four eyes glaring at them. Finally, one spoke. It was a woman's voice. "Get off our train," she said with authority.

The second voice, also female, said, "Strangers aren't welcome here. So, prepare to get pushed out of the car, all three of you."

"We ain't done nothing wrong," Jim said. "We have just as much right to the car as you."

"But we were here first, and you're trespassing," the female voice said.

"We'll keep to our corner if it's all the same. We won't bother you," Sorrie said. Jim was surprised she spoke up but couldn't decide if she was making the situation better or worse.

The second female voice spoke: "What if we told you we had a gun and could force you off the train, maybe when it's going fifty miles an hour."

"That would be murder," Jim said.

"Not if you're intruders, which you are."

"We're all intruders. The car doesn't belong to any of us."

"Just start making your peace with God."

Jim moved closer to the woman, his fists at the ready. "What in the hell . . . ?" he started to say, but the two women began laughing before he could finish his sentence.

"Scared you, didn't we?"

"Ricky Blue Pants, is that you?" Jim asked.

"Right, you are James, and here's my new girlfriend, Boopy."

"Call me Boop," the woman said. She extended her hand to shake Jim's, then turned to Ricky. "Name's Jim? Was this the guy you were telling me about? The one whose father is Jim Morrison?"

"Born and raised, that's him," Ricky Blue Pants said.

"Why do they call you that?" Dweeb asked.

"That's a rude question, and who in hell are you that you need to know?"

"Just passing through," Dweeb muttered.

"Go on, pass down the line then. Jimmy can tell you." Ricky Blue Pants turned to Jim. "By the way, we ran across someone not long ago who was looking for you. Called you by name, too."

Jim's ears perked up. Was this the Stranger who told Junkman he was traveling the highways? "What did he look like?"

"He was tall and dark with curly hair, kinda like yours. He didn't tell me his name; he just said that if I saw you, I was to let you know he's out there looking for you."

Butterflies raced in Jim's stomach. Was this his father or someone looking for Sorrie? He didn't know but hoped his dreams were finally coming true. "Did he say where he was going—a route maybe or a town?"

"Only to say, a man's looking for you. Not much after that. My advice would be to keep searching, Jimmy. If he knows you're out there, then he also knows you're going to meet up sooner or later, so just keep on truckin'."

Jim's mind started racing. It would be easier if he had his father's things and spread the word. His urge to get to Montana was more vital than ever. It was Sorrie who brought him back to reality.

"So, what do you do while you're on the road?" Sorrie asked Ricky Blue Pants.

Jim perked up. "Don't you know Ricky's an artist? Got big pieces of art stretched from New York to Cali. She's shown in some of the most famous places I know."

Sorrie was intrigued. "Where?" she asked.

"Oh, Five Points, schoolyards, every barn and closed hopper from here to L.A., Disneyland, Dogtown, you name it."

Sorrie looked disappointed. "You paint graffiti."

"Don't sound too let down. Best street art in the world," Jim said.

"Best *art* in the world, and you are?" Boop asked.

"Sorrie," Jim broke in. "And that's not an apology; that's her name."

"Well, don't be sorry," Ricky said, then giggled. "Be proud of being Sorrie. That's all I have to say."

"I am."

"Me too," Dweeb broke in. "Reminds me of the time I called up my girlfriend, who asked me to take her to McDonald's. She was nice. No stupid stuff. Also, an artist. She took pictures. Anyway, she asked me to take her to McDonald's, and then halfway through the meal, she told me she was breaking up with me. I ask her what are we doing breaking up at McDonald's. Why couldn't she have broken up with me on the phone? I could've saved money, but then she told me, 'yeah, I wanted a Big Mac first.' I didn't care. I was in love, you see."

"You in love anymore?" Ricky asked.

Dweeb sat back. "Nah, she was a real disappointment. It cost me eight bucks of food so she could break up with me."

They spoke for an hour before encountering a pause in the trip where Jim told Sorrie they had to get off. Sorrie agreed but asked if Dweeb was coming with them, to which Dweeb replied, "No, I'll stay with my new friends for now."

"I don't know whether to thank you or insist you come," Sorrie said.

"Nah, I'll stay."

"Ricky and Boop look like tough customers. I hope they don't kill him," Sorrie whispered to Jim.

"Well, he's not coming with us," Jim said. The train slowed to a crawl; they jumped off, walked through a small freight yard, and boarded another car. "We never have to go back, and we never have to turn around. Besides, I didn't ask Dweeb to come. He made peace with the world. So, if they throw him off the train, that's his fault."

"You don't mean that, do you?"

"Nah, he's okay. Funny sometimes. Most times, he's pretty right in the head, but not this trip. Maybe the drugs got to him. But let's just say he doesn't care about death. I thought I was saving him from drowning, but it was all a big joke. I should have left him there. He almost got me killed." Then Jim paused, and his voice got soft. "By the way, I never did thank you for helping me in the camp. I'm mighty grateful."

Sorrie laughed. "Really?"

Jim closed the distance between them. "Yeah, really," he said as he wrapped an arm around her shoulders and gently kissed her forehead. Jim removed his arm, stared down at his hands, then looked at the afternoon sky. "I kind of have a confession to make."

"Yeah?"

"I wouldn't have brought you, but I felt sorry for you. You paid and promised to read the book, so I let you tag along, but now I like you. The problem is that I never had feelings like that for anybody except my angel in school. But you saving my life made me change my mind. I started believing someone in this world cares. I used to think there were no friends short of food, booze, and a warm place to sleep, but now I'm not so sure. You could be my first real friend."

"Do you need a friend?" Sorrie asked.

"I guess you're my friend now. Before you, I wanted to be with Jim all the time because I knew he still existed. I feel it in my heart because he's my dad. His energy still circles the world. I feel doors opening and closing all around me, and sometimes, he slips through and whispers he's here. He might be anywhere along our route now that I heard what Ricky Blue Pants said. I hope for my sake that he's still out there."

Sorrie hesitated. "Are you sure he's real?"

Jim thought for a moment. What was she saying? Was she telling him she thinks he's crazy? "Of course, he's real. Ricky met him. Junkman met him. I think maybe he's looking for me just as hard as I'm looking for him."

"I'm not sure. Are you sure it's him and not the man my parents sent to find me?"

Jim's voice softened. "We don't even know if they sent someone to find you. That could all be something you made up, just like you say I might have made up that Jim Morrison is my father. But here's something else. Did you ever look at my father's book?"

"I'm reading it to you, aren't I?"

"But I mean, really look through it." And with that, Jim fished the book out of his knapsack. In wonderment, Jim gently flipped through the last few pages. "My Momma used to read this to me all the time, so I got it memorized." He held out a page with a poem about a child and someone named Choktai. Scrawled on the page in black pen was a note that read, "Rose, Thanks for total freedom. You're my baby. Love, J. M." in a childlike scribble.

Sorrie extended her hand and read the passage, silently at first, then to Jim, who mouthed the words as she read it. Sorrie looked at the photo on the cover. "This is really your father, then?" She asked.

Jim lightly skimmed his fingers across the words as if pressing too deep would erase the letters. "People ask me how I know," he whispered, "this is how I know."

* * *

There was a ring of yellow beef fat around the edge of the metal rim when Sorrie opened a can of stew. She told Jim it was cold, but it was the best stew she'd ever eaten, and even the tough beef fibers wrapped around her aching teeth were rich with a smoky flavor. Jim could have been more enthusiastic. He struggled to chew it, then swallowed and tried licking the beef tallow off his hand but found it had hardened into the lines of his fingers and under his nails. He cursed and flung the empty can into an adjoining field.

They exited the train when it stopped and found a clearing by a farm in the fading sunlight. Jim thought about Sorrie reading the book and seeing the passage. "I never let anyone see what my father wrote. It's a secret I've shared with only one person, and she's dead," Jim said.

"Who was that?"

"My sister. She died of cancer when I was younger. I thought I could cheer her up, so I showed it to her when she was dying."

"How did she take it?"

"She smiled and then fell asleep. That was the last smile she ever gave me."

Sorrie nodded. "Thank you. I feel honored that I could see it."

"Well, there's one more secret to be shared, and I think you know what it is," Jim said. "We're almost at an end, but it looks like it's going to have to wait just a little while longer."

* * *

They woke up in a field and walked to the nearby farmer's house, asking if there were any chores they could do in exchange for a shower and food. The farmer and his wife were just a little older than Jim and put them to work cleaning a barn covered in mud. They also cleaned the farm stand and prepared baskets of fruits and vegetables to be sold that day. They helped with carting gallons of juice and goat cheese. The farmer thanked them by offering a hot shower, a meal, and a promise that they could stop by for additional work if they were ever in the area again.

Jim knew North Platte was only a hop away, so when they were finished, they grabbed their gear and started back, and in the time it took to move from the field to the freight yard, they were on a car going west again.

Once settled, Jim said, "Maybe we should talk about what's coming next."

"What's coming next?"

"Like your dreams. What dreams do you have from here on out?"

"I don't know. I've had my whole life to think about it, and I'm still wondering where I'll end up. How about you?"

Jim thought awhile. He could ask Sorrie to stay with him, but he also had a mission to finish. "I got to finish what I started. See it through to the end. You're welcome to come with me, but we're on different levels."

"We were on the same level when it came to growing up and being lonely." Sorrie continued. "When I talk about my dreams, we can paint a straight line to anywhere besides where I grew up because it hurt so much when I was there."

"I had a mother on drugs, so yeah, I know. Maybe that's why I got no feelings."

"Well, I don't feel anything either," Sorrie said. "I haven't felt anything for a long time."

Jim watched the light flicker off Sorrie's hair as she sat beside him. He realized they were alike in so many ways. For days, he'd felt burdened by her, only to discover he was traveling with a mirror, someone with the same aches. The rage was gone, replaced by overwhelming sorrow. Jim realized Sorrie was the closest friend he'd ever had. "I'm here to protect you until you get to your family. But maybe I'll come back. We shared some good secrets, you and me," he said.

"I'd rather be nowhere than be back in that prison with my parents."

Jim huddled next to Sorrie and put his arms around her shoulders. "Sometimes nowhere is a good place to be."

13

Nebraska

THE RIDE TO North Platte was bumpy and cost them the comfort they'd had with similar boxcars because the flooring was grooved and hard. Both of them were sore after sleeping on pebbles and dirt. They huddled together and dozed throughout the trip, and when the train came to a halt, all they could see across the landscape were miles and miles of tracks and freight cars.

But they weren't on the main line. Jim peered out of the car and guessed that the train engineer must have pulled into a side yard. Sorrie stood and stretched and cleaned her eyes of sand.

"Best not to stand up now, " Jim said. "We might still be jerked around."

"I'm achy and have to stretch from laying in that one position."

Jim began gathering the contents of his knapsack. "That's an even better reason not to stand."

Sorrie wiped her eyes. "More sand."

"You were crying in your sleep again," Jim said. Sorrie stopped rubbing her eyes and sat motionless as Jim continued, "but then it seems you have a lot to cry about."

Once they were sure the car wasn't going anywhere, they walked a few miles and were soon dumpster diving behind a local quickie mart. Jim fetched out day-old pastries, and Sorrie scored a carton of ripe strawberries. A patch of grass provided a breakfast spot. "Where are we going now?" Sorrie asked, red juice dripping from one side of her face.

"You tell me. These are your folks. I'm just the pilot."

"It would help if I knew where we were."

Jim laughed and lit a cigarette. "North Platte, if we're lucky, in the middle of nowhere if we're not. It looks like North Platte, but even here, the only thing you'll find for the next hundred miles are cattle, corn, and trains to haul them." Sorrie looked forlorn, and Jim continued. "Where'd you say the people you were looking for were from?"

"A place called Paxton. It's off Route 80 going west, but I only have an address: 300 Lovett St."

"You got a name?"

"My mother's last name is Southard. Her older brother and his wife live there. I only met them twice, but they seemed like family even back then," Sorrie said. "Three summers ago, they came to spend the night but spent four. He's a farmer, and she's a teacher. Both offered to take me to Nebraska, but my mother wouldn't allow it. They asked the following summer, and my mother still wouldn't allow it. But while they were with us, they took me places to buy books. I'll never forget that."

Jim surveyed the landscape. There wasn't much movement in the yard, and even if they got lucky and grabbed a train, it might overshoot the town, and they'd wind up spending half a day getting back to where they needed to be. "It's probably easier to hitch from here, so get your gear. If we're lucky, we'll catch a ride; if not, then the way things are stretched out, we might have to walk 20 miles."

"We've come all this way only to hitch 20 miles?" Sorrie said. "I've been waiting on this day for four years now, and it's less than 20 miles away, and you're telling me I might have to walk it?"

"Well, we can always go back," Jim said as he reached for his knapsack. Of course, he knew she'd never agree to that, but in the pit of his stomach, Jim felt nervous thinking about when they'd have to say goodbye.

Sorrie let out a sigh and picked up her gear. She stiffened and willed her tired legs to begin the trek west. The journey was almost over, and she wanted the strength to see it through. "Let's go," she said.

* * *

The first car to pick them up wasn't a car at all but a truck hauling rocks—not just small, hard-to-notice pebbles—but massive boulders that made the back tires sink into the mud. The driver explained he was only going up the road a few miles. They threw their packs onto the floor and climbed into the bench seat in the front, with Sorrie sandwiched between the driver and Jim.

When the driver pulled away and onto the highway, the truck jerked forward, and Sorrie's body alighted into the air, nearly causing her head to smack into the top of the cab. She extended her arm and held onto the dashboard. "You can hold onto my arm," the farmer offered, but Sorrie ignored him.

"You can hold onto me," Jim said, and Sorrie hooked her finger into the notch on his belt to steady herself. Lack of food and a proper place to sleep left Jim and Sorrie tired. Jim scanned Sorrie's face and thought about the secrets she'd shared. He guessed that she was a jumble of numbing sadness just like him. She didn't like being touched, but Jim noticed that he could hold her arm or stroke her face, and she didn't complain.

Though Jim acted like he didn't care, he felt everything, especially the presence of his father. He was always hovering like a shadow in the air. Always present, but never really there.

Then Jim remembered: he was going home soon, and he would get to open that chest containing his father's things. After that, he would start by checking out the highways in Arizona and New Mexico. If that didn't work, he'd look for new places to search.

Jim lay against the truck's door, closed his eyes, and envisioned his father onstage, snarling into the microphone and looking at the audience in ways that excited girls. The girls—Jim saw them in his sleeping and waking dreams. His hand tightened around the edge of the seat as he wrapped himself in the warmth of the summer sun cascading through the window. It was like being surrounded by a great crowd of women admirers—their heat was everywhere, pressing into his body. He made himself comfortable against the seat and felt their hands reaching to caress him. They were getting closer to his body now. He reveled in it until he opened his imaginary eyes and saw Sorrie in the distance. She looked numb. Panic set in; he didn't want her to see him like this. He started pushing the girls away and reaching out his hand. He watched her turn and walk away. *Don't go*, he was saying, *don't go*. Then, suddenly, a gruff voice brought him back to consciousness. "You kids traveling far?"

Jim snapped to wakefulness and sat up straight as the driver repeated his question. "Just up the road, maybe 20 miles or so," Jim said as he stared out the window. The truck rolled along the highway, cutting the daylight into vast expanses of blue sky and yellow carpets of pasture and barren fields. Jim saw truck after truck of 18-wheelers heading in the same direction they were. He'd driven a pickup once as a 10-year-old. His foster father had put him in the seat of his prized '72 Chevy. Jim thought he was all Boston bum sitting up in the place of honor, gripping that blue leather steering wheel, trying to get enough height to see out the front window. On most occasions, Jim would sit there waiting for the old man to tell him to scoot over to the other side. But this time was different. He was surprised to see the old man get in on the passenger's side, pluck the keys from his pocket, shove them into the ignition, and wave his hand as he said, "Drive," pointing into the distance.

Not one to disappoint, Jim's legs struggled to reach the clutch and start the truck. Finally, he managed to get it into gear and go, but he couldn't shift fast enough and drove into a pig pit down the road, getting mud all over the old man's wax job and stalling the Chevy. When Jim couldn't start it again, the old man bound out of the truck, ankle-deep in mud, threw open the door and tossed him out. Jim was so embarrassed that he never drove a car or truck again.

The man with the green overalls and heavy rocks left them miles from where they needed to be. He turned onto a long dirt road and peeled out in a trail of dust. Jim circled back to the main strip and began hitching again as Sorrie pulled a canteen of water out of her knapsack and washed her face. "Why are you wasting water like that?" Jim asked.

"I'm not," Sorrie said as she took a few gulps and snapped it closed. "I'm cleaning my face and having a sip. I want to look presentable after all."

Jim thought a moment. "What do you know about these people anyway?"

"My Uncle Ross is my mother's brother. They never spent much time together because he went into the Army around the same time she was born. When he got out, he came to see her, but by then, my mom had left home, and he moved to Nebraska. She talks to him every now and again and sends him Christmas cards. He sent me a birthday card once with twenty dollars in it. Momma got mad about that, but let me keep the money."

"Are you sure you want to go live with these people? You don't seem to know them very well," Jim asked, then added, "And what about this so-called private investigator that might be trying to track you down? Aren't you afraid your uncle will turn you in?"

"He said I could visit anytime, and I don't think he'd turn me in. It wouldn't matter if the PI showed up. I'm not going back to my parents. I'm eighteen and my own person. I could probably make it alone, but I need some time. I need to be in a place where I feel safe."

"Then what?"

"I plan to go to college. I have a fund set up through my grandfather, and my parents can't touch it."

"What college? Out here in nowheresville?"

"I've been accepted to colleges in the east. I want to study psychology."

Jim squinted in the morning sun. He vaguely remembered Sorrie telling him the word meant studying the mind. He hoped she could go with him instead and could be there when he finally met his father.

Sorrie kicked up some dirt with her foot. "We're different people, and I know the itch to be on the road will never go away. I'm sometimes afraid to be alone, but I won't be if I'm with my uncle. Can you say the same?"

Jim didn't know the answer to that. He walked to the Interstate on-ramp, extended his thumb, and took a different approach. "Is he decent? Does he drink?"

"I know he doesn't drink. Is there anything else I need to know?"

"Do you trust him?"

"Yeah, I trust him."

Jim stopped to take a quick gulp from his canteen. He thought a moment between swallows. "What about his wife?"

Sorrie walked along the paved shoulder with the sun against her back and extended her thumb. "I've only known her from the times she came with him. What's the matter? Don't you approve of marriage?"

Jim imagined being married, then let go of the thought. "Married? Not in a million years." He stuck out his thumb even higher. "You know, my father used to hitchhike all the time."

"Who told you that?"

"My Mom. But he wrote a song about it—it's creepy."

"What makes it creepy?" Sorrie turned around and walked backward with her thumb out.

"It's about death."

"Is that all he ever talked about—death?"

"He was always trying to grasp the unknown, and death just happened to be part of it. So maybe you can use some of your psychology to figure out what that means."

"I might be able to if you sing me some of it."

Just as Jim began to sing the song, an Oldsmobile Vista Cruiser pulled off to the side of the road. Two young children sat in the second row, strapped into their seats.

"I'm only going a little further than Paxton," the brunette woman behind the wheel said as she opened the passenger side window.

"That's good enough for us," Jim said. The woman reached over to the toys on the front bucket seat and threw them onto the floor behind her. She patted the space for Jim to get in, and just as he readied himself, Sorrie shoved him aside to sit in the front while Jim was left to unlatch the tailgate and climb into the back with his knapsack. No sooner had Jim clicked the door closed than the woman peeled out of the dirt and onto the highway so forcefully that Jim's backside jolted up, and his head hit the side of the window.

"Where y'all from?" the woman asked as she floored the accelerator and began zigzagging around cars. "Better grab your handles," she said as she continued weaving from lane to lane. Finally, she reached a stretch of highway without traffic and began driving faster. They were going nearly one hundred miles an hour, and the woman let out a war whoop. Sorrie clicked her seatbelt closed and gripped the side of the door, and as she did, she could hear Jim laughing at the other end of the car. The turbulence of the rear shocks and the swaying had him crashing side to side against the tailgate and the backseat cushions. Instead of holding onto something, he threw his hands in the air and let out a thunderous laugh.

"Now that's what I like to hear," the woman roared, "a straight-from-the-belly laugh. You keep it up, honey. I like to hear piss-assed hootin' and hollerin', especially if it's coming from the back of my car. Ain't that right, kids?"

The boys in the backseat said in unison, "Yes, mama."

Jim glanced at the two boys, who looked about four and six, and noticed that both had unbuckled their seatbelts. "Your kids aren't strapped in," Jim said.

"Kids are meant for bouncing, and bouncing is all they do. So, I take rides with 'em when they get out of hand, and it calms 'em down right straight away." The driver glanced into the back and waved at the two children. "Ain't that right, boys?"

They replied in unison, "Yes, mama."

Jim laughed and then, with a smile, asked, "They twins?"

"Nah, just two out-of-control kids about to feel their Momma's wrath for messing with the garden hose."

"Garden hose?" Jim asked, but the driver said nothing. Instead, she revved the engine harder and let out another war whoop.

"Where you heading anyway?" The woman asked, then added, "By the way, my name's Adelaide, but you can call me Addie. Has a nice ring to it. Where are you going?"

"If we tell you, will you slow down?" Sorrie asked.

"Oh hell, it might make me want to speed up. Ain't that right, boys?"

The boys replied in unison, "Yes, mama."

"They robots or something?" Jim asked, but before the woman could answer, one of the boys stood up and yelled, "Highland steer, Highland steer," at the other boy, who stood up and began yelling louder, "Highland steer, Highland steer." They both drew fists and started knocking each other around, and each time one of the boys tripped over a toy on the floor, he'd get back up and start swinging again.

Suddenly, Addie swerved onto the zebra-painted shoulder and slammed on the brakes. "Now, Dawg," she yelled, "you sit down. I swear one of these days I'm a gonna send you to that marble orchard. And Bear, you sit down too, and don't pretend you don't know what I'm talking about." Addie swerved the car back onto the highway and gunned the engine until they traveled faster than before.

"They always like that?" Sorrie asked.

"Oh, hell no. Sometimes, these boys are the worst. Makes me want to kill both of 'em and tell Jesus they died."

"Is that their names, Dawg and Bear?"

"Not their born names, but I forgot what I used to call 'em—you know, their Christian names—I been using those names since they were just young bucks."

Sorrie turned to one of the kids and asked, "Do you know your name?"

"My name's Bear," the child replied.

"Do you know your real name?" Sorrie asked.

"What's a real name? They call me Bear."

"Where you from anyway?" Addie said.

"Why do you want to know?" Sorrie said.

"You asked for the ride, not me, sister. I'm just making a little conversation to pass the time, you might say."

"We're from Virginia," Jim yelled from the back.

"Virginia, but we're going to Paxton," Sorrie added. "I'm feeling a little sick. Is it possible to slow down?"

"You guys eat anything?" The woman asked, and when Sorrie shook her head, the woman drove the car with her left hand and reached out her right hand to one of the boys in the back. "Dawg, now give me that box of wafers I gave you this morning."

"Awe, mama . . ." the boy said.

"Come on now. This girl's your guest, so it wouldn't be proper not to share. I swear he's about as useful as a pogo stick in quicksand." The boy handed her a box, and she turned to Sorrie. "You better open these up, child, and get something in your stomach." Sorrie grabbed the vanilla wafers, hurriedly unraveled the plastic bag inside, and began munching on one. "Thank you," she said between bites. One of the kids in the backseat demanded a cookie, but Sorrie didn't notice, and the boy began bouncing in his seat. Then the other boy started acting up until both jumped up and down and chanted, "We want cookies. We want cookies."

Sorrie offered some, but neither paid attention as the ear-splitting chant took over. Dumbfounded, Sorrie glanced at Addie until Addie yelled, "You want cookies? You want cookies?" then she suddenly veered onto the shoulder, slammed on the brakes, threw the car into park, leaned over, and began slapping both of the children on their heads as she recited, "You want a cookie? I'll give you a cookie. Do you want a cookie? I'll give you a cookie." She grabbed the box from Sorrie and began raining the children with bits of cookies.

But the boys didn't stop. They kept bouncing up and down, yelling, "We want a cookie," until some unseen rage took over. They began punching each other, yelling, "I want a cookie, I want a cookie."

Jim took it all in, laughing and, at the same time, shielding his face from the punches. Amid all the chaos of the boys hitting each other and the woman throwing cookies, Sorrie spoke up. "Stop, stop," she said while reaching back to offer her arm as a barrier between the two kids. Instead of slapping each other, the two began slapping Sorrie's arm. "Hold on, hold on, hold on," she said as she got them to stop. Addie ceased flailing, but now there was a standstill over who had won: the kids, the mother, or Sorrie. As if in silent agreement, Sorrie took the box from Addie and dropped it into the backseat, which quieted the kids. Addie peeled away from the shoulder, and where there had been chaos just moments before, silence overtook the car—except for Jim, who was still roaring with laughter.

Sorrie looked annoyed, but Addie remarked, "At least I brung happiness to someone."

The ride ended just as abruptly as it had begun, with the woman leaving them at a juncture of a major interstate. Before she peeled out, she reminded them that Paxton was a mile up the road. She turned north, and Jim saw the kids bouncing up and down, flailing their arms in each other's direction. "That was some trip," Jim said as he continued laughing.

"Do you know where we're going?" Sorrie asked.

"It's your show," Jim said. "This part is all yours. You're almost at your new home."

As they walked, the dirt kicked up along their boots, creating a dust storm; Jim coughed, but Sorrie stared ahead, looking for where her uncle lived. "I kind of feel sad now," Sorrie said. "I almost don't want to leave you. It will be hard saying goodbye. But maybe we can keep in touch."

Jim blushed. He'd spent the better part of the trip trying to get rid of her, but he'd grown fond of Sorrie, and it would be hard to see her go. "I come this way all the time, and when I do, I'll look you up. Maybe I'll pass by more regular now."

They came to a street and finally made out the silhouettes of trees and roads, and before they knew it, they'd reached Paxton.

Soon, Sorrie found herself knocking on the porch door of the uncle she hoped to live with while Jim sat in one of the two white rocking chairs. First, they heard footsteps; then, an elderly man appeared at the door.

"Mister Ross Southard?" Sorrie asked in a timid voice.

"Yes?" The old man said, a bit bewildered.

"I'm Sorrie, your niece from Virginia."

The old man stared at Sorrie. She waited, not saying anything. Maybe he hadn't heard her. "You know, Julie's daughter."

Jim expected the man to open the door and invite her in, but instead, he looked puzzled. "Julie's daughter?" Suddenly, there was a hint of recollection from a deep place of remembrance. He lifted his head. "Sorrie?"

"Yes, it's me, Uncle Ross." A smile crossed her face as she held out her arms for a hug. Instead of the door swinging open, Uncle Ross just stood there saying, "Sorrie? Sorrie?" then, as if remembering a dream, "Oh yes. Julie's daughter. Your mother called not too long ago wondering if you might be headed this way," he said in a gravelly voice.

But something wasn't right. Jim noticed the man wasn't smiling—the same way his mother didn't smile when she was deep into one of her fits. "What did my mother say?" Sorrie asked. "What's wrong? Remember you promised I could stay with you?"

Suddenly, the man's wife came up behind him. She was petite with salt and pepper hair and large hazel eyes. Dressed in white cotton, she was intimidating in a way her husband was not. She didn't look familiar to Sorrie. She remembered her Aunt Barbara being tall. "Yeah, well, we're not going to invite you in because we don't need any kind of trouble," she said.

"Who are you?" Sorrie asked. "You're not my Aunt Barbara."

"I'm your uncle's wife now. Your aunt died." Sorrie was perplexed. "Didn't I hear from both of you at Christmas? How could this be? There isn't any trouble. I don't know what you're talking about." Jim was caught off guard by the conversation and could see Sorrie was too.

Sorrie gulped hard. "What trouble? What did you hear?"

"She said you were crazy—that you caused trouble and were out of control. We don't need that kind of upset in our home." Uncle Ross looked at his wife, and then they both looked at Sorrie.

"But I haven't done anything. What's wrong with you?" Sorrie said, tears welling in her eyes. "What did my mother tell you? She'll make up any type of lie to control me," Sorrie said in a more insistent tone. "She doesn't want me living anyplace but home. Have my parents threatened you if you take me in? Have they bribed you with money?"

The woman hesitated. "No one tells us what to do."

Jim stood up and could tell the woman was lying by the way she spoke. "Tell the truth," he said. "They gave you money, didn't they?"

"At least take the time to listen to my side." Sorrie grabbed onto the edge of the screen door and tried to open it. Her uncle's wife gripped the knob harder.

"We've got to close the door now," the wife said as Uncle Ross backed away from the screen.

"But I'm cold, and we haven't had anything hot to eat. We're filthy. Couldn't you just let us in for a shower and to clean up? Uncle Ross? Uncle Ross? *Uncle Ross?*" Sorrie pleaded as she grew more desperate.

Suddenly, the old man stood up straighter and, in a monotone, said, "I got nothing to say to you except that you're a stranger and you're disturbing my time." Before Sorrie could say more, Ross and his wife disappeared behind the screen and the white front door.

Suddenly, Jim became animated. "Well, I got something to say to you," he said as he started banging on the door. "You sonofabitch, you're nothing but ashes, old man. You broke my girlfriend's heart; now I got to do the same for you." Jim grabbed a piece of wood lying in the grass and began smashing the rocking chairs and screen door. He heard the old man say, "I'm calling the police," but that didn't stop Jim from clawing at the pillars on the front porch and smashing the wooden plank against the door. Jim tore through bushes and ripped apart the split rail fence lining the driveway. He looked like a madman in his ripped jeans and white T-shirt, his curly hair bobbing in the sunlight, and his tanned face beet red with anger. Jim grabbed the fence rails and crashed them against the posts, reducing the wood to shards of razor-sharp kindling. When he finished with one, it was onto another and another and another until half the fence was gone.

Sorrie tried to stop him by yelling, "Jim, Jim" whenever she could, but he was possessed, like a demon born from the cold, hard stares he saw daily, and in one fell swoop, all of the frustration bundled up into a fierce rage that tore at each rail of fencing.

Jim clawed at the mailbox and smashed it to the ground before abruptly stopping as if a lifetime's worth of rage had lifted from his thin body. He dropped to his knees and began to sob. Sorrie leaned over him and cried too. She rubbed his back and ran her hands through his hair. It was as if the entire universe melded into this moment, linking their souls together for all time. He took her hands and stood up. Like two magnets drawn together, they kissed and felt each other's gaze and exhaustion, as if the entire trip had led to them converging into one thought, one spirit. They gripped each other's arms and embraced, tears streaming down their faces, and just as they realized they had closed one door only to open another, a police car rolled up. Two officers stepped out and grabbed Jim and Sorrie by the arms.

As they were being led to the car, Sorrie yelled, "What's happening? All I wanted to do was see my uncle."

"He doesn't exist," Jim yelled back. "He was a dream, an illusion, a part of the parade." Both were led in handcuffs and placed together in the backseat.

* * *

The police officer led a handcuffed Jim into the front part of two small rooms that made up a part of the town's police station. Jim smiled as he was shoved into a wooden chair near the room's only window. He glanced outside and saw the sun reflecting off the hood of the police car. It was a good day to catch a hot shot to Cali, but his thoughts were interrupted by two angry eyes staring at his face. "What are you, the village idiot?"

"Where's my girl?" Jim demanded.

The Sheriff leaned in. He was a burly man in his fifties. He smelled of cheap aftershave and smoked a cigarette as he backed off and sat on a wooden chair opposite where Jim sat.

"Looks like you've been having a good time in the attic," the Sheriff said as he tapped his forehead. He got up, moved his chair closer to Jim, and put his boot on the space between Jim's legs. "Well, boy, your good times are about to end."

"I don't know what you mean."

"I mean, your head ain't focused, or you wouldn't have been breaking down fences and wrecking people's yards."

"Where's my girl?"

"Never you mind. It's you we're concerned about for causing all that ruckus," the Sheriff said.

"No ruckus. My girlfriend's family insulted her. I had to defend her honor," Jim said.

"Hell, no," the Sheriff responded. "You don't piss off my friend. The friend whose wife gives me a tasty cherry pie each month. I might not get any pies for a year if I don't do something about it." He pointed a stout finger in Jim's direction.

"Well, that wasn't my intention, officer," Jim said politely. "Looking back, maybe I was acting kind of stupid." He'd dealt with the law long enough to know that the harder you pushed, the more they pushed back. "By the way, is my girlfriend around?"

"You'll be together soon enough, like maybe in forty or fifty years," the Sheriff said. He looked at the deputy and made a sudden jerk, and Jim grabbed for his crotch.

"You could be looking at years," the deputy said. "Disturbing the peace, destruction of property, harassment, assault."

"What assault? I didn't touch anybody."

"You don't have to. All the person needs to do is feel like their life is in imminent danger, and my friend's wife is pretty shaken up right now," the Sheriff said.

"That old battle-ax? If anything, she threatened us."

"That isn't the way I heard it. I heard that that girlfriend of yours isn't really your girlfriend."

"Yeah, you're right. Sorrie's my money ticket, you know?" The officer's eyebrows perked up. He was intrigued. "She's been financing this trip since Virginia, and we ran out of money, so she thought that because we were near her relatives, we could get some."

"You mean like steal some, don't you?"

"No, it's not like that. She's close to this uncle, and he invited her to stay with him. She was going to give me some money for getting her here—like payment. Coming to Nebraska was some kind of crazy dream of hers—and they told her to go away, at least the wife did—so I had to make it look good for the sake of the cash, you know, to keep her moving on with me. Otherwise, I'd be broke from here to the West Coast, which might mean I wouldn't get to move on. I'd be stuck in this town holed up in some hobo hotel, bringing my stench and stuff," he said.

The officer squinted and looked mean. "You threatening me?"

"No sir," Jim said as he straightened up, "just telling the truth is all."

The officer kept still for a moment, and then, with a clap of his hands and a smile, he stood up. "Well, we got to change things," he said as he led Jim into a back room and lowered him onto a wooden stool. Jim was happy to see Sorrie, but she was handcuffed to a metal chair on the other side of the room. Her eyes questioned Jim about what was going to happen next.

Jim looked around. The scene reminded him of the principal's office.

Jim had been in this setting more times than he could count, usually in school. When the principal was tired of yelling at him, he'd get shipped off to the guidance counselor, who'd ask him why he never showed up for school if he was so bright.

"Because I can't hardly read. The letters get all mixed up," Jim would say. He couldn't even read his father's lyrics; he could only listen to the songs.

"What are you gazing at?" The Sheriff asked, noticing that Jim was staring at a book poking out from his knapsack, which was sitting at Sorrie's feet.

She reminded him of his twelve-year-old foster sister, Lally. Lally could read. Jim recalled long afternoons sitting outside by the tire swing and Lally talking about traveling around the world. Of course, it was always Jim and Lally discussing the trips they wanted to take, but right after he lit out, he heard that Lally got shipped to another home; he regretted not saying goodbye.

In looking at Sorrie, he said, "You okay?"

"I'll survive." She glanced at the book and tried to push it back into the knapsack with her foot. The Sheriff noticed her movements.

"Well, now there, little lady, what you been looking for in that knapsack? A gun? A knife you can spring on us?" Then to another man, "Damn it, Dave, I told you to search the knapsack."

"It's a book," Jim said.

"What kind of a book?" The Sheriff reached into an outside pocket of Jim's knapsack. "Pornography, maybe?" He pulled out *The Lords and the New Creatures* and glanced at the picture of Jim Morrison. "Hey, wait. I know this guy. Jim Morrison. I remember him," the Sheriff said as he tore off a part of the cover. "He was a regular pervert in the day. We'll put this picture on the rifle range for target practice."

The thought that the Sheriff had defiled his father's image infuriated Jim. "Hey, that isn't yours. Stop destroying my father's book," Jim yelled.

The Sheriff folded the book with the ripped cover and shoved it mistakenly into Sorrie's knapsack. "The way I hear it, this guy died in France."

"He's alive," Jim said, "He's out there, and I'm looking for him, and nothing you're saying is going to tell me different. He didn't die in Paris."

"Well, I got another town I'm thinking of, and it's right here in the U.S.A. As a matter of fact, I'll write it down for you." The Sheriff took out a wallet-sized pad, tore a piece of paper from it, and began writing in bold block letters, "Paxton."

"Stand up," the Sheriff said to Jim. He folded the piece of paper into a series of squares. The deputy stood a few feet away, trying to get his attention. The Sheriff ignored him and continued the conversation. "That's right, stand straight up. You are the most pathetic piece of crap I ever did see lying in the road and about as dumb as a bagful of weights. Got that?" The Sheriff asked.

"Yep," Jim said.

"Well, then, you won't be surprised to learn that I think what this town needs from you is a little justice." With that, the Sheriff rammed the piece into Jim's mouth and clamped his hand around Jim's head, forcing him to gag as he attempted to swallow the paper. "Normally, I'd have you catch your breath, but in this case, I'll let you think about how you ruined my day while you're fighting to live."

Jim struggled to get free. "You're killing him; you're killing him. Stop it! Stop it!" Sorrie yelled.

The Sheriff loosened his hands just enough so Jim could catch a breath through his nostrils. "Normally, I'd let you spit it out, but seeing as how you just gave me a year's worth of hurt Sundays, I think you need to get that thought inside of you." Jim tried to free himself from the man's hands; the Sheriff gripped tighter. "Now, stop struggling. Stop struggling. The more you struggle, the harder my palm gets against your mouth." Jim continued to resist, and seeing how hard he was fighting, the Sheriff grabbed the back of his head and cupped his hand tighter around Jim's face, once again cutting off his airflow.

Jim felt dizzy, and the room spun in front of him. Was this what it felt like to die? Would the world turn from red to black, just like people said it had for his father? And what would happen to Sorrie? Jim stopped struggling. He summoned his courage to calm down and remained still. A gush of spit washed over the paper in his mouth, making it moist and allowing it to soften.

The Sheriff loosened his grip and looked Jim in the eyes. "Tell you what we're going to do. You're going to chew that piece of paper and swallow it like a good boy, or I'm going to clamp my hand back over your nose and say you died from an asthma attack. You cost me a whole month of trouble over that stunt, and now you'll have to pay for it." The Sheriff relaxed against a metal desk, took a pack of cigarettes from his shirt pocket, lit one, and blew smoke in Jim's face. Jim attempted to open his mouth, but the Sheriff said, "Keep your mouth closed; otherwise, I got another piece of paper ready." Jim rolled the mush in his mouth until it began to soften. He angled his tongue, felt the scratchiness of the corners of the paper, and tasted the bitterness of the black ink. He suppressed his gag reflex as he chewed the mush, then swallowed it in front of the Sheriff, the deputy, and Sorrie.

When he was finished, the deputy clapped. Jim opened his mouth and showed his tongue, then sat expressionless, waiting for the Sheriff's reaction. Finally, after a long, slow silence where the only sound in the room was the shuffling of the Sheriff's soles against the linoleum floor, Jim asked, "Is that it?"

The Sheriff took a last drag on his cigarette, let it drop to the floor, and stomped on it, extinguishing the glowing ash. He leaned over and noticed that the butt of the cigarette clung to the bottom of his shoe. "Well, I'll be damned," he said, looking down. The corner of Jim's face turned up a little as the Sheriff bent down and flicked the butt off his shoe, and as he came up, he backhanded Jim hard across the face. Sorrie let out a cry, but Jim seemed to expect it. "Now, I don't think you heard what I said. You just cost me a year of pies." Jim felt the warm taste of blood trickling from the edge of his mouth. A few drops splattered onto his hand. He tried to wipe it away, but the handcuffs made it impossible, so instead, he just smiled. He stared at a drop of blood on the edge of his thumb.

The deputy, who had witnessed the whole scene, suddenly seemed uncomfortable and walked to the outer room. A minute passed before he was back. "Uh, Buck, I think there's something you need to know." The Sheriff didn't pay any attention. Instead, his eyes were fixed on Jim. "Buck . . ."

"What the hell do you want?" The Sheriff asked.

"The old man's here with his wife, and they don't want to press any charges."

The Sheriff looked stunned. "What?"

"Yeah, they're sitting in the front room, and they say to let 'em go cause they don't want to press any charges—to just let 'em be on their way."

"Bring 'em here." The Sheriff had the face of an angry bear, and beads of sweat formed on his forehead. "Let's get this thing straightened out once and for all."

The three waited until the deputy led the old man and his wife into the room. The Sheriff faced them. "Afternoon, Mister and Missus Southard." The Sheriff nodded and smiled. "I understand you don't want to press charges against these two for busting up your property, am I right?"

The wife looked up. Her face held a defiant glare. "We need to talk, you and me. We need to see about these two hoodlums."

"Now, wait a minute," the old man interjected. He let out a cough; his words were slow and deliberate, as if he was wading through a cloud of faded memory. "Let them go," he said. "No charges. No shame in that. Maggie will make it up to you, and your brother Sully might get some work out of it." The short woman tried to speak, but Ross held up his hand. "Are we clear?" He said, staring at his wife.

"Clear," she repeated and looked down at the floor. The deputy walked over and removed the handcuffs from Jim and Sorrie.

"Well, if you're feeling that way, we can give 'em a ride out of town."

"That'd be nice of you."

"You don't worry none, Ross. We'll treat 'em right. You just get better from your stroke." The Sheriff waved them off and watched the couple turn to leave, but the old man circled, and without saying anything, he fished out a wad of $20 bills from his wallet. Once he did, he held it out for Sorrie. "For getting home," he said. Sorrie gently took the bills and glanced at them as the pair prepared to exit.

The Sheriff walked them to the door and then turned back to Jim. "Well, what'd I tell you? I guess you were right, her being your meal ticket and all. Looks like everything turned out okay. You're no worse for wear," he said, a wide grin etched from side to side. He walked up to Jim and went nose to nose as the smile disappeared. "Now, Mister Ross says to let you go, and we're going to get to it, but before we do, I want you two sorry sacks to know I don't ever want to see you in this town again because the next time you're stupid enough to ride through here, you're going to get tossed into jail for sure." The Sheriff walked over to Sorrie. "I think this is mine," he said as he snatched the money from Sorrie's hand and put it in his pocket.

"We're not leaving," Jim said, "without going back to that farmhouse and telling the old man what you did with his money."

The Sheriff and deputy looked at each other and started laughing. Jim stood motionless while Sorrie hung her head. Was this all a big joke? "Well, listen now," the Sheriff said as he bent his head low next to Jim's ear. "I just happened to hear a rumor from someone working the railroad lines who told me a man and a woman—both young—were seen running from a train yard after stealing a wallet from a railroad cop. It may have been in another part of the country, but I'm a servant of the law, and I have a duty to report the culprits if you know what I mean."

"I don't know anything about that," Jim said casually.

The Sheriff sighed and then looked Jim in the eyes. "I see your kind all the time. You're like cancer coming into a town and bringing drugs, tramps, and vice into decent people's lives. But I'm a generous man, and I'll tell you what I'm going to do. Dave and I will drive you to the edge of town and let you catch a freight out of here before I change my mind about locking you up." Jim felt a glimmer of hope, and Sorrie stopped fidgeting. Was it possible they were letting them go? Jim suppressed a smile.

"Either that, or I can have Dave here shoot you."

"You can't do that; we got rights," Jim said.

"You got no rights where I'm the law," the Sheriff said. "But I'll tell you what. I'll make a deal with you. I see a bunch of punks like you every year, and the last place I want them to stop is in my town. So, do me a favor and pass the word down the line." The Sheriff looked up at the deputy, who was waiting for instructions. "Dave, my friend, let this boy and his girlfriend go."

"Right away," the deputy said.

The Sheriff smirked at Jim. "It's going to be good escorting you out of town," he said.

"It's going to be good getting out of here," Jim shot back.

"Hey, Dave," the Sheriff said, "I wonder what kind of sad dingle this boy's got between his legs. Fetch Mississippi Mike, and let's find out."

"Right away," the deputy said, but the Sheriff called him back before he could leave the room. The Sheriff leaned close to Jim's ear. "I just did you a favor, boy. You owe me."

* * *

Once they were out of the police station, the knot in Jim's stomach loosened, but the feeling that something was about to happen kicked around inside his head. Were they really getting out so quickly, and just as important—how would they get the money back?

He tried to relax and rubbed his arms and wrists as the two men carefully led him out of the police station, which struck Jim as odd; usually, they liked to rough him up a bit.

"Get in the car," the deputy said as he opened the door to the police cruiser.

"You aren't getting me in one of those. It's not as if I was born yesterday," Jim said.

"It's the only way out of town," the deputy insisted.

"I'd just as soon walk out," Jim countered.

Then the burly-voiced Sheriff chimed in. "You don't get that choice. We drove you here; we'll let you out nice and quick on the edge of the county line where the train goes slow enough for you to hop on."

"I don't believe you."

The deputy sighed. "You want me to put them cuffs back on, don't you, boy? I can have 'em digging into your wrists enough to cut off your circulation."

"I guess we have no choice," Jim said as he glanced at Sorrie. The deputy placed both of them into the backseat of the car and then got into the driver's side. As soon as the Sheriff got in, he started the car and pulled out. While the deputy kept glancing into his rearview mirror, the Sheriff leaned over and looked through the steel mesh that separated him from Jim and Sorrie. He didn't say anything but just stared; Jim began laughing.

They rode on past tidy houses and open pastures until they came to a clearing along the side of a dense patch of grass and trees. There was a dilapidated red picnic table in a roadside clearing. On the other side of the road lay a ribbon of railroad track stretching off into the distance. The deputy swung the car in a semi-circle, and as he stopped and threw it into park, he said, "Time to get out and run, little kiddies."

"What do you mean?" Sorrie asked.

"Why do we have to run? We got time," Jim said.

"No, you don't," the deputy said. Jim and Sorrie exited the car and hesitated. Jim glanced back and saw the trunk hood fly up and the two men leaning in to retrieve something. As the deputy looked up, Jim grabbed their knapsacks and yelled, "You wouldn't dare shoot us. We didn't do nothing to you. You got no cause."

The two men pulled rifles from the trunk. "Is that so?" The Sheriff said.

Jim could hear him click a magazine into place. Jim turned. "You don't have the balls to shoot. Folks around here will know what you did."

The deputy cocked his weapon and broke out in a belly laugh. "No, they won't. They'll think I was hunting vermin, and you got in the way."

The deputy aimed in Jim's direction, and Sorrie grabbed Jim's arm. "Shut up and run!" she yelled as the bullets began to fly. Bam! A click, a moment of silence, and then another bam! "Oh, God, please run! Please, dear Jesus, save us!" Sorrie yelled as both of them took flight. Jim shouldered both backpacks and tried to balance them as they ran. He could hear the whistling sound of a bullet whiz by. They ran as fast as they could, finding a path to the other side of the train tracks and into a thicket of nearby woods.

Jim paused. How many shots had he heard? Three, four, five? No, six. Were they reloading? He knew a magazine held more rounds than six, so why did the cops stop? Jim waited for another round, but it never came. Instead, he heard the sound of car wheels against gravel and, in the distance, a maniacal, ho, ho, ho, like some crazy Santa. Would it be murder or insanity? Wasn't that what Jim's father said in one of his songs? It was all a crazy blur now. Jim looked around, and from the dizzying way he felt, he didn't know if he was alive or dreaming.

They came to a clearing to catch their breath. Sorrie grabbed Jim's arm only to discover blood on her fingers. "You're hurt," she said.

"I'll be all right. Better to keep going." Jim was out of breath, but he urged Sorrie on, pushing her deeper into a thick maze of trees.

"How's your arm?" Sorrie asked.

Jim glanced down at the line of blood on his T-shirt. "I'll be okay."

"You need to take your shirt off," Sorrie said. They stopped, and Jim removed his shirt, revealing a red ribbon where the bullet had grazed the top of his arm. Blood trickled down toward his elbow, and there were crimson smears all over his skin.

Jim emptied the water from his canteen onto the wound while Sorrie cleaned it. She applied pressure, and when the bleeding stopped, she dabbed on some antibiotics and bandaged it with Jim's blue and white bandana. "I'll be okay," Jim said. "Doesn't hurt much."

"It looks like you need stitches."

"It's fine. I've been hurt a lot worse."

"Either way, you might need to see a doctor to stitch it up," Sorrie said.

"No doctors, no doctors," Jim insisted.

"Okay, I won't insist." Sorrie changed the subject. "Do you know where we're going?"

"Sure, I got the directions right here in my back pocket," He said. They sat on a nearby rock.

"Oh, God," Sorrie said as she began crying. "What am I supposed to do now? Everything's all shot to hell, and I don't have a prayer now of doing anything. I can't go back home, and even if I could, I don't want to go there *ever, especially after what my mother told my uncle*," she cried.

"Come on now, it's not so bad," Jim wrapped his arm around her shoulders. "Who says you got to go home anyway?"

"You're going to Montana, but me? I don't have anywhere to go anymore. I don't think I ever had a family." Sorrie lowered her head and sobbed into her hands. "What will it take to make you understand? I'm alone now. Eighteen years old with no money and no family. I feel so afraid."

"Nobody said you couldn't go with me," Jim answered. "I wasn't going to stay at my Mom's forever. I was just going to settle some unfinished business."

A ray of hope flashed across Sorrie's face. "You really think it's okay if I come with you?"

"Sure, we got lots of traveling to do together. I know my dad's out there someplace. It would be a shame knowing he's in some bar waiting for me to show up and me not coming." Jim hugged her and wiped the tears from her cheeks. The man who once despised being attached to anyone extended his hand.

"A few days ago, you couldn't stand me. Now, you want me to go with you? I don't understand."

"Look, I won't say we'll stay together for life, but I think I owe you this one until you find your way."

Sorrie laughed through her tears. "Find my way? We don't even know where we are."

Jim stood up and brushed some wet leaves off his pants. "It won't be hard to figure it out. We've probably run into one of the only stretches of woods in this part of Nebraska." Jim helped Sorrie up and reached into his pants pocket. "Oh, and here's the money from your uncle. I picked it from the Sheriff's pocket while he was escorting me out." Sorrie stared at him in disbelief. Jim pointed in the opposite direction from where they'd been dropped off, and together, they walked arm and arm out of the darkness.

14

Nebraska Through Wyoming

THEY FOUND A stream to wash up, and it wasn't long before they were hopping freight going west out of Nebraska and into Wyoming. "Looks like we're cookin' with gas now," Jim said, and sure enough, it was one of those hot shots Jim dreamed about. The boxcar rattled along while Sorrie and Jim sat staring out the door. "Is this your first look at the prairie?" Jim asked.

"When we'd travel, the plane would fly over places like this, but it was hard to see any of the details. Up close, it's more than what I'd imagined from books. It's fresh air and cattle and red barns against blue skies that seem to go on forever." Sorrie turned to Jim. "I finally understand why you want to be so free. It's like nothing is separating you from the electricity of experience. No regrets between your skin, the sky, and the cool of the earth."

They celebrated their freedom by reading more of *The Lords and the New Creatures*. Sorrie removed it from her knapsack, and Jim looked at the ripped cover. A wave of sadness swept over him. He tried repairing it by piecing it together with a few clips he had but wound up just folding it in half and securing it to the first page. "I'll tape it when I get to my Momma's place," he said.

"I feel bad," Sorrie said.

"Me too," Jim said. He was about to hand the book to Sorrie, but she pushed it back and insisted Jim try to read it. He sounded out the words and read some of the love poems, then returned to passages about death and aloneness. "I wonder how lonely my uncle in Paxton is? There was no life in his eyes. There was no thought until he handed me the money as if to say, 'Forgive me.'"

"I'm sure they got money for telling you to go away."

"That would be typical of my parents. They don't think I can make my own decisions, so I'm convinced they think I'll come crawling back to them."

"Don't worry about them. He's got his wife to tuck him in. There wasn't any sense in staying there. She was a real pistol and probably would've waited for me to leave before kicking you out."

"I didn't recognize her. I don't know her. My uncle called her Maggie, but I only remember my Aunt Barbara, who was sweet and gentle with me."

"What do you suppose happened?"

"I don't know, and I don't remember my mother saying anything about it. She probably kept it from me to punish me for loving them more than her."

"He didn't seem right in the head either."

"The Sheriff said he'd had a stroke, only my Mom never mentioned it. But why was it so easy for him to reject me? For what? Money? How can people throw other people away like that?"

Jim shuffled the bottom of his shoe against the hardness of the car's floor. "I see it all the time. Just look around the jungles. Do you think most of those bums got born with loving families? There isn't but a one of 'em," Jim paused, then added, "Well, maybe one or two. But the rest got flung onto the heap of hurt."

"That's very profound," Sorrie said. "But I was raised in a house with money, and I still felt that way. It was always about expectations and what other people would think."

Sorrie held her face against the sky and closed her eyes. Her face grew light with the sun's rays, and her hair whipped against the current of the wind. She looked beautiful. Jim reached out and took her hand.

"If anyone calls you a tramp, then better to live a tramp's life and hold onto what you got that's real rather than being owned by somebody else. But we got each other now, right?" Sorrie didn't answer but kept her face turned toward the light. Jim looked out the door. The same currents of air that blew through Sorrie's hair thrashed the strands of Jim's dark curls against the side of the boxcar. Though he closed his eyes from the force of the wind, he could still see the light of the day on his irises. It was so warm and inviting, and he felt cleansed by it. He was used to rejection. But seeing Sorrie get rejected bit into him like a mad dog. It was one thing to feel excluded; it was another to see it happen to someone you cared about. And he had to admit to himself that he did care about her.

They rode in silence until the sun sank behind the horizon. As the train passed into the night, they crawled into a corner of the boxcar, where Sorrie used a flashlight to read more poems. The words spoke about cinema and alchemy and had meanings Jim didn't understand.

"What's alchemy?" Jim asked as he leaned over the book, and Sorrie pointed out the words.

"It has something to do with turning metal into gold."

"You mean like a wizard who zaps a frog and makes him a prince?" Jim smirked.

Sorrie put the book down. "It's more like chemistry," she said.

Jim remembered back to his science days. He only remembered the creation of the universe and wondered where his father was in it. "I never took chemistry. I'm not even sure what it is," he said.

"It's like two atoms making a connection by being attracted to each other because of the properties they possess."

"Like the way fate put us together? Like the way a small thing becomes a more valuable thing when it's paired with something else?" Jim said while nodding his head. "I can live with that."

"I guess you can say the same thing about me. I had no value until you turned me into a princess."

Jim was embarrassed by the moment and decided to change the subject. "Okay, what's cinema?" He asked.

"You know, the movies."

"Like what they do in Hollywood?"

"Yeah, but only more sophisticated, like art."

"My father used to say he created art. He went to film school, you know."

"What film school?"

"Someplace in California. He even made a film about a mysterious stranger who hitchhikes along the highway."

"How did you find out about the film?" Sorrie asked.

Jim leaned against his backpack. "Once and a while, I'd ask a girl who showed interest in me to look stuff up, but there weren't many of those growing up."

"Sounds like you had a lot of charm." Sorrie reached into her knapsack and pulled out a bag of potato chips.

Jim smelled the salty flavor in the air. "Gimme one, okay?' Sorrie placed some chips into his open hands. At the same time, Jim continued, "My father used to walk down Sunset Strip in Los Angeles, and I hear he couldn't move because of the crowds of girls following him." Then, seeing Sorrie's bored expression, Jim added, "Aren't you just a little interested?"

Sorrie scanned his body with her eyes. "Maybe," she replied.

Jim lay on his back and placed his Boonie hat over his face. "Thought you'd say that," then he began singing about bliss, light, and nighttime.

"That's pretty," Sorrie said, reaching over to play with Jim's hair. "Delight or night?"

"Night, of course," Jim said as if it was apparent.

"Why's that?"

"I guess I just like being part of the darkness, but delight's pretty good too."

"Is that why you always wear black?"

"I'm like the shadow you see down an alley. I may be okay, but I may be dangerous too."

"Like your father?"

Jim began singing about a highway into the night.

"Are those your father's words?" Sorrie asked.

"Yeah, he's a great poet, don't you think?"

"It just seems to repeat a lot."

"You don't understand," he whispered through the Boonie hat.

"I don't know much about his music. All I know is what you told me." Sorrie tossed her knapsack against the boxcar wall and laced up her boots.

Jim removed the hat from his face. "It's like darkness. Is it bringing you into hell, or is it on the edge of light? Or is it an empty closet? Are there secret compartments and other things in there with you, or just air? My father asked all those questions." The click-clack of the wheels against the rails and the shifting boxcar made the car jerk, bringing Sorrie and Jim closer. "I'm serious about my father. He was a genius and a poet, and that's something I want to be someday. You see? I'm not just a pair of dirty boots and stringy hair. And another thing, I'm serious about you too. I thought you'd understand that most of all."

"I do," Sorrie said, "because I want a future too." Jim hung his head and picked at his fingernails while Sorrie stared outside into a world that failed to understand them.

Jim sat up and moved toward the opening. The pale moon in the distance reminded him that if there was a favorite time of night, this was it: glowing moon, flat land, the smell of wheat, the grating of the train wheels on the tracks. "My father once said we were all bystanders—that's what things like television did to us—made us onlookers in our own lives. Well, I don't want to be an onlooker. That's why I do what I do. He used to say that he reached the inside from the outside. Well, isn't that what we do? We ride the rails, feel the wind in our hair, and live in the moment. Aren't we taking what we see and hear and smell and touch and bringing it into us, bringing it inside? Like eating the moment? Like living each second of today inside, where no one else can touch it?"

"Don't you want a future? Don't you ever wonder where it's all going?"

"Is that what you thought when you knocked on your uncle's door? That he was going to give you the childhood freedom you never had?" Jim looked into Sorrie's eyes. She hesitated, and just as she was about to respond, he said, "Face it, the way we were brought up means that if there's going to be a future, we have to make it for ourselves. The only thing those people were good for was telling us about our mistakes and how we weren't good enough. They didn't help; they made it harder."

There was a momentary lapse of silence. Sorrie spoke first. "Do you ever lie to yourself?"

This puzzled Jim; he didn't know what she meant or where she was going with the question. He chose his words carefully. "It seems that if you lied to yourself, you wouldn't know it. So why would I tell myself something that wasn't true if I knew it wasn't true?"

Sorrie lowered her head. "Come to think of it, you're right. How could you lie to yourself if you weren't aware of the lie?"

"It's like the lies other people tell you that they believe. It seems everyone's got free advice about how you should live your life when they're in a heap of mess in their own lives. So, they lie to themselves, thinking they're better not realizing all the deception that's going on around them."

Sorrie shook her head yes. "Even when my mother got mad at me for not following her instructions and yelled and kept me up at night, what were her biggest complaints? All my faults: clean up your room; you'll never amount to anything; you're no good; clean up your face; you overeat; there are too many books in your room; throw some away. You'll never amount to anything if you don't follow directions and live up to expectations. Even after I got two scholarships to college, she told me my grades sucked. But she never looked in the mirror. Instead, she made me feel so worthless that at the end of all things, I'd still be that sad little girl in her room listening to her rant and rave and slam her fist against the wall. I used to want to ask her, 'Why do you hate me so much?' but I knew I'd never get an answer." Sorrie closed her eyes as streams of tears ran down her cheeks.

"What're you crying for?" Jim asked.

"You're right. I think you're absolutely right," Sorrie said. Then she settled against her knapsack and sobbed quietly as the emotional pain of a thousand sleepless nights came rushing back. Jim moved to where Sorrie was and gently wrapped his arms around her midriff, cradling her. He kissed her, and instead of resisting, she received the kiss. "It's all just shot to hell," Sorrie said. Jim held her closer in his arms. She offered no resistance. "You say I can come to Montana, but do you want me to, or am I just another girl? Won't you be off again looking for your father?"

Jim searched his heart. She was unlike any other woman he'd ever met. "No, you're not just another girl. In fact, if I'm off looking for my father, I hope you'll be there with me," he whispered. She wrapped herself around him and clutched his broad shoulders. "There's nothing you can trust in this world," he said. Then Jim raised his head and looked at Sorrie's ashen skin against the pale of the moonlight. "You really are beautiful," he said.

"Thank you for saying that."

Jim smiled. "You don't have to thank me. You really are, you know. I knew that way back. Maybe that's why I called you names. Maybe I was afraid you'd know I liked you." And as Jim gently stroked her translucent skin and hair and hugged her, they both sank into the moment. Jim wanted her to be comfortable in his arms. He didn't want to rush anything.

* * *

It was Jim who awoke first. He crawled to his knees and, for an instant, forgot his surroundings until the noise of the wheels brought the world back. The train wasn't far from the freight yard, which meant crossing paths with unpleasant visitors. He didn't want to spend more time in a police station.

Jim made his way over to the boxcar door and looked outside. Sorrie lay in the corner asleep. The memory of her tears came back. Wasn't this the way he found her the first time they met? Her hair was red, but in his mind, he could see distinct traces of blond. She started out stout and thick but now looked gaunt and frail.

The honesty of the night drew him to reflection. Could he leave his father in a bar somewhere? He didn't know. He knew it was time to make a choice. How long would it take before he found his father? Would he be old and bent, unable to climb a ladder or hop a train before he was down-to-the-bones tired?

The train slowed, and he only had a few minutes to wake Sorrie. He felt his face and realized he needed a good shower and shave.

Jim turned to Sorrie and said, "Time to rise and shine." Sorrie stirred, and just as Jim swung his legs back into the boxcar, a hanging signpost went by. The car was slow, but the post would have hurt. He shook her into wakefulness. "We have to go," he said as he picked straw out of her hair.

"Where am I?" She asked.

"I think we're outside Cheyenne. Time to get off the train." Sorrie rolled over, and Jim shook her some more. "Come on, Sorrie. Come on and get up." The train stopped; the freight hands would be coming to check the cars soon. Maybe the railroad bull would show up. That might mean visiting the local jail or a long trip back to where they started. "Come on, Sorrie. Come on," he said, more rushed. "We can't afford to get caught. You don't want to get arrested."

"Where are we?" Sorrie rubbed her eyes and brushed more straw from her jacket; Jim helped her to her feet.

"We got to get off." Jim took Sorrie's hand and led her to the edge of the boxcar. It was an easy jump as the car crawled along. They wriggled under a chain-linked fence, and Jim guided Sorrie to a nearby house with a picket fence for a quick shower, food—and a meeting with Frankie.

Jim rang the bell and hid behind a bush. Sorrie didn't notice and waited for someone to answer. When the door opened, there was a tall, muscular woman dressed in black slacks and a glittering T-shirt that said, "Punk Bitch."

"My name's Sorrie."

"I'm Frankie," she said as if she weren't surprised to see a stranger knocking on her door. "I never saw you before. Are you with anyone?" Then, without waiting for an answer, she said, "I can see from your clothes that it's been at least a thousand miles."

"I'm just going to Montana with Jim," Sorrie said.

From his vantage point, Jim could see Frankie stiffen up, which made her look even taller than she was. She towered over Sorrie, and her voice got low. "Now, who's Jim?"

"I am," Jim said, coming from behind the bush.

Frankie clutched her chest. "Oh, my God, it's like seeing a ghost. We all thought you died from that bad hooch they passed around by the hobo camp near Stryker two months ago."

"Nah, that wasn't me. I was nowhere near that trashy place. It's filled with a bunch of *ladrones*."

Frankie laughed, but Sorrie didn't get the joke. Frankie looked at Jim and rubbed the back of his neck. "This is my man," she said, giving Jim a sloppy kiss on the cheek. Frankie turned to Sorrie. "You know what? He says he's the son of Jim Morrison. Got to treat this boy with some respect. There may be some fame in it down the road." Jim laughed, and Sorrie looked uncomfortable. Frankie led them into the kitchen and, without hesitation, said, "Hungry? I got chicken, pork sausage, and leftover mashed potatoes and, oh, yeah, some apple pie made to order." But before they could eat, Frankie insisted they take showers to wash off the dirt.

No sooner had they climbed back into clean clothes, thrown their dirty ones into the washing machine, and walked into the kitchen, they were surrounded by food: chicken, mashed potatoes, a dollop of sour cream on each plate, butter and butter and more butter beside a basket of homemade bread. Frankie sure knew how to cook. "Eat up, my children. Time to get nice and fat for the next ride."

"Why do you do this?" Sorrie asked.

"Do what?"

"Take people in. Feed them. Let them wash up."

"I'm just nice, I guess." Frankie wiped her hands on a towel.

Jim looked up from his plate, and with potatoes still in his mouth, he said, "Frankie likes to take care of us."

Frankie waved her hand and pulled a cigarette from her pocket. "Oh, honey, don't be telling stories so every bull artist and bum can come to Frankie's place and get a hot platter. You just pass the word that Frankie's retired now."

"How did you meet Jim then?" Sorrie asked.

Jim stopped eating to explain. "Ricky Blue Pants introduced us, and I've been coming here ever since. Frankie's like a hobo angel."

"Oh, hell, honey. I'm no angel, though I do like to serve things bottom up. Cook my ass off for twenty years selling fish." Frankie stopped and thought a moment. "No, no, looks like I'm mistaken. I've been cooking like that for more than thirty now. Which is where I got my hands," Frankie held out her arms and hands. They were hydrated and translucent as if they'd been moisturized with an expensive cream for many years. "I used to ride with them hobo tramps sometimes for the thrill, not for a living, but it's not like a poor man's transit system anymore, where you jump on and off without a whisper from the brakemen or the bull. Now you got them computers controlling everything, not like before. It's a lot harder these days with all those cameras and sensors. Makes my living more difficult."

"You were a hell-raiser in those days," Jim said.

"Still am." Frankie bent back, let out a hoot, then extended her hand to touch Jim's shoulder. She revealed a roadmap of black ink tattoos up and down her arms as she did. There were etchings of a skull, a bird, and a rat's face with the word "voleur" underneath. "So, tell me, honey, when you going to come 'round to Frankie's place and play?"

"I'll let you know when I flip," Jim laughed.

"Well, you know what I'm looking for, and it ain't no virgin meat," Frankie said. "It's information, James, information. The last time you whispered to me, I got myself a truckload of scrap steel. Kept me in lettuce and cabbage for a month."

"I got nothing for you today, Frankie."

"Well, tell me, and let me decide. What routes have you been traveling lately?"

"Coal mostly and some empty boxcars, some lumber and crops, nothing you'd be interested in." Jim finished his plate of food.

"Slim pickings, I agree. Bums, not too far back, told me to look out for an auto rack coming west filled with used and new models. Seen anything like that?"

"Haven't been near it," Jim lied.

"If you see something, say something, especially to old Frankie here." Jim scooped up the gravy on his plate with a piece of bread and said nothing more.

Frankie took Jim's plate. "Let's get your clothes in the dryer," she said, and Sorrie nodded in agreement.

After their knapsacks were loaded with clean clothes and food, Sorrie started to thank Frankie for her kindness, but Frankie held up her hand. "Best to leave conversation behind. Just remember that people will say anything to get in good. Watch the train routes and the shadows lurking behind the big containers in the yards. They're my people. It's a growing business."

Once they left, Sorrie asked Jim about Frankie's parting words. "Well, that's how she stays in business," Jim said.

"I don't understand."

"She has people lift things from the freights that pass through," Jim answered. "She feeds the hobos and lets them take showers, but she expects them to tell her what's in the yards and when the trains get loaded so her people can steal the stuff on board or get one of the yard hands to cut the train and hide it someplace to be offloaded."

"But why did you lie to her? You told her we hadn't seen any autos."

"I don't want to get involved with Frankie's business anymore. I feel like I need a change."

"What kind of a change?" Sorrie asked.

"Like maybe settling down a bit. Choosing my routes more carefully. I met dozens—maybe hundreds—of people like Frankie. They're only in it for themselves and to use everybody else to get what they want."

"But she seemed so sweet," Sorrie said as they returned to the freight yard.

Jim stopped and turned to Sorrie. "That's the way it is with most people. They'll look at you sweetly and tell you how much they like you while their buddy comes up behind you to snatch your knapsack or pick your pocket. That's what I thought you were going to do when I first met you in that patch of woods. Do you want a piece of advice? Trust no one."

"What about you?" Sorrie asked.

"Nah, you shouldn't even trust me. I'm only in it for myself, too. But lately, I been in it for both of us."

"Why's that?"

"You saved me in the jungle. You haven't lied to me like most girls. And one more thing."

"Yes?"

"I don't think I can part from you," Jim said.

15

Wyoming to Montana

THEY HAD NO trouble hiding in the well of a 100-car train, and once it was out of sight of the crews, they sat up. The noise of the cars made it impossible to talk, so Jim was content to lay against the metal and watch the passing scenery of brush and mountains. At one point, he took Sorrie's hand and squeezed it. Along the way, they passed a freight hauling metal rods going in the opposite direction. "Looks like Frankie's people missed that one," Jim shouted as he peered at the blue tops of the mountains in the distance. Jim pointed. "Homeward bound!"

The ride was anything but smooth, though. The bends in the route left them hanging on for dear life, and Sorrie got sick and leaned over the shallow sides to empty her stomach, complaining that she had food poisoning from the chicken. Jim laughed, knowing she might be right; there was no telling how old Frankie's food was. Frankie usually cautioned those she liked best, but Jim wasn't one of them despite their friendliness toward each other.

Jim held on to the well and thought about what to do when he got to Montana. Owning his father's stuff was at the top of his list. Helping Sorrie was next.

The train moved into stark terrain. It wasn't gray like the soot of the mines or tinged with rust like the outside edges of the factory fences lining the route in the cities. It didn't hide anything; it revealed its naked self against the vastness of the sky: dead foliage, grey underbrush, lonely telephone poles, and the bluest sky Jim had ever seen. Jim looked into the distance and felt content with the thought that he had everything he needed—except his father.

As the altitude changed, so did the sights: from brush to spiked trees to views of flowing rivers and iron bridges. Sorrie couldn't help but be struck by the expanse of it all. They passed through flat areas where locals sat near the tracks, waving and whistling as the train flew by and sped past huge log cabins jutting from the sides of mountains.

At one point, the train paralleled a highway where a truck full of old men waved and blew kisses. Sorrie blew kisses back. Her smile told Jim she was happy, and he wondered what he could offer her now that she could pick any life and go anywhere. Inside, he didn't want to lose her, and in his heart, he thought she didn't want to lose him. Jim gazed out onto the fields and smiled. As soon as he found his father, it would be goodbye to his full-time life on the road with all its wayward stops and aching loneliness and hello to a new adventure. After all, weren't new beginnings something his father was trying to do in Paris?

The train lumbered on for hundreds of miles. It was a long trip as the train climbed, dipped, straightened up, and veered along jagged cliffs. The rocking threw their balance off, so they snuggled in a corner, and as they held each other, Jim's breath brushed Sorrie's forehead, and his eyes peered into hers. "I feel safe in your arms," Sorrie whispered. "Like Edna was free."

"Who's Edna?" Jim asked.

"She was a poet who lived her life freely, not like Emily, who was too afraid to go out of her house. I feel like I'm an Edna now. She wasn't afraid of anything, except maybe of losing a lover." Tears formed in Sorrie's eyes. "But I don't know what that feels like—loving someone so much that you care if they're no longer there. Except, perhaps, until now." Sorrie looked up at Jim; her blue eyes resembled full moons glistening light above a dark earth. He held her closer.

In the distance, sunlight illuminated specks on the mountains. Jim heard the click-clack of the steel wheels and smelled the dust as it kicked up from the train's underbelly. At one point, he began singing his father's songs. Sorrie joined in by repeating the lyrics after he sang them, their voices blending into harmony.

The travel was pleasant and uneventful, which was how Jim liked it. During a patch of track where the train rode smoothly, he and Sorrie got up to peer beyond the train. He enjoyed exploring the scenery, seeing a distant mountain or a lone electrical tower on a cliff. At one point, the railroad tracks paralleled a river, and Jim and Sorrie marveled at the rapids and clear water. Turning northward, they were deep in the heart of mining country again, which made Sorrie fearful that the train would suddenly stop. Jim reassured her it wouldn't; soon, the landscape reverted to grassland.

They passed a vast freight yard and waved to the yard hands, who waved back with their track tools. Even the junkyard dogs didn't seem to mind seeing them. Along the way, they went by a massive southbound train filled with rocks, which looked like it would topple onto its side at any moment.

As they passed into Montana, they were greeted by the sight of elk on the side of the road, which scared Sorrie and made Jim laugh. "Aren't you afraid of them? They look so big," she said.

"It isn't anything to be afraid of unless you're up close, which I don't intend to be."

"Come to think of it, what are you afraid of?"

Jim didn't see the question coming and was genuinely surprised. "Nothing, really." He leaned back and thought again. "Maybe the tricksies in my head that talk to me sometimes. I drown 'em out with alcohol. Otherwise, they won't shut up. Sometimes I drink so I can think straight."

"Do they frighten you? It sounds like maybe you have some type of mental thing."

"We all have mental things," Jim said. "Don't you have times when you hear that voice in your head? Like Emily and Edna and all the other characters that live inside you from your books? We all have it, but mine keeps at it most of the time like I'm back in that foster house with the old man yelling at me all hours of the day and night." The voices came more frequently during the day when there was a lot to do and disappeared when he relaxed and watched the stars and the full moon with a gentle breeze that only seemed to come after the sun went down. That's when he felt closest to his father, knowing his father was out there, eyes in the dark, staring into the distance, waiting for him. But sometimes, the voices were helpful. They whispered what direction he should go, and when Jim listened, the voices turned out to be right.

Until Sorrie, Jim was always up for another adventure but usually came home disappointed. Once, there had been time to discover the night sky, the yards, and the pretty women in bars, but now the sounds and places were so familiar that each moment ran into the next, and he had trouble remembering a particular day or month. He wondered if, in the end, it would all be worth it—that he'd find his father and feel complete. Then, Sorrie snapped him back to reality. "When will we be getting off? My hair's all tangled, and my skin feels grungy."

Jim glanced back at her. She tried to drag a comb through her hair while the train's speed whipped it into a frenzy. "Still the princess after all this time?" He smirked. He glanced back at the scenery, looking for any telltale sign that he was close to home. They passed through a series of shantytowns and an old Union Pacific underpass, and he knew it was time to get off. Anticipation filled his heart; he was less than 50 miles from his mother and his dream of owning his father's things. He hoped his mother would remember their phone conversation—and the promises she made.

16

Montana

I T WAS ALMOST dark when they arrived outside Laurel. The sun clouded over as it set in the west, and rain moved in, pelting them until their clothes were soaked. Jim knew it was time to hunker down for the night rather than wander around and risk getting lost or stumbling into a swollen creek. "We have to get some shelter." Jim surveyed the glistening streets and the stream of water running down the center of the road.

"Where are we going to stay?" Sorrie asked.

"I was hoping you might want to spring for a motel room for the night. No funny business. I just want to get out of these wet clothes and get cleaned up so I can be ready for my Mom tomorrow."

"How much will it cost?"

"There's a cheap one in town—the Rodeo Motel. It should be reasonable, and it's clean and respectable."

"Well, okay. No funny business."

"No funny business, I swear."

* * *

The Rodeo Motel was in a converted elementary school and had a neon sign outside that glittered in the rain. The clientele were mainly elderly lodgers and a group of men in cowboy hats sitting in a small alcove near the office where the rain couldn't reach them. They dipped their hats when Sorrie walked by, which made Sorrie smile but annoyed Jim.

True to Jim's word, the price was affordable, and the room had white linens, towels, and hand soap that came in a box.

"Soap in a box," Sorrie said, grabbing it from a welcoming basket in the center of a table. "For the price, I didn't think I'd get much except a bed and a light." But there was a television, a separate clock radio, and a phone with a cord that you could plug into several outlets.

While Sorrie fingered the little packets of soap and other sundries in the basket, Jim sat on the edge of the bed next to the nightstand. "Got anyone you want to call?"

Sorrie's face soured. "No, you?"

"I could call my brother, but it would probably be extra."

"Does he live far?"

"A few country miles from my Mom."

"And your sister?"

"She died a long time ago—after I got put in foster care. She passed away from cancer." Jim hung his head low. "My mother couldn't help her, and she died slowly." Though crying wasn't in him, if there was one thing that could summon tears and sadness, it was the death of his sister. "I wasn't there to see it. Like most news, I got a letter delivered to the foster home. Not even a phone call. Just a letter a few weeks later."

"Would you like to visit her grave while you're here? Pick some flowers? Say hello?"

A low, steady clump of sadness sank from Jim's heart to his stomach. "Momma couldn't afford a funeral. So, my sister was cremated with her ashes sprinkled outside of town. She was like a young colt and loved to race through open fields. I can see her to this day, laughing and running with me, trying to catch up. Her brown hair blowing against the wind, and her arms flapping like a bird ready to take flight."

"What kind of cancer did she have?"

"Something with her brain. Years later, Momma told me that during her last days, she would ask for the time all day long. Finally, Momma bought a bunch of clocks and put them around the room, but my sister

kept asking all the same. Momma got so mad—like my sister wasn't trying—and she asked her why she didn't know the time. My sister said that
she could see the clocks and understand the numbers, but she couldn't
make sense of them, the same way I can't make sense of letters."

"That's so sad. What was your sister's name?"

"Deirdre, her name was Deirdre. Momma said her name meant 'sorrow,' and that's why the sadness came to her."

Sorrie sat down next to Jim and put her arms around him. Jim smelled
the scent of lavender as Sorrie's hair brushed up against his cheek. She
must have dabbed on perfume, probably to make herself feel clean. "I'm
going in to take a shower," he said.

Sorrie released her arms and held up a box. "You'll need soap."

* * *

The shower was warm and enticing. Jim stood under the water and
let the day's mud trickle past his chest and stomach and sink into the
drain. He had never felt so worn out and took his time. Jim wanted to be
pure and not stained with axle grease and dust from the road. He often
wore the grit like a trophy, showing how much of the world he could
take on without being beaten. But after the last bout at the hobo camp, it
was clear there was nothing worth fighting for except his father's things,
Sorrie, and the Stranger. Everything else was just the ghost of memories
that weren't important anymore.

Jim wondered too about Sorrie. Would she stay with him? He'd never
let anyone affect him the way she had, and he asked himself if, after their
time together, he could ever be apart from her.

After showering, shaving, and brushing his teeth, Jim emerged
wearing a clean pair of jeans. He glanced at Sorrie, who was reading the
emergency instructions on the back of the door. He didn't want to tussle
with her tonight; his only desire was to lie on a soft bed, close his eyes,
and relax.

Sorrie stopped reading when she saw Jim and went into the bathroom. Jim could hear her turn the lock as soon as the door was closed.
He thought he'd give her some privacy and wandered outside. There were
two metal chairs a few feet from where they were staying, so he sat in one

of them. The white paint was chipped in places, with a few signs of rust, but as uninviting as it looked, he needed a smoke and time to arrange his thoughts. Jim looked toward the horizon and traced the outline of the mountains in the distance. The air was fresh with a scent of pine, and despite a slight chill, it was still warm enough to enjoy the outdoors without a heavy coat. He wasn't long into thought when the chair next to him was occupied by a tall man wearing a black fedora with a feather in the hat band. His shearling coat looked inviting, and Jim wished he had a coat as thick and warm as this one appeared. "You're not from around here," the man said. "I can tell from your clothes you've been traveling." His voice was soft, and he pronounced each word perfectly with no hint of an accent as to where he might have come from.

"You could say that," Jim said. 'My girl Sorrie and I have been riding freight, so I guess you can tell I feel a bit worn."

"Me too," the man said. He extended his hand. "I guess no conversation would be proper unless we introduced ourselves. My name's Douglas."

"Jim," Jim said. He felt the stranger press his palm against Jim's. It was rough, as if the man had been working in the fields all his life. Jim had the same type of hands.

"So, you got a girl?"

"She's in the room taking a shower. We're just passing through to see family then we're back on the road."

The stranger sat back and looked at the horizon. I used to travel all over the world, but now, I mostly walk the highways. It scratches the itch, you might say."

"Where's home then?" Jim asked.

"When I'm not roaming, I feel most comfortable here where the ghost of the shaman whispers into the ears of the living."

Jim was intrigued and turned and looked at Douglas, whose expression hadn't changed. "What do they say?"

"That all depends on how close to death you are." Jim was confused by this, but Douglas continued. "My soul is that of a shaman, which is why I'm drawn to this place. I'm attracted to the animals who live here and the solitude, but mostly, I'm drawn to the balance and reason of it all. Native Americans talk about harmony. This is where I find harmony, but my spirit's restless."

"I live here off and on, but I'm restless too. I wish I could find a place of peace."

"You'll get there," Douglas said. "You're young and have plenty of time. When I was younger, it was always work, travel, and people. There were a lot of demands, but I left all that. My soul wasn't free."

"Coming here made you free?"

"Coming here gave me purpose."

"What's that?"

"A joy for life. Finding answers in the wind and the mountains. Not being in pain."

"My only purpose was to find my father until I met my girl. Now, I'm not sure."

"You'll find him, and you'll find your purpose through your girl, too. Don't stop looking." Douglas tilted his head. "It looks like the wind is calling." He stood up. "Just remember to take care of that girlfriend of yours. I sense she'll bring you some peace. Maybe we'll meet on the road again. Until then . . ." Douglas extended his hand, and Jim shook it, tilted his hat, and walked into the distance until Jim couldn't see him anymore.

Jim returned to the room just as Sorrie emerged from the bathroom wrapped in a green towel. She sat at the edge of the bed, still grasping the towel around her. "The clothes Frankie dried aren't dry," she said, "So I hung them on the shower rod."

"You're clothes weren't dry?" Jim laughed. "That's just like Frankie. Why didn't you say something to her?"

"I didn't want to be there any longer; I think she's creepy. Besides, some things are too big to wear now. They'll fall off if I put them on."

"Do you want one of my shirts?"

"I'd appreciate that."

Jim was surprised at Sorrie's response. He reached for his knapsack and pulled out a red flannel shirt. "This should fit."

"I'll wear it, but I still hate grunge." Sorrie took it into the bathroom. When she came out, Jim noticed the shirt was loose, and the bottom hung below her hips. It reminded Jim of the Christmas cards he'd seen where the whole family dresses up in red tartan pajamas—only now, the plaid was so bright against Sorrie's skin that she nearly lost herself in it.

"You look pretty," Jim said.

"Thank you. No one's ever said that." Sorrie lay down on the bed.

"You do, and I like you. Do you have any plans after I see my Momma?"

"I haven't thought about it."

"You could come with me," Jim said matter-of-factly. "You're eighteen and legal, though the smell of milk isn't gone from you."

"What about milk?"

"You're still young and don't have much experience, but you can make your own decisions now."

"What would you do?"

"Find my father. I'll go to the desert highways in the Southwest."

"You're just going to light out and get swallowed up in the bars and alleys again?"

"I think maybe I need to focus a little on where he might be—that traveling isn't as important as thinking and mapping it all out. Maybe you can help me. Maybe we could stay together."

"Does that mean I'm your girlfriend?"

"If you want to call yourself that, then it's okay with me. I'd like it if you were something more than a hobo buddy."

"You mean that?" Sorrie asked.

"Of course, or I wouldn't have said it, but something still bothers me."

"Yes?"

"Will your parents be sending someone out to look for you?"

Sorrie shifted her position to face Jim. She avoided his gaze. "We haven't seen anyone yet, so maybe they just gave up. Maybe they figured I was legal, and I'd discover that living was a lot harder than being alone in my room."

The silence that followed Sorrie's comments swirled in the air. He closed his eyes to absorb what she said. Then suddenly, he felt Sorrie's lips on his. He opened his eyes, and she withdrew. "I had to do that," she said, "for freedom . . . and as a goodbye to Emily."

Jim gazed into her blue eyes, then moved toward Sorrie and wrapped his arms around her. His hand stroked the outside of the shirt, and then he slipped it under to caress her back. She was bare underneath; this puzzled him, but he started feeling comfortable with the movement of his body against hers. There was no resistance.

Jim sat up, lifted the blanket from the bed, and placed it over them. As he became more amorous, Sorrie slipped off the shirt. Jim glanced at her body. Except for the places burned by the sun, her skin was milk and soft and smelled sweet. Jim kissed her neck, shoulders, and breasts, and she didn't resist, as if the tenderness in his touch melted away her fear. He worried that the coarseness of his hands would make her withdraw, but she didn't, so he touched her arms until he noticed a musky smell. She hadn't shaved her armpits, but instead of feeling repulsed, he was glad: this was like most of the girls he'd met on the road.

Sorrie responded to him by letting go, and Jim could feel her muscles relax as she wrapped herself around him. Her hands ascended his bare back, first hesitantly, then with a sense of curiosity, and finally, an acceptance that he wouldn't hurt her. "Be gentle," she whispered.

"I promise I will," he said as he slipped off his jeans. Jim felt Sorrie's legs intertwine with his, and as he did, he heard his father's voice singing sweet and low. It was a slower version of a Doors song about a couple who had come too far to turn back. The music filled his mind, and something changed. The gulf between them melted, and the only thing that mattered was the blending of flesh. The beat took over his mind, and he reacted by feeling Sorrie's body against his, knowing they would forever be connected. The fierceness of showers pelted the tin awning outside. Sorrie sucked in the air and let out a deep exhale as her body melted into the mattress. "It's raining," Sorrie whispered.

"I know," Jim said. "Some people say it's good luck."

* * *

They awoke entangled in each other's arms. The sun crept through the slats in the blinds, and Jim could see it was late morning. Fully awake, he squinted and gazed toward the window. The sleep left him aware and present. It was the most restful sleep he'd had in years. He saw Sorrie stir as he made his way to the bathroom. When he emerged, she sat up, Jim's red flannel shirt covering her body. "That was a beautiful night," Jim said.

"Yes, it took all my tears away."

"How do you know that?"

"Because my eyes were clear this morning, no fogginess."

Jim smiled and sat on the bed. He reached for Sorrie's hand and kissed her on the cheek. "Time to awaken, my lady. We should be hitting the road to get to Laurel."

Sorrie paused and lowered her head. "Listen, before we go, I just wanted to thank you for rescuing me from that ditch and bringing me along. I wasn't your first choice for a traveling buddy, but I wanted you to know I feel grateful for making me realize something."

"Realize what?"

"That it was important for me to have someone know I was here, I existed. And you've done more than that. I think I feel something again when I'm with you. I now know why Edna cried when her lovers left. I understand the depth of her heart because mine has grown just as deep."

Jim hesitated. This was a discussion he didn't want to have. "Maybe we have more in common than you think, but we can figure the rest out later. So, let's be on our way. I'm anxious to see my Mom."

The cowboys were gone, including Douglas, and in their place were a few elderly renters wearing sun hats and khakis and sipping coffee. Jim grabbed two free cups from the office and handed one to Sorrie.

They began walking north, and Sorrie noticed that Jim was shaking. "Perhaps you should wait to see your Mom. You're all fidgety."

"I got to get there just as soon as possible," he said, guiding them from the town to an open field. "We still got a way to go. We got to hump another couple of miles, but on the way, we're going to stop and see my brother."

"Couldn't we hitch or something?" Sorrie asked.

"Yeah, we could. But these roads are barren most of the time. A truck here or there. Don't worry; I won't lose you," Jim said.

After a few miles, they found a local coffee shop with chairs and a view of the street; they settled in with a dozen stale donuts the clerk offered for free because they were from the day before and couldn't be sold. He also gave them coffee and let them sit at a table near the front of the store.

"Where's your Momma live from here?" Sorrie asked as she attacked a donut. Glaze stuck to the sides of her mouth, and she gingerly licked it from her lips and hands.

"A few more miles," Jim said. He stopped eating long enough to swallow some coffee and take a drag of a cigarette. He stared out the window.

"What will you say to her when we get there?"

"I'm not going to say anything. I'm going to ask to see my father's things—the things she promised me when I called her. By the way, a funny thing happened while you were showering yesterday." Sorrie nodded her head. "I went outside to have a smoke, and this older guy comes and starts talking to me, asking me about where I been."

"Did you know him?"

"No, but I got a strange feeling that I'd met him before. He was a little weird, but he told me to stick with you because you'll bring me peace."

"Did you believe what he said?"

Jim swirled the spoon in his coffee. He gazed into the blackness and, without looking up, said, "Maybe. I mean, I think so. We'll see." He let his voice trail off. Jim raised the spoon to his lips and made a smacking sound. "It's time we go see my brother."

* * *

They left the donut shop and started walking the dirt paths of the backwoods before coming to a clearing where there were tiny houses in a series of rows. They descended a hill and found a flock of sheep behind a fence. "Moo," Jim shouted from a distance. "Moo."

"Why are we seeing your brother?" Sorrie asked.

"Because he's my brother. Also, to make sure my Momma's still alive," Jim said. "I don't want to walk in and find a corpse."

"Have you ever seen a dead person on the road?"

"A few times, nothing big. Mostly, I saw a lot of hurt: fights, missing arms, missing eyes, the whole damn stew of sadness. I'm no enforcer, so I just ignored that shit, but once I met a one-eyed truck driver who got stabbed in a bar fight and had a patch where his eye should've been. I felt bad for him, but he still had his trucker's license. How he kept it, I'll never know. That's what happens on the road. Most of us sleep where we fall. But some have wanderlust. They come from good families but never fit in. They're not always the happiest, but they go through the world walking tall, knowing they always got a bed to go to when they get tired. I used to pride myself on being a wanderer—no plans, no direction—just light out at daybreak and see where my travels take me. If I wound up sleeping under a bridge, then I'd be content sleeping under a bridge. But this time was different. It was off in some way. So, I think there's a message there. This trip has made me more tired than all the other trips combined."

"But you're only twenty-three. How do you know? I think you just need a bit of a rest."

"It's the cold," Jim said. "It's the chill in the mountains before daybreak. It sinks into my bones, and it gets a little harder each morning to stand up straight. So, maybe it's time to give away the spurs, but I got to find him first, and I got some good leads to go on."

Sorrie stopped by the side of the road and picked some wildflowers. She made an arrangement that fit nicely into a rung on her backpack and twisted more flowers into a circle to put in her hair. She looked up at Jim. "Have you thought about just staying here and taking a break? If he's out there, he'll be out there next week and next year. Why don't you wait until you feel rested?"

"It's like that thing deep inside you that you can't get rid of—like an animal craving. Could you go through life without books?"

"Of course not."

"It's like a demon takes over and just wants to drive me on through until I either find my father or die." Jim shook his head. "I hope death's not in my close future."

* * *

Jim's brother's home was set back from the rest of the other houses and was smaller than most in the neighborhood. The yard was clean, and the place was cared for, but the car in the driveway was old. Either way, Jim hardly noticed as he bound up the concrete steps to the front door. Sorrie ran behind him. He knocked, then waited, then did it again. There was a swing set off to the side and children's toys scattered in the driveway. A roped tire hung from the branch of a tree. "Are they home?" Sorrie asked, her eyes squinting through the front glass window.

Jim knocked louder, then waited. "I don't know. Maybe we should just take a walk around the back of the house." Jim turned to leave when he heard someone unlocking the white door.

A gray-haired woman said, "Can I help you?" At first, Jim thought the woman resembled his mother, but then he noticed she was younger. Her complexion and hands were smooth and youthful; the only thing that looked old was the color of her hair. "Mollie, it's Jim, John's brother. Do you remember me? I haven't been by in quite some time, but I'm on my way to Ma's place." Jim stretched out his hands and was ready to embrace his sister-in-law, but she drew back.

"Jim? John's brother?" Then, a look of familiarity crept across her face. Sensing this, Jim again stretched out his hands, and she took them into a hug, slapped him on the back, and kissed his cheek. "We weren't expecting you. We thought you might be dead because we hadn't heard in so long." She led them inside, and a few minutes later, a figure appeared. He was wiping grease from his hands with a blue bath towel. "Jimmy?" the man said.

"Yeah, it's me," Jim said with a smile, and the brothers embraced. The door opened again, and Jim watched as a young girl, perhaps three, wrapped herself around Mollie's leg. In the distance were the sounds of television cartoons.

The brothers continued embracing until Jim noticed Sorrie standing there. He broke his grasp and said, "Johnny, here's my girlfriend and traveling companion. Her name's Sorrie."

John extended his hand. "Pleased to meet you, Sorrie." He hesitated, looked down at his fingers, then shook her hand. "You've been tramping around the country with my brother? Bumming rides and riding the rails? I hope he's been treating you right."

"Yes, he has," Sorrie said.

A few minutes later, they were sitting in the kitchen, and as neat as the outside was, the inside was clean and orderly. Not a dish in the sink, not a toy on the floor.

Mollie insisted on making coffee, and Jim couldn't stop talking about the aroma—or the flavor. "That's one mighty fine cup of coffee, Mollie. I wouldn't trade that coffee for the best ride I ever had." She offered crumb cake and sandwiches and showed Sorrie where the bathroom was.

Once Sorrie was out of sight, John said, "You can cut the B.S. Jimmy. Why did you really come here?"

"No B.S., John, none whatsoever."

"Then tell me why you're here. We haven't seen you in two years, and suddenly, you show up out of nowhere with some girl and expect me to believe you were just dropping by?"

"I came to see Momma and was passing through with Sorrie. We were heading to Momma's place because I called her, and she told me she was sick and wanted to give me some stuff from my father before she kicked off."

"She's always saying that. Hell, she's been sick for as long as I been alive, at least." John laughed and looked at Mollie, then shook his head. "My little brother. He isn't right in the brain. She told you she was sick? I don't believe it."

"She told me she was dying," Jim said. He ran it over in his mind. The phone call. Her desperate pleas to come home. The annoying cough through the phone lines.

"She's been back and forth from who-knows-where going on three months now. I think she's home, but it's hard to tell for sure. She moves in and out so much. Sometimes, she hides from me when I go calling. I think she lit out for Arizona because I haven't seen her lately. I did get a phone call a while back from those foster people down in Florida telling me about how you lifted some money from the old lady."

"Lifted money?"

John laughed. "You don't think those people you were staying with weren't going to try to find you after you stole fifty dollars from the old lady's purse, did you? She says you stole all her grocery money."

"I don't rightly know how she got your number. I've been on the road going on eight years now. They collected more than enough from the state for me. I haven't seen either of them for years." Jim caressed his coffee mug. What the hell was going on here? Mom not being sick? His foster family calling his brother? Sorrie returned to the room.

"I told her I haven't seen you, and I haven't heard from you, and that's the truth."

Jim swirled the coffee. "Yeah, John, you were always good at that: covering for me even though you hated my guts." Jim decided to change the subject, especially with Sorrie in the room. "And who is this beautiful little girl I see hiding behind her mother's skirt? I think it must be Mary." Mary came out from behind her mother, sucking on her finger. Mollie tried to coach her out of her shyness but couldn't. Jim looked at his brother and tried to make light of things, but John wouldn't let it go.

John then turned to Sorrie. "Let me tell you about what you got hooked up with. My brother's nothing but a liar and a thief, and he has no good bone in his body worth talking about."

Sorrie stared at John. "Why do you talk mean to your brother? I heard you grew up together in awful circumstances. He should be your best friend."

"Well, we used to be." John stopped and looked down at the wooden floor as if to recall their days together. He lifted his head. "Jim's loony tunes now. He has been for years. Always talking about the voices in his head. He got voices all right. He belongs in a booby hatch. Did my brother tell you how he got his name?"

"I don't think that has anything to do with anything," Sorrie answered.

"Well, did he tell you? Did he tell you all about being Jim Morrison's son?"

"Yes, but I don't think that has anything to do with you. Jim and I are going to be together."

"You keep on believing that." John shook his head and took a sip of coffee. "Our mother—if you can call her that—is crazy, just like Jim. Jimmy here would believe anything she told him."

"Why are you so afraid of him? "Sorrie asked.

"What are you afraid of?" Jim repeated.

"Not you, little brother. Now, to finish my story. You see, our mother's just a little schizoid, and she had Jimmy believing from when he was a baby that his daddy was the great Jim Morrison. The only problem with that is he isn't. Jim's daddy—just like my daddy—is a common barroom bum, like all the bums and trailer trash my Momma hung out with over the years. Nothing but guys who had no place to go, no bed to sleep in, and no woman to pass out with until Momma came along, offering wherever she was staying and everything else along with it. When Momma was finished partying and drinking, she'd see how much money was left for food and rent, at least when we had enough to afford a place. Sometimes, we made it, and sometimes we didn't, but there was never anything left over for food, and we kids would have to go and beg a neighbor to feed us. Either way, she'd be drinking and screwing around, and we'd be stealing milk and shoplifting crackers."

"You and Jim?"

"Oh no," John continued. "Jimmy got dropped off into foster care when he was eight. Momma got caught for leaving us in a supermarket, and the state had him taken away and into foster care. My sister Diedre and I got shipped off to our dad's, but then she came to get us. We stayed with Momma because we were the older ones. We babysat Momma's hangovers and kept her from putting both feet into the fire. Once and a while, she'd leave us with our real daddy, but then we'd be back taking care of her. Yeah, it was fun and games, but Jimmy didn't have any of that. He had a good life in Florida with those nice foster folks."

Jim couldn't control himself as his rage began to boil over. Not only had John spread lies, he'd embarrassed Jim in front of his girl—the only girl Jim had ever allowed to get inside his head. "Shut up, liar!" Jim yelled. "You and Diedre didn't live with Momma. You both got shipped back to your daddy and grew up there while Momma went off on her own."

"We lived with Dad for a year, and then Momma took us back."

"Well, while you were dealing with her hangovers, I lived with a stupid old man who wasn't nice. He wasn't nice to any of the foster kids."

"And you don't know the hard times I went through," John yelled. He stood up from the table and slammed his fist hard, so hard it startled his daughter, and she began to cry. Mollie bundled Mary up and took her from the room. "A drunk mother, staying in trailer park after trailer park until we were asked to leave. Kids made fun of me because I got my shoes and clothes from the trash nobody else wanted. Watching our sister die at seventeen because Momma had no money for the medicine that would've kept her alive. I barely got through school and had to work long nights so I could feed myself. What the hell do you know about it?"

"I know about it because I lived it, too. Are you the only one who ever had to wear second-hand clothes? All of us foster kids did. The only thing we got worth remembering was a pair of shoes at Christmas. I had to get away from there and find my father. He was the only thing I could believe in. That's why I've been traveling. When you see something worth grabbing, you go for it, even if the sun blocks its view. You have Mollie here and a life; I just had the dream of finding my father until Sorrie came along."

They both took a moment. Both shaking, exhausted, re-living their hurts and anguish. Jim was too young, and John was too exhausted to try to recount every moment that sliced its way into their spirits. It was all just memory now, and as Jim and John looked at each other, they realized it too. They saw each other's tears, and without hesitation, they embraced.

* * *

Jim and Sorrie stayed longer, each brother holding out the hope that they understood each other's pain. They spoke of their travels and the funny stories they'd taken with them, and John talked about how he'd been working a job at a local warehouse.

The conversation slipped into the pranks they'd pulled on each other ("Remember the time I put gorilla glue on the toilets?" Jim said, to which his brother responded, "Momma was so mad."), but no mention of Jim or John's fathers came up again. Jim felt genuine warmth for his brother as they talked and a glow formed around him. They discussed getting together again.

Jim and Sorrie left with apples and a full canteen of water, with Jim's brother telling Jim to "Go find the documents. Momma has them. They will tell you who you really are, but don't be disappointed with the answer."

After they left, Jim pointed Sorrie toward a path away from town. It was the kind of late-summer day that surrounded them in light. Jim had known these days, but now, with Sorrie, it seemed even more memorable.

"Was that true what your brother said?" Sorrie asked as she kicked up the dust from the side of the road.

"One thing you have to learn about my brother is that he's always got to be right, no matter the truth."

"But is it true? You're crazy, and your father's not really Jim Morrison?"

"I know who I am and who my dad is. He's in my blood, and I know who I belong to."

Sorrie stopped walking. "It wouldn't make a difference. But is it true? Is what he said true?"

"No, it's not true," Jim said, quickening the pace. "Can't you see my brother hates our mother so much he'll say anything to get me to hate her, too?"

"But is it true what he said?"

"If he's right, what have I been doing for the last eight years? Chasing a shadow? I'm not crazy. I know what I know in my heart." Jim walked faster.

"It didn't seem like he was crazy either."

Jim suddenly stopped. "Don't you know that a person can seem normal, but deep inside, they're crazier than a crap house rat? Don't you know my brother hates me because I'm somebody's kid and he's just an old man with sour memories? Of course, my Momma had to travel. Of course, she had to work at different places. Momma had to hide the fact that Jim Morrison was my dad. She had to hide it; otherwise, people would've come after her—and me. Don't you see my brother's jealous?"

"John didn't look jealous or that he was trying to hurt you. He seemed to be telling the truth. It's like the cave story. Are you the prisoner looking at shadows against the wall, just saying what you think they are? I didn't know what to say when he started yelling at you the way he did."

Jim grabbed Sorrie by her shoulders and shook her. "What do you want from me? What can I say to make you believe I'm telling the truth?"

"What will make me believe you besides a couple of initials in a book?" Sorrie asked.

"My mother," Jim replied. "I have my mother. And she was a witness to all of it. She was there."

* * *

Jim navigated through the backwoods until the space opened to a clearing and a trailer park. It was unrecognizable from every other trailer park. Still, it was clean, so much so that it resembled a middle-class neighbor in any suburb in America. Only the rusting cars in the driveways and a piece of metal banging on a roof made the place feel different.

Jim walked down the line until he found the pathway to where his mother lived. They walked halfway to the end of the road before stopping at a powder-blue-colored trailer with a makeshift wooden porch in front. A rattan rocker creaked as the wind made it move back and forth, and a wind chime danced to its own music. Jim knocked a few times, but no one answered. He reached for the door. It was unlocked, and as he turned the knob, he felt afraid.

No lights were on in the living room, not even a nightlight plugged into a socket. "Momma," Jim yelled, but there was no response. "Momma, I'm home," he said, walking through the trailer with the fear of a man who didn't want to accept the inevitable. He looked in her room, glanced around the floral bed comforter to be sure she hadn't collapsed onto the floor, looked in the closets, and then went into the bathroom to check if she was there. Sorrie waited in the living room.

"She's not here," Sorrie said.

"She's got to be here." Jim quickened his steps. He looked in the hall closets and the kitchen and walked out behind the trailer to see if she might be there. "Momma," he said as he circled the metal frame. He glanced around for any neighbors who might have seen her, but no one was around; he couldn't even hear a dog barking. He returned to the house where Sorrie sat on a green cushioned sofa. Jim glanced around the room again. Even though the furnishings looked undisturbed, everything had a layer of dust as though no one had lived there in months. Dried leaves gathered in the corners, and a crumpled blanket lay on the kitchen table. Jim walked over and lifted it. A few mice scurry from underneath it and disappear behind a crack in the floorboards. He checked the cupboards, but they were empty except for a half-eaten box of crackers. There was nothing in the refrigerator; even if there was, it would have spoiled a long time ago as the appliance wasn't plugged in. Jim walked over to a light switch, but it was clear that the electricity had been turned off. No power meant no heat, and Jim hoped the temperature wouldn't drop too far during the night. He checked the water, and it was working. *At least their pumps are on*, he thought. He walked back into the living room and sat next to Sorrie. "She's not here and hasn't been for a while." Jim surveyed the room again to verify what he was seeing.

"Didn't your brother say that she took off to travel? It doesn't look like anyone's been here for a couple of months."

"But I called her. She told me she was sick. She told me she was dying. She told me I should come." Jim crossed his hands and placed them on his head. His eyes widened, and he felt his nerves tense up and his mind go blank. "Why would she say that if she was going to take off? I don't understand."

"Maybe she had an emergency that required her to go to the hospital or something."

"For months?" Jim asked. Then the thought occurred to him: perhaps she had gone to the hospital because of the cancer and was too sick to come home. "She might be in a nursing home somewhere," Jim stopped as the possibilities ran through his head. "Maybe she died," he told Sorrie.

"Who put the blanket on the table?" Sorrie asked. "Could she have called an ambulance, and they did?"

Jim walked over to the phone on a wooden side table and picked it up. The line was dead. "The phone's not working, so who did I call when I was in Florida? It was only a few weeks ago, not months, but now the line was dead."

"Are you sure you spoke to someone?" Sorrie asked. "Maybe it wasn't her. Maybe it was a wrong number who thought you were someone else."

Jim looked behind the table and noticed the line wasn't hooked up. It had been ripped out of the wall. He held up a frayed cord. "Looks like someone might have been here besides your Mom," Sorrie said.

For Jim, that meant only one thing: his father's things might have been tampered with, even stolen. He searched the bedroom, the closet in the hall, and the closet in the living room, where he found a blue trunk. He dragged it out, set it near a window for light, sat next to it on the floor, and opened it. It was clear that someone had gone through it: photos of Jim's mother, Rosemary, and Jim Morrison were scattered haphazardly around the contents, a yellow poster with a red border advertising a concert in Berkley, California, was ripped in half, and the prized leather jacket that his mother had shown him was missing. Only the crumpled tissue paper it used to be wrapped in was there. Sorrie walked over and sat next to Jim. "They've taken it, they've taken everything," Jim said.

"What did they take?" Sorrie asked.

"His jacket. My father's leather jacket is gone." Jim buried his head in his hands. He resisted an urge to cry.

"Maybe your brother has it. How do you know your Mom didn't sell it?" Sorrie said.

"It wasn't him. He would have taken everything and burned it. He wouldn't have left the pictures or the poster. Momma would have never sold something that meant so much to her. Someone must have stolen it." Jim sifted through more items. There was a comb and some drawings but nothing to convince Sorrie that Jim was who he said he was. He handed her the photos. "See here," Jim pointed to his mother. This is Momma standing next to my father at a concert. "And there's some other ones." Jim handed a stack of photos to Sorrie. As she shuffled through them, he began tapping his fingers on the side of the trunk. The sound became loud.

"That's really distracting," Sorrie said to Jim. He continued to do it, though, and she moved away from him and returned to the couch.

Jim stood up and sat in the chair next to Sorrie. Instead of banging on the side of the trunk, he examined the inside lining. It was a fine blue burlap with a slight bulge in the middle. Jim noticed tiny threads around the perimeter. Almost unconsciously, he began pulling any loose threads until they moved through the weave, and when he gave them a good yank, they slipped all the way out of the fabric.

"Jim, what are you doing? You're going to ruin the lining if you keep doing that," Sorrie said.

"It's old," Jim said. He pulled more threads until he had a stack of five or six beside him. "Besides, it helps me not to be so nervous and to think about who might have taken my father's jacket."

"You need to forget about what just happened. You need to focus on finding out where your mother is and if she's okay."

"Not before I ruin this trunk," Jim said. He grabbed more and more threads at a faster and faster pace until whole chunks of fabric were loosened. After pulling as many strings as possible, he latched onto one that went down the center to where the bulge was. He was finding it difficult to pull it through the fabric, so he pulled harder, and instead of it gently traveling through the weave, it ripped the burlap down the middle until it stopped at a small piece of paper inside the lining. Jim maneuvered it out and unfolded it. It was an official birth certificate from the state of Montana. It had Jim's name on it, and in the box for the father's name was someone Jim had never heard of: James Morley.

Sorrie glanced at the piece of paper. "Who's James Morley?"

"I don't know. It says here he's my father, but that's not true. My real father is Jim Morrison."

Sorrie glanced at it. "Not according to this," she said.

Jim looked at it again. Under "mother's name," it had Jim's correct mother, but he had never heard of the man named as his father. The address was a Montana town, but even that was foreign to him. "There must be a mistake," he said. "This can't be my birth certificate. This man isn't my father. I need to find out where my mother is so she can straighten this out."

"It was under the fabric in the trunk, right?" Sorrie explained. "Maybe she was hiding it from you. She lied to you, Jim. Your dad isn't some famous rock star. He's just the man who made you."

"You're lying to me. My Mom was right, but you're trying to convince me my father isn't famous. You always doubted me. You never believed." Jim slammed the top of the trunk closed, which startled Sorrie. She moved away from him.

Sorrie got up from the sofa. "I didn't lie to you; your mother did. She saw an illusion that's not there and convinced you it was real. She's been lying to you all these years. I think it's time to face the fact that you're someone you're not. Just like the prisoners in the cave, you're chained to the shadows you see, but they're not real. You're a prisoner just as much as they were."

"But it's just a story," Jim said. "The cave dwellers aren't alive."

"And neither is Jim Morrison. He's not roaming the earth looking for you. It's all in what we perceive. You want your freedom, but all along, you've been stuck in a hamster cage spinning on a wheel that's not really there. I followed you, and at one point, I believed you, but you lied."

"Stop what you're saying. Just stop it." Sorrie stood her ground. Once Jim noticed she wouldn't budge, he pointed to the door. "You're not telling the truth. Someone brainwashed you. Was it Church? Or Dweeb? It's all a setup, so I don't look for my father. You want me to stay here. You want to chain me up and control me just like your parents are controlling you."

"That's not true. You know that. I came this far with you, and I'm willing to go the distance, but you have to promise to give up this crazy dream of being some rock star's son."

"I don't need your help. You're just one of those people who's trying to convince me I'm wrong about my father, but I'll prove you wrong. I'll prove all of you wrong."

"How do you intend to do that?" Sorrie pointed to the birth certificate. "Here's proof."

"I don't care what you say. I'm going to find out where my Momma is, and then I'm going to find my father on the highways in the desert." He sat down and stared at the certificate, running his thumb over the name James Morley. He sat for an hour believing that at any moment, the door would open, and his father would walk in and tell him the document was all a big fraud meant to cover up the fact that he had a famous father.

Jim thought. "What about the man on the porch? Or the Stranger? Or the man Ricky Blue Pants met? Were they all just ghosts?" Jim looked at Sorrie.

"I don't know," she said. "I can't explain it."

Then Jim remembered Douglas, the man at the motel. What was it he said? That he was drawn to the balance and reason of it all? That was his father's message: balance your life and think it through. Make sense of it. "I don't know how to make sense of it all, but I'd like you to stay with me."

"After you lied to me?"

"I didn't lie. It's like those prisoners. I was seeing shadows, and now I have to find out if it was real. You're the best thing that ever happened to me, and I'd like you to help me sort it all out."

"I remember Church said that we should all live our own version of life. I'd like to come with you, but I'm scared. I need to know you won't go crazy or anything."

Jim walked over to the kitchen and took the blanket from the table. He was hungry but decided to take a nap first. He needed to think about who his real father was. "I won't go crazy. I plan on tracking down the address on the certificate and talking to the guy whose name is on it. It could be he just put his name there to shield me from everyone finding out the truth. Will you come?"

"Can I go rest on your Momma's bed for a while and tell you in the morning?"

"Why don't you do that?" Jim said. "I'll be here on the couch waiting."

It was still dark when Jim heard a noise. Sorrie, maybe? No, it was like shoes scrapping against a wooden floor. "Who's there?" he said, but no one answered. He sat up and thought he saw a figure moving in the darkness. "Who are you?" He asked. With no lights or candles, Jim used the moonlight to see if anyone had come into the trailer. He looked around and thought he saw a shadow in the kitchen and got up to look, but no one was there. "It was all an illusion," he said out loud, expecting someone to answer, but no one did. It was then that he heard an 18-wheeler going down the highway and a train whistle in the distance. He packed what little he had and told Sorrie to gather her things because they were leaving. They walked out the door together.

* * *

Somewhere in America, two people are looking for the truth: one is searching for reason but can't escape the prison of what he believes; the second, a woman, is desperate to preserve her freedom at all costs, even if that means traveling with a prisoner who lives in illusion. Then there's a third person, a shaman who walks the highways, ensuring Jim and Sorrie stay safe from the shadows. He knows it is a long and lonely highway.

Acknowledgments

MUCH THANKS TO my editor and publisher at Sunbury Press as well as my guardian angel, Eileen Obser, who always helped me keep the faith. I'd also like to acknowledge the staff of the MFA program at Lindenwood University, especially Dr. Wm. Anthony Connolly and Tony D'Souza who served as my mentors during my time in the program. Lastly, thanks to my writing and memoir students for keeping me positive and hopeful.

About the Author

Jill Evans is a Long Island-based freelance writer and editor with a bachelor's degree from Stony Brook University and an MFA with a concentration in writing from Lindenwood University.

Jill has been an editor and writer for several trade publications and her memoir pieces have appeared in several newspapers including *Newsday* and *The East Hampton Star*. In addition, she was a nonfiction finalist for the 2016 Christopher Hewitt Award in A&U magazine for her memoir piece about the beginning of the AIDS crisis entitled, "It Started with a Phone Call."

Jill has taught creative writing classes at Suffolk County Community College on Long Island and currently teaches a memoir class at Connetquot Library.

Jill has a passion for telling stories about the common man or woman who often remain unhear and unseen as they deal with the struggles of how to survive life's challenges. Many of her story ideas come from personal observations or musings on how each of us journeys through a dignified life often facing joy and tragedies unseen by our fellow humans. *Travels with Jim* is her first novel.